Hoʻolulu Park and the Pepsodent Smile

and other stories

Juliet S. Kono

ISBN 0-910043-70-1

This is issue #85 (Spring 2004) of *Bamboo Ridge, Journal of Hawai'i Literature and Arts* (ISSN 0733-0308).

Copyright © 2004 by Juliet S. Kono

All rights reserved. This book, or parts thereof, may not be reproduced in any form without permission.

Published by Bamboo Ridge Press

Printed in the United States of America

Indexed in the American Humanities Index

Bamboo Ridge Press is a member of the Council of Literary Magazines and Presses (CLMP).

Cover: "Heliconia Season" by Roger Whitlock; watercolor, 20" x 28", 1999.

Parts I, II, III: "Orchid Window I, II, & III" by Roger Whitlock; watercolor, 6" x 9", 1999.

Design: Rowen Tabusa

Bamboo Ridge Press is a nonprofit, tax-exempt corporation formed in 1978 to foster the appreciation, understanding, and creation of literary, visual, or performing arts by, for, or about Hawai'i's people. This project was supported in part by grants from the National Endowment for the Arts (NEA) and the State Foundation on Culture and the Arts (SFCA), celebrating over thirty years of culture and the arts in Hawai'i. The SFCA is funded by appropriations from the Hawai'i State Legislature and by grants from the NEA.

NATIONAL
ENDOWMENT
FOR THE ARTS

Bamboo Ridge is published twice a year. For subscription information, back issues, or a catalog, please contact:

Bamboo Ridge Press
P.O. Box 61781
Honolulu, HI 96839-1781
(808) 626-1481
brinfo@bambooridge.com
www.bambooridge.com

Acknowledgments

Bamboo Ridge, Journal of Hawai'i Literature and Arts:
  "Anniversary"
  "The Cardinal"
  "Ho'olulu Park and the Pepsodent Smile"
  "Rock Fever"
  "Small Rebellions"

Hawai'i Herald, 1991
  "Soup"

Aloha Magazine, 1985
  "The Pond"

"Soup" was the winner of the American Japanese National Literary Award, 1991.

"Educating Amy" was an honorable mention in *Glimmer Train Stories* short-story competition.

"Boys' Style" was an honorable mention in the 1998 *HONOLULU* Magazine Fiction Contest.

"Rock Fever" was a runner-up in the 2001 *HONOLULU* Magazine Fiction Contest.

Some of these stories appear here in slightly different versions. Written over a span of twenty-five years, they are about Japanese immigrants who came to Hawai'i to work on the sugar plantations at the turn of the century, and their descendants.

I wish to thank my grandparents and parents, who are here in spirit, and all my aunts and uncles for their incredible stories. To the editors and staff of Bamboo Ridge Press—Eric Chock, Joy Kobayashi-Cintrón, Darrell Lum, and Wing Tek Lum—for their help in making this book possible, to BR study group for the many years, to Darius Kono for his steadfastness and love, to Kathy Meyer for her editorial suggestions, to friends at Leeward Community College for their encouragement, and to teachers of the entrusting mind for their guidance, grace, and spiritual support throughout my life, my deepest appreciation and sincerest gratitude. And as always, to David, for his devotion.

This is a work of fiction. Names, characters, and incidents are used fictitiously and any resemblance to actual persons, living or dead, is entirely coincidental.

Table of Contents

Part I

Hiroshima Peasant 11
The Doctor 29
Educating Amy 43
Pake Zaka 57
Japanese Tea Garden 69
Koi Pond 87

Part II

The Motonaga Women 101
Soup 111
The Cardinal 123
Boys' Style 137
Hoʻolulu Park and the Pepsodent Smile 147
The Wall 161

Part III

Small Rebellions 181
Ahukini Landing 193
Web 207
Anniversary 223
The Grandfathers 235
Rock Fever 251

For Shannon and Stephen

Prologue

Communities. Small communities.

Isolated, coastal, conservative, mixed, plantation, poor, insular, backwater, without pity, full of rumors, full of stories, full of secrets, full of shame. Full of lies.

Years of lies. How in the world—why did everyone lie so much? But everyone lied, didn't they. No one told the truth.

People lived in houses filled with lies. They worked their way around the accumulation, the layers and layers, the dust of them stacked like tofu blocks or futon in the closets. Small and white, lies lived in the maggot shadows, in the lowering of voices, the showering of tales, the seams of their frumpy clothes, the mop-stained baseboards, the bottom of the rice bin, the scum of the tea kettle, the dirty cupboards, and, like the grass broom propped in the corner, concealed themselves until disturbed or forgotten. In the silences.

As someone once said, "People are so clever, lying by silence, lying by leaving things out." They lied, too, by what they did or did not do. No one had a claim on the truth in these small communities. No one escaped never having told a lie. Everyone had something to lie about. Everyone had something to hide.

And people lied because of shame. No one wanted to be found out or ridiculed. No one wanted to see the repeated rubbing of one index finger by the other thrust into their face indicating: "Shame, shame, shame." Shame became the house that lies built. Shame in all its permutations penetrated their pores, covered them over like mold or seeped in like high water, smoke in the hair, or cheap perfume on their clothes.

Shame made people conscious of their bodies their thick legs, short hairy arms, buck teeth, slant eyes, pigeon-toes, flat noses, thick hair, yellow skin, moon faces, fish lips. Shame placed the hand over the mouth to hide the laugh and bad teeth. Shame pulled in the thick sweaters across the chest to hide the breasts. Shame crossed the legs at the ankles to hide what was soft and warm between. Shame dragged hair over the face to conceal the eyes. Shame flowed into their ears, flashed out of their eyes, blew out of their noses, heaved out of their breath, festered in their sores, the gurgling of their bad stomachs—the voices of their bodies. Shame bled from between their legs.

Shame rolled over the Hamakua hillsides down through the small villages of Pāpaʻikou, Kaiwiki, Wainaku, Pepeʻekeo, Hakalau, into Hilo town. One day, it forced Shigemi Takemoto to silence herself after she'd been raped. She wasn't the only one. There were others like her. Made the Okinagas beat up their son because he was a pervert, showing his privates around town. Sent the Motonaga girls far away when their mother kicked them out of the house.

Shame was everything. Shame was everywhere.

And if you didn't want to "make shame," you kept secrets. You held on to them as tightly as you could, and if you were lucky and not found out, you took your little secrets, sweet and cruel, with you to your grave.

Part I

Out of nothingness, something is born.
—Japanese proverb

Hiroshima Peasant

"Tomo-chan, show me your face."

"Oh, Mother," Tomoko Morishige said with a daughter's exasperation and moved her face away.

But her mother gently palmed Tomoko's cheek and turned her face toward her. Delicately placing her fingers under Tomoko's chin, as if it were made of fine porcelain, her mother examined it this way and that. She then tilted it higher into the light, out of the shadows cast by the dim kitchen lantern.

"You have the face of a typical Hiroshima peasant," her mother said, smiling. "But yours is a nice face. It's round and bright like the moon."

With rare enthusiasm, her mother stepped back to look harder at Tomoko's face. She then put her hands up to her mouth in delight. "Yes, it's as I thought. I'm happy for you, your features like those on my side of the family. See these lines, going across? You'll grow into them. That means you'll be an agreeable person."

Between the wooden tub and a meal preparation table in the narrow sunken corridor where the women washed the rice and vegetables for the day's dishes, Tomoko's mother often studied her daughters' faces. "Reading the face," she called what she did, her hands still moist from the water-soaked ferns or the mountain yams she had just washed, when it moved her to take one of her daughters' faces into her hands. Although Tomoko and her younger sister, Yuri-chan, were irritated at first, they were quick to give in, the girls giggly and ticklish beneath the touch of their mother's interpretations.

Mother, your eyes light up like coals in the brazier when you touch our faces. Your hands are fires, your cheeks ablaze.

The color in our faces is like what burns in autumn leaves, you say. Watch the leaves! See them change color, shape, design when they move in and out of the light and shadows.

I know you not only see the lines in our faces. You see what is beyond them. You see the years—perhaps the sorrow, the regrets. Sometimes I see a flash of pain, like a burst of smoke that clouds your enjoyment. But because I am young, I am shortsighted. I cannot imagine what you see. I can only turn my face as you direct and join you in your laughter.

What Tomoko's mother did was not unusual. After all, she was someone who worshiped the fox god, trimmed the trees with white sacred paper ribbons, and prayed to the roadside guardians. At night, she'd stop in the middle of her sewing to listen to what stirred in the dark. "Who is it that cries in the woods? Is it the white fox?" Sometimes she'd hear the screech of a night bird. "They've changed their forms to fool someone out on a lonely country road," she'd say. "The gods' altars have not been attended." The next day she'd run out to the many shrines in the countryside to give offerings of proper humility. At home, she threw salt over her shoulders, placed new rice wine on the table, mixed the hot mustard to give it her anger.

"Lines moving across the face make for peaceful feelings," she continued, welcoming this good reading of Tomoko's face that day. "If lines go up and down a face, that means it is not peaceful. It's a hard face with a stubborn streak. My daughters, may all your children have lines that move across their faces." She laughed, deep within her throat, and slid a gentle finger across Tomoko's forehead.

Once, when Tomoko's mother talked in this manner about Tomoko's face in front of Tanaka-san, a family friend who frequented their home, the old man got into the act and laughed at them.

"Let me see for myself," he said and stared at Tomoko. "Your face is too round, the roundness narrowing the forehead. Only smart people have wide foreheads, so you can't be very smart. Sending you to school has been a waste of time. I'm going to tell that to your father. Look at you. Actually, you're only good to wash fish, work in the rice field, and scrub a husband's back. Make lots of children. Yes, very good to make lots of children." He hissed as if in satisfaction through a mouth of bad teeth.

"Hebi, snake," Tomoko said under her breath. She hated the scaly skin on the back of his hands and his old man, farmer smell—of sake, dirt, and dried fish. "He's not a very nice person," Tomoko whispered to her mother, noting the lines going down his face.

At one time, her mother tried to keep Tomoko at home to show her how to cut the cabbage, clean the rice, gut the fish, but Tomoko was quick to run off with her brothers. With her kimono tucked like a boy's between her legs, she played with her two older brothers on the train tracks or ran through the rice paddies, leaping over the water.

Yuri-chan often complained. "Why is it that Tomoko can do almost anything she wants to while I have to stay at home?"

"We can't have two girls like Tomoko running around like boys," her mother said.

In her worry, Tomoko's mother admonished her oldest daughter. "Something's going to happen to your legs. They'll crack like fire sticks beneath you. They'll crumble like salt. You shouldn't be running like your brothers in the rice fields. Rice is sacred. Stretching your legs over what is sacred is bad luck. You should be at home, doing what girls do."

"How is it that my brothers can toss mud into the air, leap in the rice water like frogs, but I cannot?" She was annoyed at her mother who tried to separate what she could or could not do with her brothers.

"Boys are boys. You are *different!*"

"How?"

"You're a *girl*. Don't you know that?"

But she did not see the difference. She could do many things better than her brothers. She could fly her kite higher, spin her top faster, net more fireflies; she could call out like a frog, whistle like a bird, swim like an eel.

In 1910, when Tomoko was thirteen, her father, a successful rice farmer and merchant, suddenly sent her brothers to America. The real question that went begging under the gathering of Tomoko's brow was, how could she have been so oblivious to all the comings and goings in her family, to all of her father's and brothers' plans, until her brothers were almost on board the steamship that took them away?

One day, three years after her brothers had left, Tomoko was on her way home from high school when she met up with her sister on the road. Yuri-chan had been on an errand for their mother. It was presumed that she was the daughter who would take care of their parents in old age.

"Yuri-chan. You are no longer going to school," Tomoko remembered her father announcing one day.

Her sister cried all that night. From then on, Yuri-chan stayed at home. It was, again, one of those times when a decision was made and Tomoko had no idea how or where it had come from—like the sudden flight of a bird or the leap of a fish. A father's whim. With that, Yuri-chan was fated to be the daughter who would marry young, raise a family, and live nearby her parents' household.

Dear sister. Poor sister. I can see it clearly. Father will match you to a spoiled merchant boy from a nearby town as in a transaction for sacks of barley tea or corn for the chickens. The boy you marry will become a drunk like so many men here. He will want the best suits, a gold watch, and keep a woman in town. He will despair of filling the rice houses, dislike his children. Your marriage will sour like fermented beans.

If she could help it, Tomoko vowed never to enter a fate she envisioned her sister falling into. Feeling luckier in life, she looked over at her sister with pity as they walked. She aspired to become a teacher, thinking always that this would save her from the village boys. Soon, she would be one of a few girls taking their college exams.

"Tadaima, we're home," the girls said their voices in harmony.

"Welcome back," their mother said. But Tomoko was puzzled. It was clear her mother was trying hard to match her daughters' exuberance.

"Yuri-chan, the things I sent you out for?"

Tomoko thought it strange too that her mother kept her head down, busying herself with making some tea. Her sister handed their mother the pearl-shell buttons and thread needed for sewing. Still looking down, her mother took the notions from Yuri-chan's hands and said to Tomoko almost inaudibly, "Your father wants a word with you. Change your clothes before you go to see him."

"What does he want to see me for?" asked Tomoko, for she was summoned before her father only if it was important.

Her mother did not answer her. She looked away from Tomoko's inquiring looks and remained solemn as a sea bream, the lines of her body swimming in what looked like sadness. The puffiness around her mother's eyes indicated that she had been crying. Tomoko wanted to say something, but the angle of her mother's body forbade her from speaking. She wondered if it had something to do with her brothers; the family had not heard from them for the longest time.

Mother what is it you are not telling me? I'm like a hooded falcon. I'm like the cow they walk to market to be slaughtered.

Show me, mother! Show me your face. Show me what the lines on your face say!

Yesterday, I stepped on Yoshio's, older brother's, comb and the cold burned upward into my body. I want to run in the grass again with my brothers. I want to wade in the cold stream where the pebbles sing. I want to fling the stones, high, and into the wind, so my brothers can hear me. Mother, for you, losing them to another country must have been like having them die.

As always, I learn of things too late. I am like the leaf on the tree that must wait for the snow or the wind or the sun or the rain.

"Yuri-chan, how is it that things happen around us and we never know about them until it is almost under our noses?" Tomoko asked her sister one day.

"Because Father makes the decisions."

"Do you think Mother knows about things beforehand?"

"No, she's like us, always surprised by what Father does. She does what he says."

"I don't believe it."

"I do."

"You sure?"

"Oh, I'm certain."

Men moved in a mysterious world of their own, Tomoko thought.

"Our brothers were sent to America in order to make 'better lives' for themselves, mother told me. Father had a *feeling* that no one could go against," Yuri-chan said.

"A feeling—that's all?"

"Yes, that's all, from what I can gather. According to Mother, he feels there is something in the air. To him the birds fly north earlier, the bees turn away from the flowers, the well water turns brown. That's why he sent the boys away."

"What does that mean?"

"I don't know. I think he's worse than Mother in his superstitions. At least Mother's superstitions are harmless. She isn't compelled to send her children away."

"Isn't anything real? First, Mother. Now, Father."

Tomoko did not understand her father's wish to *better* her brothers' lives. Life in Hiroshima was very comfortable for them, so why? The brothers had good jobs in the city. When their father retired, they could take over his business. Life was never better.

What did you see for my brothers in their new country, Mother? I know they wished to turn back when they could not land in California. New laws had restricted their entry, but Father insisted that they stay, and they could not turn against him. He took them down to Mexico, then left them there. Those days you dreamed of slit throats and bowels hanging from the trees. I heard you cry at night.

Mother, you were like a caged animal when you heard that Father left your sons in Mexico. You paced to the rhythm of that name: Mehico, Mehico. Back and forth, the halls of the house beat like a drum under your feet. Later, you packed up the boys' clothing into a wicker trunk like dead children's.

The fox god received many tokens and coins of favor. Wish sticks burned every day in the brazier. The tree outside was covered with white ribbons of prayer. The ribbons quivered in the breezes, delivering their prayers across the ocean.

Tomoko learned from her brothers' letters that they had disguised themselves as Mexicans and walked their way up into California. Once there, they found jobs as migrant workers picking apples, cherries, strawberries, and oranges. The pay was poor and blisters broke open on their feet. "We implore you," they had written to their mother. "Please send us some comfortable grass slippers."

She wanted to believe that her brothers were much safer and better off in America, as her father seemed to believe. There, they didn't have to be conscripted. They could do as they pleased. But Tomoko felt uncertain. She had heard in school that many Americans did not like the Japanese—the "yellow bellies" they were called—with their slant eyes and buckteeth. Monkey people.

Tomoko's father had his back to her when she entered the dark, cool room, his form in the shadows, dark as a door opening to an unknown place. He was distant and cold; she could feel it in the length of his back.

"Father?" Tomoko said, as she shuffled on her knees across the tatami floor and sat at a polite distance from him. She folded her legs under her body on a floor cushion and waited. Her father nodded, acknowledging her presence, but he continued his silence, as if pondering the issue he wished to discuss with her.

Tomoko studied her father. He had on a blue and black checkered yukata, a low black belt which rode his hips and further lengthened his long, lean body.

Father, I look at your back before me and I can only see a difficult door I cannot open. It is dark beyond that door, and I am afraid of its lines. They are sharp, can cut deep.

When I look at your back, I realize now that I have never ridden on it like other children I have seen. You have never offered your hand to me, or touched my face in a caress or affection. I do not know what your body feels like. I've never touched you. It would have been better had I been able to touch you rather than only respect you.

As I look at your arms and hands which slide out of your kimono sleeves, green veins wrap like wires around your muscles, muscles that twitch and twist hard, like a rope—wound and wounding in what is male, you, my father.

After some time had passed, her father cleared his throat and turned to her in profile. He did not look at her. He began by making an effort to speak, then stopped. He cleared his throat several times. Although Tomoko found her father's behavior strange, she did not interrupt him.

"Tomoko," he finally said. "I've—" He stopped to rub his chin. Then, with what must have been held back by suppressed emotion, he said, saliva spraying with the intensity of his words, "I've accepted an inquiry of marriage for you. You're going to Hawai'i."

It was as if he had dropped a bag of rice on Tomoko's lap. A long, stunned silence followed. Tomoko was so surprised she couldn't make a sound. She opened and closed her mouth like a fish, struggling for oxygen in the water.

Summoning courage, she spoke, the words faltering, as if she had not spoken for a long time. She could hardly find the words in the ocean of her surprise. "Father, you can't mean this. I never wanted to go there."

No one spoke against their fathers like this. Discouraged when he said nothing more, Tomoko turned aside, smoothed the lap of her kimono, then looked outside at the serene waterfall in the garden. She couldn't recall how long she watched the water or how long they sat there in silence.

After a while, unable to contain herself, Tomoko said in a rush of words, "You couldn't have, you just couldn't have." She listed as many reasons as she could think of as to why she shouldn't be sent away. "I'll be more useful here. I plan to become a teacher. What will I do, married, and so far away? You'll never see your grandchildren. I'll never see you or Mother again."

Between reasons, she kept repeating, "How could you?" Between reasons her father grunted.

Tomoko saw his face grow longer.

"Please, don't ask me to do what I can't. My life is here, in Japan."

From then on, Tomoko could not stop the words that flew out of her mouth, bad now in their impudence—lizard tails, dog paws, sow ears.

What made you accept this marriage proposal? I do not know what the answer is. Is it just another one of your feelings? I understand why you sent my brothers away. They are men and men need new roots. But I bring nothing to you. My bride price is negligible. I do not know how to work in the fields. My feet and hands are awkward and large. I don't know how to dry the fish or strip the gourd meat or plant pumpkin seeds.

If you send me away now, surely I will shrivel up like a persimmon. I will dry out like shiitake and become crusty like kelp in the sun.

I am useless. I have been schooled but not prepared for the kind of life I see you making for me. I am not prepared to be a farmer's wife in some far-off country. I don't know how to wield a hoe. I don't know how to make bathwater.

"Did I send you to school to go against me?" her father snarled. "Did I send you so you can whine like a cat, bleat like a mountain goat? Then the schooling has been wasted. I never promised you anything."

"But I thought you always understood what I wanted? I would have done well as a teacher. I would have made you proud of me."

"It was a silly indulgence on my part, to have sent you to school."

"Sending me to school was the best thing you could have done."

"Yame. Enough of this. You will do as I ask!"

"It's no good, I can't."

"You dare go against me? You will not shame the Morishige family! Our word is our word, and I will not tolerate this insolence. I will disown you, if you don't listen. You will never be able to set foot in this house again." He stood up and towered over Tomoko.

If I go out of this house forever, it would only hurt my mother, my poor mother. I cannot do this to her. I cannot bear to see the tears swimming in her eyes and her powerlessness to stop my banishment. It would break her heart more than if I were to go to another country, although going to another country is like death.

For her sake, I will go away.

Her father said in a quiet, resolute voice, "I struck a bargain with this man and his go-between. You will do as I ask. I will hear no more."

Her father sat down. He slammed his fist on a table before him, angered by the impertinence of his daughter. A small, unlit brazier overturned, and charcoal dust coiled into the air.

Tomoko was shaken. Her strength and spirit fell like a flimsy millet-thatch cottage.

So you struck a bargain with a man as if I were fish or vegetable for the table. How easy it must have been for you to do this, as if I were one of your bags of rice.

Too, you have put me in my place by the thunder of your anger. I am frightened by it. Your temper has silenced my mouth in this first swallowing of my tongue. And you feel nothing for me, you feel no pity. There is only hardness in your face, in the wanting of your way.

Mother fought for me in the best way she knew how. That is why she sent Yuri-chan out of the house earlier in the day. I understand now why my mother has been crying. But she swims alone in her fight with you. She skirts the dark rocks, fights the swift currents. She is a lonely fish in this house.

Outside a fine rain began. Tomoko no longer pushed the matter with her father. She was left with the sounds in the room: the pattering of rain on the rooftops, its sweep on the stepping-stones, its escape through the trees, and the sound of her father's heavy breathing. She saw the straining of his muscles beneath his skin, the anger in his body that she had aroused.

She knew that the situation was hopeless. The matter could no longer be negotiated by her arguments. She sat there without a sound and stared at his back. She swallowed her cries. Tomoko felt the earth tilt and yaw, a crevice open, and widen forever, her father standing on one side, she on the other.

I look up at your face and I must turn away. There is no tenderness when I look at you. Your iron mouth, your rock chin, your ice eyes, your curled fists, your granite will.

Something happened to Tomoko at that moment, when she held back her crying, when she held back making a sound. She learned what was in keeping with the withholding of one's wishes. She thought of her mother and understood why she worshiped her gods and read faces, a pastime to cover her own, unstated wishes.

Tomoko used to laugh at her mother—at her mother's frog charms, the word charms, the bird charms, hanging from her wrist, above the beds, on doorknobs. But no longer. Tomoko knew that she, too, would carry these charms with her to the new country.

In the privacy of her room, Tomoko dropped to the floor and cried. Yuri-chan stole into the room after her.

"Don't cry, Tomoko," she said. "When Father stopped me from going to school, I cried, too, remember? But I couldn't do anything."

"I know. But why is Papa like this? Why is it that he wants to send me away and you get to stay?"

"I don't know. Maybe I'm not as smart or as brave as you. Mother says that in the end it will be good for you, to get away from Father. From Japan."

"You believe her?"

"Yes, I do."

"Why?"

Her sister shrugged her shoulders and left the room.

In the morning Tomoko's eyes were swollen like the rice terraces after a hard rain, and for the first time in her life she felt as if she were floating without purpose. Now, even the thought of school seemed remote, as far as the foreign country she was going to. Some people said it was a place where men became rich and mud grew between their toes. She didn't believe it.

They had come one evening not long ago, the group of men. It was not unusual. Men had frequently come to the house on "men's business." Tomoko remembered having served them tea. Mr. Tanaka was there, a Mr. Sakata from Yamaguchi-ken, Tomoko's Uncle Terao, and some others. The women knew nothing about what went on behind these doors.

Mr. Sakoda, Tomoko learned later, was the go-between who initiated the transaction with Tomoko's father. Tomoko could envision it, the men talking in their negotiations, arranging her marriage:

"Mr. Hayashi from Hawai'i wishes to marry your daughter."

"That so?"

"Yes."

"Where does he come from?"

"Yamaguchi. He's a good man, but needs a wife."

"But my daughter, she's not a farmer's daughter. She is useless. I sent her to school and she has learned only book work."

"He understands that. He will try to give her a good life. While he is only a farmer right now, working in the cane fields, he plans to become a merchant like you someday."

"Saaa. As I said, my daughter is useless. She cannot cook. The chickens she goes to kill will run from her, and the cows will kick her chair when she goes to milk them."

"Mr. Hayashi understands that. He sends you this sake, this bushel of rice, and twenty American dollars for good faith. He will take good care of your daughter."

"But it's not the money. I just think it's a good idea for Tomoko to get out of Japan. I want all my children out of this country except for my youngest one. A strong wind blows against my back. I see it in my wife's eyes. Difficult times are coming our way. Nobody understands this, least of all my daughter."

The negotiations had gone on into the night. Tomoko remembered falling asleep to the drone of men's voices in the meeting room, and later, when the men got up to leave, she found herself sleeping on her arm.

Tomoko remembered how everyone had stopped talking when she entered with the tea and rice cakes. She was introduced to the men by her father but did not find that any different from other meetings held at the house. He often had men there when they negotiated the price of rice.

If the men scrutinized her at the moment as someone's future bride, she was not aware of it. Even Mr. Tanaka's comment, which made her blush, did not seem out of place. "Someday, you'll make someone a good wife," he had said. It was nothing new, coming from him. He always said things like that to her, the snake that he was.

Tomoko felt a stab of anger when she thought of the men plotting their wishes against her. "Once the rain pushes against the floodgates of the rice paddies and the gates cannot hold back the water, there is no way to stop the flooding of the fields," her older brother once said when she asked why he had to go away. Now she understood what he meant.

Her father had arranged a marriage to a man twelve years older than Tomoko. According to the Japanese, it was good for a man to have a younger wife; a young wife could take care of her husband in his sickness and old age. Though the man was an only son, he had moved away. Only sons did not go wandering off to other countries unless something awful made them leave. She wondered what this man was running away from. And what kind of man was he, that he could leave his parents to face their old age alone? Who would tend their fires; who would rub their backs?

The man soon sent Tomoko his picture. He also sent money to her father to build a tansu for her. "See?" her father said when he received the money. "He is a good man. He thinks about your comfort." Inside herself, Tomoko did not feel appeased, but felt keenly the blade of her future husband and the betrayal of her father.

Late one night, soon after she received it, Tomoko twirled the man's picture in the light of the winter fire. Stern and complicated. That's what the man's face looked like. It looked uncompromising as her father's. A large man, he had an up-and-down face, the kind her mother had warned her about. Already she felt disagreeable toward him.

Her mother slipped into her room. She took the man's picture from Tomoko's hands and looked at it as if she were reading his face. Then she placed the picture between the two of them and nodded toward the mirror. Tomoko and her mother turned themselves around to look into it. Framed in the mirror like a picture, Tomoko understood all too well the moment that was held in that subdued light.

Mother, you will lose my name and face the same way you lost your sons. Soon you will be out of the picture. Instead, a strange man will be by my side. I dare not ask you what you see in his face.

The days before Tomoko's departure, her mother tried to smooth things over between Tomoko and her father. She flitted about like a spring bee among the azaleas and camellias, trying to get them to mend their breach.

"Tomo-chan, it is not good to go away without clearing things up between you two. It is like death. Make your house clean, make your soul clean. Don't leave the house in a bad way. Let in the air, let in the birds," her mother pleaded.

"Mama. I will do as I am told. Don't ask anything more of me."

As if to lessen the hurt, Tomoko's mother tried to placate her daughter by listing the concessions made in this marriage contract. "It's an easy contract. At least you don't have to go and live with your in-laws for a year. At least you don't have to cook their food, prepare their mustard, draw the water for their baths. Many girls must stay with their in-laws before leaving for America. It is customary. But I heard his father is a drunk. Your husband-to-be spared you the unpleasant task of having to care for them. All in all, I think he is kind. He doesn't want you to face the hardship of having to deal with a no-good father-in-law." She continued in afterthought. "Your father, too, has your best interest at heart. He wants you to go to America. There, life will be easier. Can't you see this is what he wants for you?"

"I can't, but it's all right, Mother," she reassured.

Tomoko, her mother, and sister filled their last days together sewing and packing Tomoko's clothing. Her mother and Yuri-chan helped to sew her wedding kimono and the American-style dresses she would wear in her new country.

The women laughed whenever Tomoko modeled this foreign clothing. Her mother cupped her elbow, rested her hand on her tilted face as she looked at her daughter in her dresses. She moved her hands over her mouth to laugh at the puffy clothes her daughter wore. As Tomoko looked at herself in the mirror, her mother shifted the fabric of the skirt this way and that. Daringly, she hiked up the length of her daughter's skirt above the ankles and the women were convulsed with laughter at this display of boldness.

"You're spending too much money," Tomoko's father said, seeing bolts of fabric being delivered to the house.

"It is none of your concern. This is women's work." Tomoko's mother said. She turned her back on him and ignored his complaints. She held him at a greater distance with each new silk kimono the women worked on. Rarely did she talk to her husband during this time.

Tomoko then had her picture taken at the Iwata Shashin Studio, one in a kimono, another in a white dress, her hair down like girls in America. Later, her mother painstakingly folded the garments and packed them away in small and special ways. She hummed as she folded them, each note taken into the fabric, a mournful chant of lament.

The women formed an impregnable world all their own before Tomoko's departure. While the rift widened between Tomoko and her father, a strange courage surfaced among the women. Three heads bent down over their sewing during their last days together appeared more formidable than ten thousand Bakufu warriors. Tomoko's father could not approach the door to the room without suffering a word of dismissal, a cold eye. He stayed away while the women worked like summer bees.

As the date to leave neared, Yuri-chan and her mother prepared some of Tomoko's favorite foods. The two women staying behind cooked as if for a banquet. Shopkeepers made deliveries of food reserved for grand occasions or the New Year. Seven good luck vegetables, buckwheat noodles, red fish, quail eggs, meat.

"Tomoko, eat to your heart's content."

"Honestly Mother, Yuri-chan, it's not as if I'm going to *die*."

"This is in place of your wedding feast. Your sister and I will not be there. We would like to celebrate with you before you leave."

"I do not know if this wedding is for celebrating, Mother."

"Eat, eat many hardship beans. Eat them away. Here, eat the sea kelp. It will keep you healthy and strong. Have more lotus root. And burdock, some chicken stew, fish, and shrimp." She heaped Tomoko's plate with food.

When once she would have been embarrassed by this display of affection lavished upon her, Tomoko no longer felt uneasy. She feasted on their goodwill.

"It will be good for you, Tomoko. You'll see," her mother said.

It was the night before she was to leave. Tomoko heard her father singing in a drunken stupor. He clapped his hands and whined. He then sang a made-up song for all of them to hear: "The moon comes out and my daughter leaves this shore. She thinks I am not sad but I cry for her—" The rest of the song became incoherent as his head rolled on his chest.

The women then heard him stagger and fall on the floor. He banged into the doors of his room and shattered the delicate paper with his flapping hands. But no one went to him. No one consoled him or gave him their pity. "So noisy," her mother said as she dismissed her husband's discordant singing as if it didn't exist.

When her mother and sister entered Tomoko's room for the last time, the sound of her father's singing drifted into the cold night filled with stars. "A good omen," their mother said, looking out, relieved and happy for her daughter. "Come here, my daughter. Let me see your face once more. I don't ever want to forget it. Let me pray to the fox god for you. Let me pray to the seven gods of goodwill. Look what the stars say. They show signs of a good life."

No one talked for the longest time, sadness pouring into their hearts. Then, as if filled to the brim and no longer able to hold themselves upright, Tomoko's mother and her sister bowed elaborately, spilling themselves onto the floor like overturned urns. Tomoko wanted to feel the warmth of their bodies in her hands. She wanted to feel their soft skin and tears on her own cheeks.

But they didn't touch. The women's heads swept the tatami as their prostrate bodies shook with sobs. Although the women did not embrace each other in good-bye, Tomoko knew that they loved each other in an abiding way. Her heart embraced them with the swell of a wave that broke over them.

In their little ceremony, Tomoko also bowed, sweepingly, before her mother and sister. "Mother. Yuri-chan." Tomoko murmured their names. She knew she would never see them again.

Mother, I wish you bright morning and sweet evening prayers; white blossoms on every tree; vibrant cicadas in the brush; large crickets in every cricket cage; mountains of rice in each bowl; the clear song of locusts in the grass; squid on your plates; sugi leaves from the mountains in your flower arrangements; combs to beautify your hair; sandals to cushion your feet; willow branches to weave your baskets; yards of silk to wear; the soothing rustle of the rushes by the river; fine horsehair brushes for your drawings; kingyo in your ponds; river-polished stones to toss; the long life of turtles; a songbird on every rafter; a colorful parasol to shield your face from the sun; fans to keep you cool; thick braziers to keep you warm in cold winters; songs to lift your heart; hours to sing your sutras, tend your flowers, pour sweet tea over the Buddha; feathers for your pillows; seashells to string, to dance in the wind; sounds of the flute at night; fireflies to light your lanterns; poems of luck against ill fortune; the fragrance of peaches in the air. I wish you silk coats and silver hair trinkets; I wish you first bathwaters; I wish you to see my brothers.

I wish you to touch my face, once more, before you die.

Outside the temple bells rang. A strong wind pushed its way through the rice grass in the water. In the light of the rising moon, terrace upon terrace shimmered in silver ripples.

The Doctor

Stirring the vegetable stew of carrots, radishes, and dasheen over a slow fire, Shigemi Takemoto peered out of her kitchen window, the view distorted by a fracture across the surface of the pane. "Mmm, I wonder what the matter is?"

Mrs. Kiyota of Kiyota Store was running toward the house. Shigemi flung open her screen door and hurried out to meet her friend.

"Hurry," Mrs. Kiyota was saying and rotating one arm in the motions of a waterwheel. She had her other hand cupped around her mouth as if to better direct her voice toward Shigemi.

Like the other families in Kaiwiki, mostly cane growers on this part of the Big Island, the Takemotos bought their staples from Kiyota Store and charged whatever they bought there. Shigemi went to the Kiyota's establishment to buy the tofu, yam cakes, bonito flakes, and 'ōpelu she could barely afford.

Shigemi looked upon Mrs. Kiyota as her best friend, this as much as circumstances allowed, their friendship largely based on obligation because the Takemotos owed food money to the Kiyotas. Occasionally, the women stopped to chat, but the talk was one-sided, usually on the shopkeeper's part. The Kiyotas also had one of the only telephones in the neighborhood and everyone was able to use the phone or be summoned by it.

"What happened?" Shigemi asked when Mrs. Kiyota reached the house. Water dripped from her hands as she spoke, a burdock root she was scraping still in her grip.

Mrs. Kiyota said between breaths: "Big trouble. Your husband was hurt in a car accident. He's in Matsuyama Hospital right now."

Mrs. Kiyota looked up at Shigemi's face, as if she were sorry for her friend's life, which was rimmed with the crust of hardship, her own circumstances more adequately fixed. Shigemi caught her friend's reaction of smugness and felt angry at first, then a surge of embarrassment for her friend. Dismissing the feeling, she asked, "When did this happen?"

"Not too long ago."

Shigemi dropped the burdock root on her foot. "And—?"

"The car your husband had been riding in fell into a ditch near Camp Two, Wainaku area."

"Is he all right?"

Mrs. Kiyota nodded. Shigemi moved up to grab Mrs. Kiyota by the shoulders. "You sure? You say he's at Matsuyama Hospital?"

"The hospital called the store. They wanted me to tell you that your husband had been in an accident. But don't worry. Matsuyama Sensei is a fine doctor. Why, just a couple of years ago—"

Shigemi wound her hands around her body and did not hear the rest of her friend's account. Her body felt light, something like freedom, when the thought crossed her mind that her husband might be dead. It was, however, a momentary lapse toward some possibility and nothing to hope for. Guilt quickly washed over her like water. Surely bachi would fall upon her for thinking these thoughts.

After Mrs. Kiyota left, promising to call a taxi, Shigemi hurriedly slipped into her day kimono. After dressing and informing her daughter about what happened, she ran out of the house and down to the Kiyota's place where the taxi would be waiting to take her to the Matsuyama Hospital in Hilo. *I wonder what he was doing in a car? He didn't say he was going anywhere. At least he didn't fall into one of the ravines or into the river below.*

The ride to the hospital seemed short as Shigemi went over the events of the day. She patted a film of perspiration on her forehead and above her lips with a handkerchief. Before long, the taxi swung into the carport in front of the hospital. She leaned forward to hand Mr. Tomita, the taxi driver, her fare and eased herself out of the heavy, black sedan. The man grunted in a surly manner, not bothering to open the door.

Matsuyama Hospital was one of the numerous Japanese hospitals that the Japanese immigrants patronized and the territorial government of Hawai'i regulated before the war. Cheap, convenient, these hospitals were popular with the Japanese, who liked being looked after by their "own kind" even if they characterized some of these doctors as "horse doctors."

Once inside the hospital, a petite nurse showed Shigemi into the waiting area. Dotted Swiss half-curtains draped the windows and a green, flower-patterned linoleum covered the floor. She waited for a long while on a hard, green wooden bench, where she could see down a long, poorly lit corridor with low ceilings. The place smelled of old alcohol and stale ether.

Finally, the doctor appeared from what must have been an examining room. Shigemi heard a barely audible click as the door closed. The doctor walked toward her.

Shigemi stood up and bowed. She had expected a much older man so was startled by his youthful appearance. The doctor looked to be in his late twenties, but Shigemi knew that he must have been at least ten years older than that. She quickly discerned, despite sagging her head to cast her eyes on the floor, that he had a tall nose, strong chin and face. She had seen him before, but from afar, and not as close as at this moment.

"Sensei," she said as she walked up to him in a half-bow, her hands folded in front of her kimono. She bowed again in respect for him and his profession.

The doctor looked at her and nodded his head in recognition, his white, heavily starched uniform crinkling, as though he had just put it on. In discomfort, Shigemi saw how he stared at her.

"I remember you. My father treated you when you had a fever many years ago. I used to make rounds with my father when he went into the camps—that is, before I went away to school." *Pat, pat, pat.*

Shigemi tried not to notice the doctor's patting of his face. And it was a handsome face despite the long scar on one side of it. The scar made his boyish face look rugged, even a bit arrogant. She tried to avert her eyes, but was compelled to look at the scar because of the unusual direction it took, making a tapering upswing toward his temple from his jaw.

As if provoked, the doctor said, "Go ahead, look at it. Everyone wants to when they first meet me."

It astonished Shigemi that he would say this on their first meeting. She gulped down her embarrassment.

People in town knew all about it. When the doctor was a young boy, he got kicked in the face by a horse while helping his father put a belligerent patient into a hospital carriage. The man's screaming had caused the horses to draw back in fear, rear, and kick into the air. While the boy tried to calm the horses, one of them pawed above his head and on a downstroke, struck his face with its hoof. The senior Matsuyama, in his haste to stitch his son's face and to avoid the wrath of his wife, botched the job, damaging some of his son's facial nerves. This, Shigemi had heard somewhere, caused the boy's face to twitch mildly and feel numb. To counteract these sensations, the doctor had apparently taken to hitting the side of his face.

"I'm sorry. I didn't mean to stare." She moved her eyes down to her feet, ashamed of herself. After what seemed to be a considerable length of time, she lifted her head to find him still looking at her, this time with an amused smirk.

Stammering, she gathered enough strength to ask about her husband, eclipsed, momentarily, by her encounter with the doctor. "Is my husband all right? Was he badly injured?"

"No, not badly. He's banged up a bit, but you don't have to worry. He fractured a rib and hit his head. He'll have to stay in the hospital for a couple of days." *Pat, pat, pat.*

"He has to stay in the hospital? Why can't he go home today? Please, you must let him go." She smoothed the front of her kimono anxiously.

"But I'd like to watch him here at the hospital." *Pat, pat, pat.*

"You don't understand. We just don't have the money. We can't afford—" She lowered her voice in disgrace.

"Don't worry, I'll arrange something."

"But Sensei," Shigemi said, extending her hand as though to touch him or to make him wait. Dr. Matsuyama simply shook his head to negate her discomfort. He patted her shoulder.

Shigemi didn't know what to make of his manner. For a second she was very aware of his nearness and felt his breath sweep across her face. If he said that everything would be all right, maybe he was going to reduce the charges or make a manageable payment schedule considering her husband's accident. Before she could ask him about what he proposed to do, he walked away.

Reassured by the doctor's solicitous manner, Shigemi decided she would let her husband stay in the hospital and not worry about the money. She walked down the hallway and proceeded to her husband's room.

She put on a cheerful face and walked in. "Papa?" She said this in a calm voice she had mastered with him. A flat, nonemotional tone worked best when she communicated with her husband, who could overreact with her.

"I was learning how to drive when . . . I wanted to surprise you. Mr. Kano said that he would teach me how to drive, so I went along with him."

He was giving something as close to an apology as was possible for him. She knew that what he had just said was difficult. "Was Kano-san hurt, too?" she asked.

"No, no. He's okay."

"Then it's all right, Papa. You can learn how to drive after you get well."

Relief showed on her husband's face. He looked glad that she had taken a different tact and was not angry with him. Shigemi had learned that her husband would only get angrier if she showed her own anger, and they would be pulled away into silence.

The next day, Dr. Matsuyama appeared, unexpectedly, at the Takemotos' front door. Shigemi had been dusting the house, her hair wrapped in a kerchief, when she spotted him. She felt flustered upon seeing him there, scuffing his shoes on the mat, his hat in his hand. He stood and waited on the verandah. After her initial surprise, Shigemi whipped off her kerchief, fluffed her hair, and poked in the wayward strands around her face.

"Gomen nasai, excuse me," Shigemi said, louder than usual for her. Rarely did anyone come to the house.

"I must be the one to apologize for this intrusion."

"Oh, no. Excuse *me* on my part." Shigemi dropped her eyes. "This is a most humble house."

Indeed, everything inside looked worn. Her years of cleaning, dusting, sweeping, and mopping merely resulted in a cycle of endless poverty with nothing to show for it; nothing ever looking different—only more shabby.

"No, no, I was in the area so I dropped by to see you." *Pat, pat, pat.*

"Thank you." Shigemi bowed down to her knees. "To have come here specially, waza-waza, to see me in your busy schedule . . . but is anything the matter with my husband?"

"Oh no. It's nothing like that. There's something I want to talk over with you. But it's a private matter, so—is anyone at home besides you?"

He loosened his tie, rolled up his shirt cuff, lifted off his straw hat at the brim, all in one extended moment.

"Yes. There's my daughter, Hanayo. But don't worry. I will send her out to do an errand for me."

Shigemi made herself small before the doctor and shuffled into the kitchen. "Please go to Kiyota Store and retrieve the mail," she said to her daughter. "And wait at the store for me. I have some business to talk over with the doctor."

Her daughter was only too glad to be released from her chores and gaily left the house, her cloth bag swinging from her wrist.

Shigemi returned to where the doctor stood on the front porch and said, "My daughter can talk to people who stop by the store while she waits. Usually a friend or two will come by. It's a lively spot."

Shigemi asked the doctor in. "You must forgive our dirty house that is not fit for your feet. Doozo," she said and directed the doctor where to go with an open palm. She showed him a zabuton beside a low table. It was the best sitting place in the house; her husband and guests sat there. The right cross breezes passed through and the sun did not get into one's eyes from the window facing south. *Pat, pat, pat.*

The doctor settled himself casually on the floor and crossed his legs. He dabbed his forehead with a folded handkerchief and inserted it into his back pocket as he lifted one hip.

Shigemi sat next to the doctor, blocking the view of the kitchen entrance. Unsightly, the kitchen was the ugliest and dirtiest room in the house so she was glad he did not have a full view of it, for form was important when having such a respected and auspicious guest as a doctor in the house. Shigemi paid careful attention to these details even if the house was probably pitiful looking in his eyes.

"I'm so sorry. We have very little to offer you, but please have some tea."

"Don't bother yourself." *Slap, slap, slap.*

"Really, Sensei, it's no bother. I am deeply honored that you are here."

"I am the one privileged." *Slap, slap, slap.*

"Please."

"Well, in that case, some tea will be fine." *SLAP, SLAP, SLAP.*

Shigemi spun herself around on her knees, stood up, and moved to make tea from water that was always simmering on the stove. She blew on a blue Kutani plate and wiped it with her kimono sleeve. She layered rice crackers on this dish that luckily was not chipped, the dish about the only decent thing she had around.

Entering the room once more, Shigemi sat next to the doctor, ready to serve him, her arm tilted in an angle of pouring of the tea. "Doozo. Please help yourself."

She gestured at the meager snack she had presented artfully on the plate on the black lacquer tray. Her mother always said that things tasted better if they were presented well, especially when there was so little to be had. She held her breath, wanting to do what was proper.

It was at this moment that Shigemi noticed the doctor following her every move as she held the teapot, her one hand holding the pot cover, then placing the pot back on the bamboo trivet.

The doctor's hands were moving more incessantly now—from his face, then back to his cup. *SLAP, SLAP, SLAP.*

Unnerved, Shigemi tucked more of her stray hair into her bun. "Sensei," she said, "is there anything the matter? Is my husband all right? Is there something you're not telling me that I should know about?"

"Oh, no." He waved his hand to calm her down. "Nothing like that. Actually, I came to talk to you, regarding the payments for his treatment."

"As I said before, we have very little . . . but I'll work out a schedule with your approval."

The doctor nodded his head but still appeared agitated. "Well you can pay me," he said.

"Oh, how?"

"There's a way." He put down his teacup and looked at Shigemi intently. Suddenly, he darted one hand out and grasped her right wrist. He hit his face with the other. *SLAP, SLAP, SLAP.*

"A-re maa. My goodness!" Shigemi, surprised by the action and the quickness of his hand, twisted her wrist and pulled back. She struggled backward on her knees like a horse that had just been lassoed. She desperately tried to tear herself away from him.

But the doctor only tightened his hold on her. Stunned, she couldn't scream. The doctor jerked her forward, toward him. She pulled herself away, but as he was so much stronger, he simply pulled her back in. Finally, when close to his face, she could smell the heaviness of his moist breath. He said in a low, flat voice, "You won't get hurt if you do as I say."

Shigemi fought to loosen her arm. The doctor tightened his grasp even more until Shigemi thought she had lost her hand; she no longer had any feeling in it.

"What do you intend to do?" she asked, her voice hoarse and raspy. She realized how strong the doctor was and remembered having heard people say that after his accident he had exercised diligently so as to be able to control *any* horse he encountered.

"You know what I want."

"I guess I don't have much of a choice, do I?" Her teeth chattered uncontrollably.

"No, you don't."

Shigemi saw him run his tongue over his lips. *SLAP, SLAP, SLAP.* "And. . .and this releases me from all further obligations regarding payment?" she asked.

The doctor nodded his head unconvincingly as he looked at her face.

Shigemi squirmed in disgust when he covered her mouth, first with his hand, then his lips. In distaste for his breath and the smell of him, Shigemi contorted her body away from him, which made him more adamant in his want of her, his arms coming over her like an octopus.

Once certain that Shigemi would comply and had stopped moving so wildly, the doctor lifted his lips to answer her. "Sure, of course, you'll be free of all obligations," he said, his voice flat, disingenuous. He slapped his face with his free hand.

He then muttered something incoherent. He nuzzled himself against her breasts. After a while, he pulled himself away, looked at her face, then brought his free hand up to touch her cheek. "You're so pretty, did you know that? Your skin, your eyes."

"That doesn't mean anything to me," Shigemi said, beginning to cry. "And I'm a much older woman. What do you want with such an old woman when there are so many young ones around?"

"When I first saw you many years ago, young as I was, I wanted you." He fumbled with her clothing. She felt his warm tea breath on the nape of her neck as he folded her down, like a fan.

Shigemi felt the weight, the dread weight of his body rise and fall on her.

It was only then that she realized that the slapping had stopped. All was quiet. It was as if she were being pulled into a terrible calm, as in the early mornings or before a storm or an evening when no wind whipped through the cane and raced through the surrounding trees. She had entered a place so still that something had shifted irretrievably in her life and she would never be the same.

She turned her face away from the doctor as they lay on the floor. Now, awakening into a different world and its sounds—the rain outside and the wind shifting restlessly through the moment—she felt herself falling over a thundering waterfall of sadness. She had no will to fight him. It was useless; besides, he was too strong for her. She clenched her fists, bit into them, and cried.

Quails and field chickens scattered as if from under her feet, and a sudden gust of wind made the curtains sail out of the windows.

The next day, Shigemi went to the hospital to take her husband out. She decided she would take care of him at home and was relieved when she did not see the doctor around.

"Shigemi," her husband said, while Shigemi helped him to dress, "I talked to the doctor about the payments we have to make. For the bill."

"Huh? I also—" Shigemi began to say, but did not continue as she lowered her head and listened to her husband.

"Didn't the doctor tell you? He said he spoke to you yesterday. He and I decided that the best way to pay him would be to have Hanayo work for him. Isn't this a good thing? Hanayo will quit school and work here, at the hospital. She will be in charge of the doctor's children and help the doctor's wife. That's how we will pay off this debt."

"Hanayo?"

It took all of Shigemi's strength to say nothing, to keep folding her husband's shirt. She draped it over one arm, like a towel, in her astonishment. She simply couldn't tell her husband how *she* had already made payment to the doctor. How would she explain what she was made to do? Shigemi, all of a sudden restless, began pacing the floor. "I forbid her to go. She's too young. She needs to go to school," she said.

"But this is the only way I can pay the doctor for his services. Don't you see?"

"Surely, there must be some other way to pay him back." Shigemi, grabbed her husband's hands and cried into them. "Please, Otōsan, I beg you."

"What's wrong?" Takeo looked puzzled. He was not very sympathetic and pushed her hands away. He said, fire in his eyes, "That's enough. Don't be selfish."

"Yes, *don't be selfish,*" Shigemi said, chastened by this turn of events—her voice barely audible, choked by having been fooled by the doctor.

After dressing, her husband moaned as he straightened himself out. With Shigemi's support, he hobbled out of the hospital into the waiting taxi. When leaving the hospital wing, Shigemi was certain that she saw a curtain part in an upper window, then drop.

That evening, before bed, Shigemi prayed to the gods of her household shrine and bowed to the west. A cruel ghost had swept through the house.

Dr. Matsuyama, one of the first of many young Japanese doctors to graduate from a big American university, had a young wife, two daughters, a white colonial-style plantation house at the edge of town, and adjoining quarters that served as the hospital in a thriving and lucrative practice. The Japanese community respected the young doctor as they had respected his father; they also liked him because he was humble, spoke fluent Japanese, and was skillful in his treatments. With such a flawless reputation, Shigemi knew she could not fight him. She heard nothing but glowing accounts from people who held him in high esteem. He could do no wrong. But Shigemi's greatest concern was that he not harm Hanayo. She went to see the doctor before bringing Hanayo to stay with him and his family, to ensure her daughter's safety. She went to his office.

"Please, Sensei, about my daughter. Out of the goodness in your heart, please don't touch her. Hanayo is still a young girl. Only fourteen. You've made a fool of me, but spare her."

Shigemi slumped to the floor. Moving on her knees in supplication up to where he sat, she took the doctor's hand into hers and said, "Promise me that much. I'll do anything."

He rose, brushed aside Shigemi's hands, then walked to the window and turned his back to the room as he looked out. "You must come to me when you can. Maybe then I will consider not touching your daughter. Also, you will pay me for what your husband owes—I will deduct it from Hanayo's wages." *Pat, pat, pat.*

"Why you despicable beast—"

"Beast, eh? There's no other way to do it without your husband suspecting something." He whirled around, braced himself against the windowsill, and looked at Shigemi without flinching. "Don't you see?"

"Why did you have to choose me? Why do I have to be the one?"

At first, she sagged her shoulders and head, but in a sudden move, she stood up and advanced toward the doctor with an open hand, ready to slap him. He caught her by her wrist. He then pulled her stiffened hand up to his face. Looking at her, he gently rubbed her hand on his scar. Shigemi hated the feeling. There was something unredeeming about how it felt. It was ugly, mean, a scar of his soul, rather than his face.

The night Shigemi's husband told Hanayo that she would have to quit school and work for Dr. Matsuyama she cried all night. "Please Mama, talk to Papa for me. Tell him I want to stay in school."

"No. We will always do the right things. In life, things take time. You can go to school later."

Hanayo was not convinced. She took her mother's reluctant manner and tone as a sign of her mother's resistance to the idea and took the opportunity to play on her sympathy.

"Mama, I'm still young. I don't want to be a housemaid. Mieko Horita says that I would be better off if I worked for her mother at their dry goods store than for the doctor. I could still go to school that way."

"Mieko this. Mieko that. Stop it. They have more money than we do, so it's easy for her to talk. We can't do what our neighbors can. You see too much. Close your eyes, don't look!"

Shigemi was now adequately stern. A promise was a promise and it was something that the family would keep.

Hanayo had already been working for several months at the Matsuyama's household. One day when Shigemi's husband had gone far afield, Dr. Matsuyama dropped by to see Shigemi, as he did from time to time, waiting for the opportunity to be alone with her.

That same day, Mrs. Kiyota came to call. Shigemi had rarely seen her friend these days, except when she rushed over to the store to buy something or to use the telephone.

"Shigemi. It's been a long time, hasn't it? I don't see much of you these days," she said at the doorway.

She had a loud lilt to her voice. However, upon noticing Dr. Matsuyama in the shadow of the small living area, she pulled herself back like a tree snail when touched, and mumbled her apologies: "Oh, I'm so sorry. I didn't mean to. I didn't know you had company, Shigemi. Please forgive me."

"Oh, no. You couldn't have known the doctor was here," Shigemi said. "But please, do come in. You don't need to apologize. The doctor is here on some business matter. He remembers treating your boy recently for a boil. Let's all have some tea."

To Shigemi's disappointment, Mrs. Kiyota quickly withdrew herself from the house. She had wanted the woman to stay, but Mrs. Kiyota moved backward in a half-bow and slid her slippers back on. She dismissed herself as was the proper and polite thing to do when other people had guests in their home, her retreat final, even if she looked curious and acted as though she wanted to stay.

The doctor had visited the Kiyotas a few times during the year to treat their son. After one such visit, Shigemi remembered Mrs. Kiyota saying briefly that she, Mrs. Kiyota, wanted the respective families to get together and to become more intimate in their relationship because they had much in common.

Today, Shigemi saw that her friend's face looked puzzled, as if she couldn't understand why the doctor was at the Takemotos for she hadn't heard of anyone being sick at her friend's house. Shigemi also knew that Mrs. Kiyota could neither think, nor much less believe, that the doctor's family and the Takemotos could be on friendly social terms. After all, they were different in *status*. Shigemi knew that her friend wanted to hurry home to consult her husband about this interesting situation.

Shigemi also speculated that Mrs. Kiyota withdrew because Dr. Matsuyama had greeted her rather coldly. She wished the doctor had been warmer to her friend. Such a special guest as the doctor in Shigemi's home would have made Mrs. Kiyota linger if he had only shown signs of being more receptive, accommodating. After all, thought Shigemi, the woman would have wanted to know more about the doctor's business, wouldn't she?

Shigemi watched her friend retreat from the house. *Slap, slap, slap.* She wished her friend could have stayed longer to visit. Maybe by that time, too, the doctor would get tired and leave, or her husband would come home, sparing Shigemi from having to fulfill her obligation.

SLAP, SLAP, SLAP. She heard the doctor clear his throat behind her and slowly make a move toward where she stood looking out. It was too late to stop him now, but not before she had seen, from the window, Mrs. Kiyota looked back while on the walkway that circled the house. It was at this precise moment that the doctor had slapped his cheek with uncommon enthusiasm.

The scrunched expression on Mrs. Kiyota's face suggested that she thought it strange, that what sounded like the doctor's slapping could be carried so far and clearly in the wind, the slapping sounding excited and unusually loud.

Educating Amy

Marrying a woman from the same prefecture in Japan should have ensured the compatibility of Bunye Sasaki and Kimie Kubota as surely as all the stars had foretold. But soon after Kimie came to Hawai'i from Hiroshima as Bunye's picture bride, and soon after the mass Shinto wedding ceremony on the dock where the couple got married in Hilo, Bunye found his new wife high-strung and difficult to please.

Kimie, on the other hand, quickly learned that her new husband was too soft for her liking and would not get ahead in life. In her heart of hearts, she entertained a desire to become high-class, rich, the lack of prospects gradually turning into resentment of gigantic proportions, her resentment taking the form of late dinners, snide remarks, money secretly saved, old water for the bath. But divorce was out of the question. Although she was independent, Kimie's sense of duty was deeply ingrained. Generations heavy, it bound her more stubbornly to the idea that she was to make the most of things no matter what the circumstances were. These feelings, however, did not stop her from mocking her husband, or Hawai'i, her new home.

"Hawai'i's too hot, too sticky. In Japan, I lived near a beautiful field and a bubbling stream. It was always cool, never like this."

"You lack reality. It was a stinky village," Bunye said of the place he and Kimie had come from. Their houses were thatched, cold, nothing but hovels. He couldn't dream of ever going back. The thought of having to return there made him shudder. He did not like the isolation, the humid summers and cold winters, the irritating sounds of the cicadas, the bottle-green horseflies swarming *zuuu zuuu*, the honey pots, and the small houses.

At first, the couple had time to be conjugal in the discovery of each other's bodies and ways—a combination of curiosity and ownership. But they were awkward partners—Bunye thin and lissome, Kimie squat and heavy. As the years passed their intimacy lessened naturally and occurred only out of need, as in the necessity to blink one's eye or to blow one's nose.

Conceived early in their marriage, their first daughter died in infancy. To Bunye's surprise, Kimie became pregnant several years later and gave birth to another girl. They named this child Amy. The couple compromised on her name, Bunye wanting to give his daughter an American name, Kimie, something Japanese.

Bunye indulged his only daughter. Days he did not work, he carried her everywhere. He visited friends with his daughter sashed across his long back. "Yasashī—a tender person, isn't he?" people said. He was seen swaying and singing with her on his back wherever he took her.

At home, as Amy grew older, Bunye would drop on all fours, have her crawl on his back for a ride, and, cautioning her to hold on, he would spring up and whinny like a horse. She adored her father. How she laughed. "Please Papa, again," she'd beg, curling her short, plump arms around his neck. Through her father's dalliances and softness, and her mother's ever-present sternness, Amy grew willingly filial.

Bunye had big dreams for his daughter, dreams that exceeded his wildest expectations, when you considered the deprivation in their lives. When he left Japan to get away from his drunkard father, he insisted that all of his children were going to be well educated. He had bragged to his best friend in Japan how, in America, all his children were going to be scholars. After having seen the mistreatment of his sister and mother in Japan, he vowed the situation would be different for any daughter of his.

"My daughters will not have to blacken their teeth to show they are married. They will not have to shave their eyebrows and draw them like leeches across their foreheads. They will not have to paint their lips green to make their faces look white. My daughters will have worthy and respectful husbands and obedient children."

"We'll see," his more skeptical friend had said.

Kimie's expectations for her daughter were lower than her husband's. She did not have the same confidence in her daughter's future that her husband seemed to have. In her view, schools in Hawai'i did not have the same discipline as those in Japan.

"Japan's schools are much better. Maybe we should send Amy to Japan to stay with my mother."

"I forbid you to send her away. Promise me you won't do that."

"Promise me, too. You can send her to school until the eighth grade, but after that, she must work, you hear?"

"I don't know if I can promise that—"

"I'm being realistic."

Kimie wanted her daughter educated *just enough* to be able to work and bring home money. By then, their daughter would be thirteen, the age most girls began work as housemaids in the haole houses or in the cane fields.

"We'll see—"

Bunye tugged the other way. He had dreams of Amy becoming a teacher. Enthusiastic for his daughter, Bunye enrolled in night school to learn English. Painstakingly, he learned how to read and write the English language.

Kimie laughed at him. "You're too ambitious for a simple man," she teased and had the greatest time making fun of his English whenever he practiced it aloud. "How wa ry-u-u," she mimicked and walked the haole way, swinging her hips, holding her nose in the air.

Bunye remained dogged about his English lessons. Before Amy went to school, he taught her the alphabet and read to her as best he could. When Amy started school, he intensified her lessons. They read stories from the school books she brought home and the discarded ones Bunye retrieved from the haole man's trash—the plantation boss's books from the big house on the hill. Bunye read these books to his daughter in the light of the dim, kerosene oil-lanterns in his halting, sputtering-like-a-flame, immigrant English.

And so the couple lived under the roof of these cross-purposes. But they managed a tenuous truce concerning their lives. Bunye disappeared into the fields every day and helped Amy with her English schoolwork during the evenings; Kimie took care of the household and saw that Amy went to Japanese language school in the afternoons. While Bunye had not solved the problem of Amy's education with Kimie, he had hoped that, in time, his wife would soften her contrary position.

One day, when Amy was in the third grade at Pa'auilo Elementary School, Miss Keawe, a schoolteacher who was educated at the Territorial Normal School in Honolulu, asked the class if anyone was able to read aloud any of the stories in the book. "Please raise your hands," she said to her students. The plantation children responded to her question with silence. Soon, much to Miss Keawe's delight, Amy raised her hand.

Many of the stories in the schoolbook were Aesop's fables, most of which Amy and her father had read before, like "The Grasshopper and the Ant," "The Dog and the Wolf," "The Lion and the Mouse." Having practiced these stories at home with her father, Amy felt confident she would be able to read any story in the book in front of the class.

Miss Keawe suggested that Amy read the fifth story in the reader. Even if this was a new story for Amy, she nodded her head in confirmation. "Go on home, practice the story tonight, and be ready to read the story to the class tomorrow."

That night, Amy asked her father to help her with the story and the two of them went over the fable word by word. They read it aloud together, several times, close to memorization.

"Do well." Encouraging his daughter, Bunye marveled at how conscientious she was.

The next day, when the reading hour began, the assortment of Chinese, Hawaiian, Japanese, Portuguese, Filipino, and Puerto Rican students assembled on the floor in a high level of anticipation for what was unprecedented. Never had anyone volunteered to read in front of the class.

"Yesterday, Amy said she would read the fifth story from the book," Miss Keawe said. "Would you like to come up to the front, Amy?"

Amy nodded and walked smartly to the head of the classroom with her book tucked in the crook of her arm. Amy looked sharp in one of her better dresses—a pink eyelet-lace dress with a large bow in the back, which her mother agreed to let her wear for the occasion.

Amy crossed her bare feet and opened the book to where she had placed her marker. All eyes were upon her. She began by clearing her throat. "Uh hum," she said. Next, she read the title: "The Hay-a and the Tot-toys."

As if not believing what they heard, the students shifted their eyes back and forth across the room. Only loudmouth George Akimsui laughed out loud, then said in his perfect English, "Hey, Amy! It's 'The Hare and the Tortoise!'" The rest of the students leaned forward on their crossed legs, looked over at Amy, then back to George. A low murmur skirted the room.

"Class, now let's not be rude. George, please?" Miss Keawe said with her eyes on him. "Go ahead, Amy. Don't be afraid."

"Once upon a time-u," Amy said, eyes pinned on her book, "thea lived a hay-a and a tot-toys."

This time the children moved uneasily in their sitting positions on the floor. A few of them had weird, uncomfortable looking smiles pasted across their faces. Others put their heads down as if to avoid each other's eyes and to keep from laughing. Someone in the back row coughed into the circle of a fist; another student stifled a snort. The students restrained their laughter that must have felt like it would burst the dam of their bodies.

But even after Miss Keawe herself corrected Amy and offered the correct pronunciations for the words "hare" and "tortoise," Amy could not help herself. She looked up and felt puzzled but continued in the same manner she had begun her reading. It was almost as if she had not heard Miss Keawe correct her.

Challenged by the sheer effort she had gathered to do this reading, and still wanting to do well, she persevered despite the mounting embarrassment. But it was too late at this point for her to change how she had learned to read the story. She was afraid that if she stopped and read it differently from how she had learned the story, how her father had taught it to her, she would not be able to read *anything*. She just couldn't change in midstream—the words swimming in a frenzy, like feeding fish before her eyes. How her father had taught her how to read the story was stuck in her head.

The students could no longer contain themselves. They began laughing harder and louder as Amy continued reading. Thereafter, whenever Amy came across the word "hare" and pronounced it "hay-a," or "tortoise" and pronounced it, "tot-toys," her classmates roared.

"Class, class!" Mrs. Keawe hit her desk rapidly with a ruler. "Settle down, please. Let Amy finish the story." But even Miss Keawe could not help but smile. Flustered and embarrassed, Amy stumbled through the words.

Amy cried all the way home that day. She felt like a fool. She had imitated her father's mispronunciations, especially the two English words she had never heard before in her life: *Hare. Tortoise.* What were these words, anyway?

When Amy told her parents what had happened, her father apologized profusely. "Papa is the foolish one. I'm so sorry."

Kimie also berated her husband. She accused him of being the cause of their daughter's shame in school. "You're the stupid one. See what you did?"

Amy felt betrayed by her father. Maybe her mother had been right all this time. Perhaps her father really was a buffoon as her mother so often characterized him.

"I no longer want to go to school." Amy hid her face in her arms.

"But you must, at least until the eighth grade. I promised your father," her mother said.

"I don't care, I'm not going. I refuse to do what you both say."

Amy sobbed in a humiliation she could not seem to surmount. How was she ever going to face her classmates? How was she going to step foot into the classroom ever again? She was so ashamed.

"I don't ever want to go back to school. Not ever!"

Her mother gloated; she was going to have her wish after all. Perhaps Amy would willingly end her schooling in the eighth grade, perhaps even earlier.

Amy's father stood by quietly. His heart was broken for his only child. In Japan he knew that people killed themselves over encounters of shame. Shame could flow deeply. He felt all the more saddened because it had befallen his daughter at so tender an age, where she could do nothing about it, and because he was partly responsible for her embarrassment. He knew how shame could burn in the core of one's bowels, how it could eat at the insides and leave one hungry for reprieve. Humiliation of this sort defied being bearable. Yet he knew his daughter had to bear it.

He tried his best to console her, but she would have nothing to do with him. "From now on," he said in Japanese, not the mispronounced English he had used with her before, "you will do as the teachers say. I will not interfere with your schooling."

"I hate school! I hate you!" Amy dashed into the cane field.

The children themselves forgave Amy easily, for they all had, in one way or another, faced these moments of humiliation. No one was immune. Amy took it especially personally, however.

From that incident on, Amy rarely spoke in class. She became withdrawn. Never smiled. Her head descended like an anchor to her chest, her face barred in long and sad lines. As soon as she reached school she dismantled her braids and pulled her hair down over her face.

When Pa'auilo School began, one woman taught grades one through three, another four through six. For many years the school remained small and unchanging. But the year Amy entered the fourth grade, the territorial government assigned several new teachers to Pa'auilo Elementary School due to the growth of the sugar industry and, as a consequence, the student population. A couple of them came from the normal school in Honolulu like Miss Keawe; the other teachers came from the states. They signed one-year contracts with the Territory of Hawai'i and had come from places people in Hawai'i had never heard of before: Boulder, Colorado; Boise, Idaho; Syracuse, New York.

These women lived in two very tiny makeshift teachers' cottages in the back of the school. And they were haole women, gaijin, with their light skin, hair, and eyes. These new teachers stood out like grass in cane that was near harvest. The children looked upon these new schoolteachers uneasily, having had very little contact with the whites in town. The children only knew haole women as plantation bosses' wives with ample bosoms, sleek black cars, and commodious houses on the hill. Plantation children never mixed with the haoles.

Miss Becker, one of the new teachers, was Amy's fourth grade teacher. "I hate this strange school. The minute I laid eyes on it, I knew I wouldn't like it. I hate the strange-looking immigrants, I hate where we live, the insects, the food and these children—they always look so filthy. How can you stand it?" she asked her housemate, another teacher from the mainland.

She kept telling herself that she had but to endure the situation for a year, and while she had resolved to put up with the work, deep down inside she felt it was her mission to go forth like a good Christian soldier and civilize these backward children, especially to teach them some manners.

"Be quiet, put your head down. No talking," she demanded. She intimidated her students with her strictness. The students themselves never looked her straight in the eye. "Never, never interrupt me," she said, when they wanted her attention. Cold, distant, she lacked compassion for anything they did or said.

The children reacted to her cold attitude by making fun of her. Because she smelled sour in the humidity—a mixture of old powder and perfume—they whispered behind her back. "Miss Becka, take one haole bath—only once a week. Try look her stocking, too, all puka. And her neck, get ole kine powda insai the lines unda her chin. Try look."

Miss Becker, on the other hand, thought the children were quite ignorant because they rarely spoke, and when they did speak, they did not speak intelligibly. "Hey, you like stay go my house, kau-kau time?" or "You like hoʻomalimali this teacha, or wat?" What was she to make of this? The language was something she found difficult to understand. It was so befuddling to her sensitive upbringing and background.

The children did not understand Miss Becker either. Her words sounded nasal. It had a twang that the children giggled at. As the days went by, Miss Becker became more and more irritated and put-upon by these barefooted, runny-nosed, mosquito-bitten children who wore bleached rice bags for clothing.

She penalized girls suspected of having ukus by having their parents cut their hair short and swaddle them in kerosene turbans before permitting them back in school. "Don't come back to school until the lice are all dead," she said. She tapped her teeth with her long nails when irritated or twisted a strand of hair behind her ear.

"And boys, comb your hair and scrub your nails," she said, although clean nails were almost impossible for boys who worked in the fields beside their parents after school or on the weekends. She put anyone on detention for talking out of turn, squirming on the classroom bench, or whistling at recess. "Give them to me!" she insisted and confiscated marbles, hanafuda, the girls' ojame bean bags, and jacks.

One day, not long after school had started, Amy went up to Miss Becker's desk and asked, politely, in her best English, "Miss Becker, can I please—?"

"Yeees?" The word *yes* climbed up the hill of her voice. Unhappy at being interrupted, her eyes widened and shifted irritably at Amy's presumption.

"'May I,' you mean, don't you?"

Amy nodded her head. "Yes. May I go out to use the obenjo?"

"We speak English here. What do you mean by 'obanjo,'" she asked and turned away.

"I'd like to go to use the outhouse . . . the toilet, outside."

"Toilet? What toilet! Don't you know we have no toilet facilities in this godforsaken place?" Miss Becker's face an explosion. "You will go only when I excuse you."

"But Miss Becker, I can't wait to—"

"Nonsense! Return to your seat and stay there until I excuse you."

She would teach them. She wanted to punish these ugly, rural girls by making them mind.

That day Amy went home with her wet underwear wrapped in newspaper and placed next to her lunch pail in her bag. A nearly hysterical Miss Becker hit Amy on the head—*smack*—with the roll of newspaper before giving it to her to wrap her soiled clothing. "You did this deliberately, you naughty girl."

Miss Becker had also pinned a note on Amy's dress. Without a salutation, it said:
> Your daughter had been disobedient in school today.
> She wet herself. Please talk to your daughter. Tell her
> that she has to exercise more control.
>
> Miss Becker

When Bunye read the note, he didn't say much. While he sympathized with his daughter, he also admonished her. "You must do better. The teacher is always right."

"I promise to do better," Amy said.

Even though the breach between them had not been healed, Amy swallowed her pride and remained respectful. In her household, she knew that a parent's or a teacher's authority was above reproach, even above one's own shame. What she truly felt she buried deep inside. She did not know how she was going to come out of this new hole of humiliation, ever.

Kimie went after her husband. "You have to make Amy behave. She's too much like you—rebellious. That's why she can't get along with anyone."

She then looked at her daughter. "Amy, you bring nothing but haji, shame, to the family. You better change your ways."

Kimie now had to think of ways to save the family's face. "First of all," she said, "you must apologize to the teacher, you must apologize to your classmates. Next time, you will wait until the teacher tells you when to use the restroom, you hear? This is more shameful for us, your parents, than it is for you. The reflection on us is as if the sun were directly above us. You understand?"

Amy bowed her head before her mother. "I will do better, Mama. I promise."

But it was not long before another accident happened. Although she tried not drinking water before school and not drinking water during school, the same situation happened over several weeks.

"What are we going to do with you?" her mother said each time Amy came home with a note pinned to her dress. Kimie became angrier as time passed—her daughter's behavior unchanged.

Soon she reached a state close to hysteria. "Are you doing this on purpose? You must be. Are you trying to shame us in front of people?"

One day another note appeared on Amy's dress and, when no longer able to contain the rage she felt for her daughter's defiance, Kimie rolled up her sleeves, hiked up the skirt of her kimono into her belt, grabbed Amy by the arm, and dragged her daughter out of the house and to a gulch nearby. Amy resisted like a tethered animal. She balked at her mother's fierce strength.

"Mama, please, what are you going to do?" Amy said as they moved along the path and down the tall grassy slopes of the area. She fought her mother's dragging her. She even sat down. But her mother, much stronger, simply spun Amy around and hauled her up from under the arms and dragged her along.

"What are you going to do with me?"

"I'm going to tie you up, and you're going to stay down in this gulch. You're going to stay here until you change!"

"But Mama—"

"But Mama what?"

"Please let me go. I promise to be good."

"Promise? It's not enough anymore."

At the bottom of the gulch, Kimie tied her daughter to the stump of a large guava tree. "You think you can make fun of us? You think it fun to mock your mother and father? Don't you know that every time something like this happens, the rest of the children report it to their parents? They're all talking about us." Kimie rattled on as she tightened the rope around Amy's belly and tied her daughter's hands securely to the back of the tree.

"Please, Mama, don't leave me here! It will be dark soon." Amy looked anxiously at the sky. "I promise I won't do it again!" Amy's voice rattled in her throat. "You don't understand."

Kimie stopped to look back. "Don't understand? Oh, I understand all right." She hitched up her kimono and walked off.

Whenever Bunye came home from work, he always looked for Amy. That afternoon, his daughter was not around, neither reading nor cleaning vegetables in her lap. Although he sensed that Amy had not quite forgiven him for the time she had read the story in school, he knew that she had softened toward him over the months. Seeing only Kimie seated on her cushion, jerking thread through a piece of embroidery, made him suspicious.

"Where's Amy? I brought her some yellow poka to eat." When his wife did not answer him but merely shifted herself on the cushion, he knew something was wrong.

"I said, where's Amy!" Because his voice sounded so fierce, Kimie had to look up at him. Her startled look, for the first time in her life, appeared to be without mockery for her husband.

"Your daughter is insolent and needs to be punished. She doesn't know true shame. Look, another note from Miss Becker." She waved, then thrust the tattered note in front of Bunye's face. "So I took her to the gulch. Tied her there until she learns."

"You did it to teach her a lesson?" Bunye said nothing more and shook his head in disbelief. A reasonable man, he still did not wish to go against his wife. But darkness was fast approaching and he was frightened for his daughter.

"Mama," he said with quiet reason. "Let's go to the gulch and bring Amy-chan home. Let's go together. We can work this out."

"It's Amy, not Amy-chan. That's been the trouble with you. You treat her like a baby."

"Okay, okay. So I'm the bad one. But let's go get Amy."

"Go get her? She will stay there until she's learned her lesson."

"But Mama, isn't what you've done, enough? I think Amy understands."

"She will stay there until I say so!" Kimie looked down and returned to her sewing.

Years of anger welled up inside Bunye's chest. Bunye walked up to where Kimie sat and swept the sewing out of her hands. "Mama, for once, let it be!"

When Kimie reached out to stop her husband, he brushed her aside. Bunye's lean arm, strengthened by years of working in the fields, became hard and defiant to her touch. Astonished by the feel of steel in his arm, Kimie fell back and let her husband pass as he gathered his hat, tabi, and cane knife and stormed out. For the first time in his life, Bunye walked past his wife as if she didn't exist; for the first time, his manner made Kimie step aside.

When Bunye finally reached Amy, he found her hands swollen and burned raw from rubbing them against the rope in her struggle to free herself.

"Amy-chan, Papa is so sorry. I tried to come here as fast as I could."

Exhausted, Amy looked sad. Bunye could hardly meet her eyes. Nonetheless, as he cut the rope, he said to her, "Amy-chan. No matter what you do, you must listen to your mother and teacher, okay?"

Amy nodded, collapsing her head on her father's shoulder, and she resolved, again, to do better for all their sakes. "Really, Papa, I will." She looked around. "But what about Mama? What happened to her? Did she send you here?" Amy was puzzled. "Isn't she going to be angry, knowing you came for me?"

"Never mind Mama. I will talk to her later."

Realizing the effort her father had made to go against her mother, Amy broke down. Between sobs of relief, and wanting to speak up for herself after months of mistreatment by Miss Becker, Amy told her father about the conditions in school. "She wouldn't let us out at recess, she threw away our jacks, she hit the boys hands hard, and worst of all she wouldn't let us use the obenjo."

"Why didn't you say something?"

"I didn't say anything, because you always said that the teacher was right," Amy said, in defense. "No matter what."

"Yes, I said that, but this is to the extreme. I am sorry we did not listen to you."

"Forgive me, too, for acting badly toward you and blaming you for my shame. I'm glad you were the one to come for me today."

Pake Zaka

Once when Sumako Tanaka's mother and father had a fight, she pushed the screen door back so hard to get out of the house that it teetered and swayed on its old and rusted hinges before it fell lopsidedly. It was not so much the shouting that scared her. "Baka. Shibaku zo! Stupid woman, you want a whack?" her father had said, and she saw her mother withdraw. It was the ugly words, the threats, the adamancy of her father's face—the way he curled his lips and widened his beady eyes, his hair moving forward and falling before his eyes—that sent her reeling. When he slammed his fist on the table and threw the teapot, it was the suddenness of it which made her catch her breath as if a bone had gotten caught in her throat. His anger, Sumako surmised, vented some of his frustration over not getting ahead, always being poor, having a leaky roof over his head, and a wife and children who rarely listened to him unless he became angry and eviscerated them with his deep, ferocious voice.

Sumako's mother had been going to the temple in the mornings, and together with other members of her church's women's club had been wrapping bandages, making loincloths, and packing cigarettes and raisins in care boxes to be sent to the Japanese soldiers fighting in Southeast Asia. The year, 1937.

"What you and your friends are doing for Japan is stupid," her father said, although the women were not political and doing this work for humanitarian reasons. It was Japan's imperialistic drive which made him hammer his fists on the table. BOOM, BOOM, BOOM, BOOM! "You have no business helping Japan, you know that?" he said.

This gave Sumako's mother a need to defend herself and her women friends. "Demooo, but—" she protested.

"Yakamashī, shut up!" he said. "Don't argue with me. You know I'm right."

"Don't you think you're being unreasonable?"

"Naaani, whaaat? Unreasonable?"

The day of the fight, Sumako ran out of the house and up to the head of the lane with her books tucked under her arms to wait for her ride. While sitting on an old stump on the roadside, she had time to get over the morning's episode, to catch her breath, and admire the scenery. It was a beautiful morning, the sky clear above the small plantation community. Further down the road, she could see one of the neighbor's houses, the Okinagas' place, with its new galvanized rooftop blazing silver in the sun.

Looking at the roof, she remembered how she had often played with Satoshi, the youngest child in the Okinaga family. She thought of how the Okinaga Mama- and Papa-san looked old, weathered like their surroundings. Their yard had the largest peach and mountain apple trees in the area, and the overhang darkened their home. Made it gloomy.

Mrs. Okinaga liked Sumako. She had intimated more than once, when the children were younger, that Sumako would make a good match for her son. "She will make a good bride," Mrs. Okinaga had said to Sumako's mother. Young as she was, Sumako hated that kind of talk between the mothers. She didn't like Satoshi very much. He was strange. He always had a runny nose, the base of which he flicked with the tip of his tongue, like a lizard, and swallowed his snot.

While Sumako had known Satoshi since they were children, she hadn't seen him of late. He was not smart enough to be in school. Satoshi was a menopause child and he was an uncle to two of his much older sisters' children before he was even born. Although Sumako and Satoshi were about the same age, Satoshi was considered taran-taran, "slow in the head," his condition becoming more apparent as the children in the neighborhood grew older.

He often hid behind his mother. He held onto her kimono, her sleeve, or the skin of her elbows, his thumb in his mouth. He was small for his age so the thumb sucking did not bother people who saw him, even if he were maybe as old as nine or ten, the time

Sumako was thinking of, and not four or five years old, as most people had assumed.

"Sometimes, Japanese look young because they are small and have baby faces. This fools people," Sumako's mother had said. But the other children knew how old he was and disliked being near him. They hid behind one another when he was around, for Satoshi carried a nasty smell of stale saliva and always wanted to hold hands.

Rumor had it that even at his advanced age, his mother let him breastfeed. People had seen him put his hand under his mother's clothing, feeling for her breasts.

"Distasteful, isn't it? The old Okinaga parents spoil their boy," Mrs. Tanji, her mother's best friend, said whenever they gossiped.

Sumako's mother agreed. "Yes, no one wants to be tied to her child the way the Okinaga boy is tied to his mother."

"That's because Mrs. Okinaga doesn't have anything better to do—like us."

Unlike Sumako's mother, who was active in women's activities in the community, Mrs. Okinaga did not seem to have many outside interests. She always carried that fresh-off-the-boat look about her, and, adhering to the typical Japanese child-rearing practice of spoiling boys, she indulged her son's every whim. Sumako had seen Satoshi kick his mother in the shins whenever he didn't get his way. She had seen him pull his mother away from others when he wanted her attention or to go home. "We go! C'mon!" he'd nag, rolling on the ground in loud fits of tantrum, or barreling his fists into his mother when she denied him something.

When the men in the fields saw Satoshi running home, his head bent down in determination, his body dwarfish with its long body and short legs, they would stop what they were doing and rest their chins on the poles of their hoes to watch. The cane men speculated that this running occurred whenever the urge to nurse struck Satoshi. "Mama's boy, that one. Thea he goes," they'd say, shaking their heads.

As he grew older, he had the reputation of being the swiftest runner in the village. The paths he made in the fields of cane formed clear, even ripples. People said that whenever he wanted his mother's breasts, Satoshi ran home through the cane as fast as he could. That was why he was such an excellent runner.

Very often, the younger boys called out to him for a challenge: "Eh Satoshi, come outside—fo' race. We like beat you." And Satoshi would come out, hitching up his cutoff pants. "Okay," he'd nod, the tip of his pink tongue sticking out slightly as if too big for his mouth.

He never said anything, but grunted, sniffled, ran his nose across his sleeve, and got ready to race, angling his body over the starting line. "On your mark, get set, go!" one of the boys would shout—the challengers off.

After beating the boys, Satoshi would say nothing, only run back into his home. Even Sumako's brother Makoto, or Mack, who was a year older than Satoshi and much taller and larger, had raced this neighbor boy but just could not beat him.

Young boys in the camp bet loose change they had in their pockets and called him out time after time. In their childish faith, it was just a matter of time, they figured, before Satoshi would be defeated.

The gambling blood had remained strong in the community. The immigrants were, after all, gamblers in their own right—for had they not gambled on their lives by coming to a new country and a new way of life? Young as they were, and in their parents' immigrant spirit, the barefooted camp boys bet on anything they could. "You wanna bet?" was a challenge, together with a crooked small finger thrust in the air. But try as they might, none of the boys could beat Satoshi. That he was the fastest of them all, no one disputed; yet they continued to race him. Only Satoshi's father's sudden appearance could make the boys scatter and withdraw with shouted-out promises to race another day: "Tomorrow, Satoshi. We going beat you tomorrow! Jes watch."

Once, Mack came running home, out of breath. "What happened," Sumako asked.

"Satoshi's father wen come out from the cane. Everybody wen run away."

"'No botha my boy,' he wen say." It was this sudden appearance that had scared Mack to near breathlessness.

"'We only like race him' I said and ran away. Mr. Okinaga wen shout something bad to me wen I look back fo' see his face."

"'You hea what I said?' he wen tell me and his face wen come big like one bullfrog—two times the size. You should have seen um."

Not much was known about Satoshi's father. "Hezu get one habut face, but him one hard-worka," her father said, when she had asked about him sometime back. "People say hezu one drinka, but I neva seezu him drunk." It was also said that he was disappointed that his youngest son was not normal like other children. A shiver ran through Sumako at the thought of Satoshi's father's mean-looking face.

Further down the road, past the Okinagas' house, Sumako's eyes rested on a small dip in the landscape covered by a bamboo grove, a wide patch of ground that overflowed into a gulch nearby. This area was called Pake Zaka.

"Once in a while, a Chinese ghost comes out," her mother said of the place. "A long time ago, a young Chinese man hung himself there. He had lost his job and he couldn't call his wife and baby to Hawaiʻi. He had no hope; must have felt like a failure. With no place to go, he made his home in the grove. He must have been lonely, thinking about his family. Not long after that, he killed himself."

Sometimes, when Sumako came upon that section of the road on her way home from school, she lingered by the place. On several occasions, she had gone into the grove to look around. Though scared, she was also inquisitive. She wanted to know if the bamboo stalk the man hung himself from was still there; she wanted to know if it had cracked when he hung himself. It surprised her to find the ground soft and dry, carpeted by layers and layers of leaves, years of dried, tea-colored leaves.

In the mornings, on her way to school, Sumako saw the gulch only in passing. A kindly neighboring family who lived further up the road picked her up in their second-hand Packard on the way down and took her to school in Hilo. Though the car was a bit uncomfortable and bumpy, she was grateful for the rides. Compared to the bus, the car ride was much faster.

In the afternoons, however, she caught the bus home. It dropped her off near a long and isolated potholed cinder road that led to her house up several small hills. While she must have walked past Pake Zaka a thousand times, the trepidation and intrigue she felt for the place was not lessened.

She felt especially scared on rainy days, when the wind whipped her oil-paper umbrella about, and the bamboo from the grove dipped into her path and made terrible squeaky sounds between the branches. Sometimes, the wind howled with a terrible moaning sound as if someone were crying. But she also knew it was the driest place in the area, the bamboo stalks weaving a natural roof high above the ground.

"Mama, does the Chinese ghost really come out over there?"

"You always ask me about that. You know I don't believe in ghosts. You only want to know about ghosts because people tell you scary stories about Pake Zaka." And yet, Sumako's mother was the very one who told Sumako not to look backward or sideways, but straight ahead, so the ghost of Pake Zaka could not catch her eyes.

Sumako didn't know what to think. It was typical of her mother to make things complicated, like not taking chances or things for granted because "you never knew" what might happen. "It was better to believe," she said, "than not to believe." In addition, her school friends told her that if the Pake Zaka ghost caught her eyes, she would die on the spot. The prospect was frightening, but nonetheless exciting to contemplate.

Mongeese, quail, and pheasants ran through the dry leaves and undergrowth whenever someone approached. These sounds startled Sumako whenever she passed Pake Zaka, but she was curious enough that once in a while she would steel her heart and walk into the grove for a look.

"It's not the ghost you have to be afraid of," her friend Shizue Kato once explained during school recess, all the girls giggling. "It's the Filipino men. You can hear them, downtown, when you pass— front of Masaji's pool hall—and they spit the juice from their Toscani into the gutter. 'Psst, psst,' they say to get your attention. That's the Filipino love call. Sometimes, they waiting for you in the bushes."

Sumako had grown tall and lanky by the time she had reached the eighth grade and started developing physically. This was also the time she and her friends talked about nothing but boys. Self-conscious, she hid herself under a large sweater behind a stack of books and a slouch. Mack, who had teased her incessantly when they were younger, no longer taunted her but took on a gruff, protective air.

One day, as Sumako and the bunch of girls she hung around with walked past the plantation store, her friends pushed her into a group of young Filipino boys who were congregated on the porch. "Don't do that!" Sumako shouted as the other girls ran off, their hands covering their mouths to stifle their laughter.

"Isus!" the Filipino boys said in loud, perplexed voices. They scattered at the unexpected intrusion that had hurtled Sumako into their midst.

After regrouping, the girls settled down. "But seriously," her friend Shizue warned. "It's not the Pake Zaka ghost or the Filipino men you have to be afraid of. It's Satoshi. He carries a long bamboo shoot in his pants—this big. No, this big!" The girl spread her hands, the same way boys spread them when they talked of fish. The girls burst into laughter. Sumako wasn't all that sure what her girlfriend meant. A bamboo shoot in the pants?

On school days, Sumako left Shizue and the rest of her friends near where the bus dropped them off on the old government road, where the macadam ended and the red cinder began. The group broke up and headed in opposite directions. Sumako turned mauka, her friends makai.

She passed Mr. Rabisa's house first, where his round-faced wife waved to her from the porch. She then walked past the Filipino houses where the children stopped playing whenever she approached, and dashed into their houses to peer at her though the windows.

After these houses and a long stretch of cane, Sumako had to walk past Pake Zaka, another stretch of cane, the Okinagas' house, and more cane before she reached her home. The sight of her house, with its familiar American guava bush on one side, a row of sugi on the other, a small bridge over a stream, and the gate to the front path, filled her with mixed feelings when things were not right between her mother and father.

That day, because of her parents' fight in the morning, the school day felt long and unsettled. She welcomed the walk home. Parting from her friends, and humming to herself, Sumako walked past the Rabisas' house and waved back to Mrs. Rabisa and past the Filipino families' houses and their staring children.

She then heard a faint rustling in the cane. At first, she thought it might be the wind and gave it no mind. But she kept on hearing light movement in the tall stalks as she walked. She had a strange feeling that she was being followed. Whoever was in the field seemed to be walking parallel to the road. "Hello," she said. "Hello, hello, who's there?" No one answered. She stopped to listen. Sumako did this several times. But every time she stopped, whatever or whoever it was in the cane field stopped walking, too.

Sumako remembered an earlier incident where she had thought someone was following her, but it turned out to be only a mongoose running in the cane. Perhaps it was a mongoose again, once more making noises in the field. She decided to dismiss the sounds.

But the feeling of being followed persisted. She couldn't shake it. In the wake of the rustling, her imagination began to run wild. She began to think that it was the Pake Zaka ghost or one of the young Filipino men. Stalking her.

"Don't be foolish," she said to herself. She tried singing, but even that didn't comfort her.

She began whistling and walked faster. Her panic rose. "Come out, whoever you are!" she yelled. She threatened whoever it was with her father's wrath: "You'd better not come near me, you hear? My father will get you!"

After shouting her anger, Sumako stopped walking and listened for signs of something in the cane. Only silence greeted her. Still uneasy, she began running again. She wanted to pass Pake Zaka gulch and the long stretches of cane between the houses. But the faster she ran, the louder the movements in the cane grew. As if to keep up with her, the person in the field ran with the same abandon. There was no doubt now that someone was following her.

Approaching Pake Zaka, Sumako saw a sudden blur, something flying before her eyes. She shielded her face as she heard a yell. It was Satoshi. He had leaped out of the cane. He held his arms high above his head as if he had fallen from a great height and landed heavily in front of Sumako. He blocked and edged himself her way, crouching his body around her in short, measured steps.

"Oh, it's *you*, Satoshi," cried out Sumako, somewhat relieved. Satoshi often acted strangely. She probably wouldn't have known what to do had it been someone else.

"Stupid Satoshi, you scared me! What do you think you're doing?" She tried walking past him.

"C'mon, let me pass!" she said, angry, more exasperated now than frightened by the boy. "Go home. Why do you want to bother me?"

Satoshi made sneering noises as he hunched his body. Moving around Sumako, he made the circle around her tighter, never taking his eyes off her face. He gave a crazed, salivated laugh and ran his shirtsleeve over his nose and mouth and snorted snot back up his nose and swallowed it.

Sumako saw that Satoshi had exposed himself. This must be the bamboo the girls had spoken of in school. Sumako gasped at its strangeness and its size. She couldn't imagine where it was hidden all the time. Her brother didn't have anything like this. She shrank back in fear, her heart beating in her ears.

Sumako turned to run the other way, but the boy was quick to follow. He sidestepped to corner her. In no time he had her spinning, all of his limbs swaying like bamboo stalks. Suddenly, Satoshi grabbed Sumako's wrist, her books and sweater sliding out of her hand as if forced away by swift current of water. She dared not take her eyes off the boy as he jerked her forward.

He was dragging her, haltingly, toward Pake Zaka. Twisting her body, kicking, hitting, scratching, Sumako acted like a crazed animal, but Satoshi seemed immune to whatever she did. Much taller and heavier than Satoshi, she quickly thought of ways she could use her height and weight to her advantage. But Satoshi was solid, close to the ground, built like an immovable tree stump.

Sumako knew that she wouldn't be able to fight him once he took her into the grove. In desperation, in a wedge of opportunity, in an exaggerated moment, she pushed Satoshi back with all of her might. She was able to shove the boy away hard enough so that he fell heavily and scrunched his face upon impact. "Humph!" he said and went down on his rear.

Sumako ran away as fast as she could.

She lost a shoe then, but her feet did not hurt on the cinders. The one time she dared look back, she saw Satoshi on all fours, struggling to get up. No matter how swift he was in his running, by this time, Satoshi was too far behind to catch up with her. She saw him make a dash into the cane in an attempt to cut her off further up the road, but she knew he was too late.

As she neared her home, Sumako came upon her father and brother who were headed in the opposite direction to work in the cane field. "Satoshi . . . he tried to—" Sumako said, out of breath.

Her father widened his eyes, the whites of his eyes becoming red at that moment, the condition never to leave him for the rest of his life. He straightened himself up, pulled back his rounded, routine-defeated shoulders, and dropped his chin onto his chest. "Mack. Go get the machetes hanging downstairs," he ordered in Japanese.

"No, Papa. No, Mack. Don't do anything foolish!" Sumako said. Her father pushed her aside as if she didn't exist when Mack returned with the sharp cane knives.

Frightened for them, Sumako watched the two men in her family swing their machetes like clubs as they walked from the house toward the Okinagas' place. Her father and brother looked savage. Sumako backed up into the house.

"Satoshi," she heard Mack call out. "Come out! We like talk to you."

She couldn't bear to listen to them as they wended their way down the road. She closed all of the windows in the house to block the commotion outside she imagined she might hear.

Later, after what seemed an interminable length of time, Sumako's father and Mack walked into the house with her books, her shoe, the sweater she lost, and the machetes dangling from their sides in long leather holsters.

"We neva find him," her brother said. "We wen chase him all over, but he too fast." Sumako sighed, happy that nothing came of their hunt.

When Sumako related the incident to her mother, her mother cried hopelessly as if the attempted assault on her daughter betrayed everything she held dear about being Japanese. "The Okinagas' boy? Such a disgrace! It can't be."

That evening, Sumako's father and brother went to the Okinagas' house, while her disheartened mother stayed at home and moved about as if she were in mourning. Once back from Satoshi's home, Sumako's father simmered some sake on the stove and wouldn't look at Sumako, as if she were to blame.

Late that night, the whole community heard Satoshi screaming. The sounds came from Pake Zaka. They leaped over the hills, dove into the gulches, and bounced off the land as if something alive was being thrashed. It was rumored, later, that Satoshi's father had strung up his son from one of the bamboo stalks and beaten him.

From that day on, Mack met Sumako at the head of the lane to walk her home. He did this for four years until she graduated from high school.

Once in a while, Sumako and Mack thought they heard Satoshi in the cane fields. When this happened, Mack turned into a madman. "Satoshi! You damn coward. Come out, show yo' face. I like kill you!" Whenever Mack yelled this way, they'd hear Satoshi give a sinister laugh and run off.

Sometimes, late at night, Sumako thought she heard Satoshi outside of the house. "It was only your imagination," her mother would say, but Sumako felt certain that Satoshi peeped through the boards of their outhouse, the ofuro, her bedroom, to watch her. At night, when the dog whined and Sumako felt trapped in her bed, she tossed about, knowing that Satoshi was out there, somewhere, wandering in the cane, cracking the stalks.

But Sumako was also confused. She didn't tell her brother or father about the nights she suspected Satoshi spied on her. She didn't understand it, but she didn't like her brother's and father's anger any more than she liked being harassed by Satoshi. She didn't know the lesser of the two evils.

And there was no one to explain to her what was happening with her father and brother. Her mother intensified the work she was doing for Japan, so she was of no help. After the incident at Pake Zaka, her mother went to the temple every day to pray, to do good deeds for Japan and promote Japanese goodwill in Hawaiʻi. "This is my way of appeasing the gods. There's too much bachi in this family," she said.

Sumako had problems sleeping. She felt especially vulnerable, often intimidated by her brother's and father's tantrums—times when, as if at the turn of the moon, they settled into what her mother called their *crazy hour*. Their drinking did not help. Drunk, her father and brother tore from the house in anger. "Bakatare!" they yelled obscenities Sumako could not shut out with her hands. They pounded their fists on the wall or flung dishes at the slightest provocation from her or her mother. "Buy mo bee-ya fo' us." "Eh, wat you said? Go run down the sto-a, quick!"

The men's barking had become more terrible after the incident with Satoshi. They became like the dogs outside, snarling and spitting. Her mother tried to console Sumako in her troubled sleep when the men had a bad day, by rubbing Sumako's face to soothe her nerves. The only explanation her mother could give was, "Sometimes, that's the way men are." Sumako suspected that her father and Mack used the incident with Satoshi as an excuse for their bad behavior.

One day, not long after the incident with Satoshi, while Sumako and Mack walked home from school, she realized she was no longer afraid of the Pake Zaka ghost. She missed the excitement that had once surrounded the place. And because her brother was always with her, she could no longer go into the grove and linger under the canopy of bamboo or to walk on the ground with its soft carpet of leaves that rustled like someone's hurried footsteps in dry grass. Sometimes, when it rained hard, she was tempted to ask Mack to stop there, but she knew she could never ask him to do that.

As she watched longingly at the place, a bird or two swept into the quiet secret of the grove in their escape from the rain.

Japanese Tea Garden

"BANG, BANG, BANG!"

Six-year-old Sandra Takahashi heard a loud knocking on the front door, her mother's slippered feet shuffling hurriedly down the hallway, her mother calling out "Hai!" as she flew past the rooms, the scraping of shoes at the doorway, people entering the house, people talking in low but urgent voices. Strangers' voices. Her parents' voices. Kenneth Ichida's voice.

"Shhh. Stay here," she said to her sister and brother. She grabbed her red sweater draped over a chair by a desk and stole down the hallway to see what was happening. She peeked through the doorway to the parlor.

In the small room, she saw her mother and father under the bare electric light bulb. They were sitting on a bench brought in from the kitchen. Two haole men in white shirts and suspenders and Kenneth Ichida from down the street stood before them.

Because Sandra's father could only speak Japanese, Kenneth had been contacted to act as the interpreter. Young as Sandra was, she could see that Kenneth liked his new role in the way that he put his hands into his pockets and puffed up his chest. "Are you a Japanese citizen?"

"Yes," Sandra's father said.

"But you lived in Japan . . . for how many years."

"For about ten years."

Japanese words, staccatolike, tumbled out of Kenneth's mouth and fell into the fear of her father's eyes.

Some weeks after that episode, Kenneth and the FBI came back to the house to take Sandra's father away. He was one of the few people in Hilo to be interned by the U.S. government. This time, when Kenneth came to the house, he had on an all-important, officious look as translator for the government. "Mr. . . . I mean Agent Carver, is there anything else you'd like to know?" Kenneth asked, politely.

"No, let's just get out of here," the agent said.

"Hurry up!" Kenneth said to Sandra's father, his voice harsh. "Don't take too much."

Sandra and her mother watched Kenneth with suspicion as he ordered Sandra's father around. Kenneth frightened them.

Sandra's mother wept quietly into her handkerchief when her husband was about to leave. She held her younger children's hands and drew them closer to her. Barefooted and standing next to her mother, Sandra dug in her heels. Watching her parents, she saw no display of affection between them, save a few plaintive directives that they exchanged.

"Take care of yourself and the children."

"You too. Take care of yourself and keep warm."

"Don't forget to tell Mr. Hamamoto that he has to close the books for the church and ask Mr. Kimoto for the—"

"It's okay, Papa. I'll take care of everything. Don't worry about us here."

Sandra's parents buried their true feelings and grief under the necessity of keeping things going. "Gambare!" her mother and father kept repeating.

Her father said the most to Sandra. "Here, keep this with you." He handed over a Buddhist dharma wheel on a chain and placed it in her hands. "You're my oldest child so you must help your mother. You are the head of the family, now. With your mother, be patient. With your brother and sister, be gentle. See that you study hard so as not to disappoint us. Make me proud of you."

"Yes, Papa," said Sandra and felt the sting. She was hostage to all that her father hoped for them while he was gone. So much depended on her and she already felt the burden of her father's words.

"Hurry up, Takahashi-san," Kenneth said, his gestures abrupt, as he showed Sandra's father to the car.

Sandra and her mother stood on the porch for the longest time and watched the car disappear down the road. They could see her father's face framed in fear, looking back at them from the rear window.

Kenneth Ichida lived in Shin-machi, on the opposite side of the village from where Sandra and her family lived. He lived with his mother, several mike neko, and two obese sisters who sat and rocked on the porch all day. Sandra had seen the family from the road.

"You want to know something? Kenneth doesn't want people to know that his sisters and mother are the ones on the porch. I think he's ashamed of them. You can tell by the way he acts," her mother said.

"Why's he ashamed?"

"Wish I knew." With a tilt of her head and a finger on her chin, her mother said, "But I think it's because he looks down on the Japanese. He doesn't want anyone calling on him at home. He doesn't want to be called by his real name, either, even among the Japanese. He wants to be known *only* as Kenneth. He's too haolefied, that's why."

"What's haolefied?"

"When you act white like Mr. Carter or Mr. Scott."

Kenneth was an accountant for Hilo Sugar Mill. The talk was that he mingled with the haoles every chance that he had, and that he always brought his bosses something to share, but his bosses seldom reciprocated his generosity. Sandra's mother and her two neighborhood friends, Kitano-san and Maeda lady, wondered if the haoles even tried eating some of the food.

"I hea he bring good kine stuff: mango, mochi, lychee, smoked pig, akule, papaya," Kitano-san said. "But poho. I hea the haoles throw out most of the food that Kenneth bring."

"You know what I tink, I tink he like marry one haole. That's why he hoʻomalimali dem," Maeda lady said.

"Dat true, but how he going find one good haole in Hilo fo' marry? Hard fo' find, especially one who going like him."

"Yeah no? You right, hard fo' find."

"Eh, how ole you tink him?"

"Hard fo' say. Thirty someting? Whatchu tink?"

"Maybe olda, eh? Maybe he gotta marry Pologee Susan down Mamo Street. Substitute." The women laughed at their wit.

"Anyway, Kenneth's fatha not his real fatha. Kenneth, Mrs. Ichida's 'love child,'" Maeda lady said.

From what Sandra understood, Ichida-san, a good man, married Kenneth's mother just before Kenneth was born. His mother's first husband, and the father of her obese daughters, had been deceased a few years back.

"Eh, you no tink he look hapa?" Kitano-san said. "He not like his sistas. Shark bait, him. Must be he get haole blood."

"Maybe dat's why he hate us pew-a Japanee. He get some long legs. I guess he no like short, bow-legged Japanee like us. I hear he wen quit Hongwanji church, too," Maeda lady said.

"Strange man, that one," Sandra's mother said in agreement with the other women.

It was not a mystery that Kenneth considered the Japanese in town barbaric. Unashamed of how he felt, he broadcasted his feelings to whomever listened to him. He said, "The Japanese should be more American. They're in a new country."

Sandra's father, who was kibei—born in America, but schooled in Japan—was especially vulnerable to Kenneth's reasoning right after the war began. When rumors hit town that he had turned in Sandra's father, Kenneth said in defense, "Mr. Takahashi was an editor of the Japanese language newspaper in town, a staunch member of the Buddhist church, and principal of the Japanese Language School. This made him suspicious to the FBI." What he said underscored Kenneth's embarrassment for those who were simply "too Japanese" in his eyes. "Don't hang on to your old ways. The Japanese people in Hawai'i will never become Americanized if they continue to support people who don't want to change and want to keep their old-fashioned ideas," he was known to say.

Sandra's father, of course, was not around to defend himself; but because Kenneth was *there*, in the community and among the people, his presence gradually diminished Sandra's father's good standing in the community and made others feel uncomfortable and ashamed of those who were interned. Sandra did not understand all that was going on, but it was enough for her to recognize the changes taking place.

Sandra had seen Mr. Kawachi watching what was going on from across the street where he lived in the park, the day the FBI came to take her father away. Sandra's family had known the park caretaker for a long time. In her eyes, the old man's jowls seemed to hang much lower that day, as he cast his saddened eyes at Sandra and her mother.

Mr. Kawachi had been a gardener all his life—mainly for the haoles in town. He had quite a reputation among them. "Ask Mr. Kawachi" was what they said if they had problems with their plants. Some time before the war, the Waiākea Japanese fishing village of Shin-machi in Hilo, decided to have a park along the waterfront for the many Japanese families living in the area. The people in town asked Mr. Kawachi to be its caretaker. Mr. Kawachi's wish had been to make the park in Hilo into a beautiful Japanese tea garden, much like those in Japan, with arched bridges and moats surrounding the gardens, red koi and kingyo swimming in the ponds, sculptured plants and stone lanterns lining the walkways, and rest houses bordering the footpaths of azaleas and camellias.

In 1939, Mrs. Anderson, a plantation matron, donated a pair of black trumpet swans to the park in appreciation for all the Japanese who worked for her. The people called them the "Anderson swans" in honor of the woman. (After the bombing of Pearl Harbor, however, she called her gift *regrettable*.)

Little did the people or Sandra know where the swans had come from, or how. The birds arrived one day and were simply placed in the park. The people wondered how Mr. Kawachi was going to handle the birds, but true to his dedicated spirit, he learned all he could about them. Soon he was trimming their flight feathers and caring for their feet. Under his charge, the birds' red beaks and legs shined and their black feathers sparkled in the sunlight. People coming around to look at the birds began calling them "the Kawachi birds," forgetting the community's haole benefactress all together.

Mr. Kawachi lived modestly with his wife in a small cottage on the park's premises across from the Takahashis. They had gotten married when they were much older and had no children but indulged any child who came to play in the park. Their cottage was barely noticeable, hidden by tall azalea bushes and a burst of bamboo.

In the heart of Shin-machi village, the Japanese families lived in salt-eaten and weather-beaten cottages, which in some earlier time had seen coats of green or red washed over their board and batten. While many Japanese fishermen lived in the area, there were others who gravitated to the bayfront because of the magnificent views of the coastline and mountains, the cheap rentals, and wanting to live where other Japanese lived. Sandra knew this was true of her father.

Before the war, when Sandra's family first moved to the village, Mr. Kawachi had just begun building his ponds and shaping the gardens. Sandra's father, often with her in hand, would stop to talk to Mr. Kawachi. He appreciated the old caretaker's handiwork. Shy and quite young at the time, Sandra hung back and hid behind her father whenever they greeted the man.

"Kawachi-san, the park looks splendid," her father said one day to praise him. "Your birds look very contented. Under your patient care the birds look handsome indeed!"

"You're too kind," Mr. Kawachi said in modest Japanese. He bowed, took off his hat and looked down. In his embarrassment, he pulled out some corn mash from his pocket and gave it to Sandra's father. Mr. Kawachi respected Mr. Takahashi and deferred to the younger man who was far more educated than he was. "Here, take your daughter to feed the swans. Put the corn on the ground and the birds will come out of the pond to feed," he said in Japanese.

"What do you say to Mr. Kawachi, Sandra?"

"Thank you Mr. Kawachi," she said politely. Back then, in the same way that Mr. Kawachi did, she liked to please her father too.

Mr. Kawachi bent down and patted her on her head. "You have a nice daughter," he said, nodding to Sandra's father.

Everyone knew Kenneth didn't like Mr. Kawachi for much the same reasons he disliked Sandra's father. "Mr. Kawachi promotes too many things Japanese, like his silly garden," he said at the kumiai, community meetings, in Shin-machi. Sandra had heard her parents talking about him. And Kenneth's disdain for Mr. Kawachi grew as he watched the man change the sea-dusted piece of land by their houses into a splendid Japanese garden. To discredit him further, Kenneth said, "Mr. Kawachi is not doing such a good job. Old age is catching up on him." While not true it did give people pause. Sandra had heard in her mother's discussion with friends that Kenneth continually thought of ways at the Shin-machi meetings to undermine Mr. Kawachi's position as the park's caretaker. "We need an American park," he had said. "Not a Japanese park." When the war started, people felt diffident about the park in their midst; they questioned if Kenneth wasn't right.

After Pearl Harbor was bombed, people guessed that Kenneth, because he worked as an interpreter for the FBI, was instrumental in having people like Sandra's father put into internment camps. At the onset of the war, Sandra heard people say, "Watch out for Kenneth." Sandra remembered how a neighbor, Mrs. Sumida, ran over to Sandra's house immediately after the bombing and declared, "Kenneth is happy because the United States has declared war on Japan. Mrs. Takahashi, your husband better be careful. Rumor has it that the kibei are being questioned."

Those who were interrogated by the FBI and Kenneth had the uneasy feeling that what he said, or did not say, to the government had much to do with who was shipped out and who was not. Sandra's father, because he had lived in Japan for many years and worked as a news editor, had been easy to commit.

At first, Sandra saw that people disliked Kenneth and feared him. In the early months of the war, people characterized him with angry pronouncements. They called him "inu," "oni," "trickster" behind his back. Gradually, however, people forgot his initial role and he became more powerful in the community. His position was transformed and grew in stature. If people shunned him at first, they gradually saw him in a different light. After all, the Japanese language schools were being shut down; anyone who already didn't have one took an English name; on top of that, everyone was told to speak only English.

One day when Mr. Kawachi was talking to Sandra's mother and Sandra at the park and they saw Kenneth pass by, Sandra's mother said in hurried Japanese: "My teachings tell me not to dislike that man, but I can't help it."

"It's all right. I dislike him too. Kenneth is osoroshī—a very scary man."

Sandra ran as fast as she could. That awful boy from school was chasing her again, hitting her with his terrible words.

"Traitor, traitor," the boy said and came after her with a stone in each hand. "Your papa's a traitor." He flung a stone and barely missed her head.

"No, he's not!" Sandra whirled herself around to face the boy.

"Your father's a bad man. He's a traitor."

"No, he's not, I said!"

Mr. Kawachi, hearing the commotion, materialized from between the hedges. "Oi-i-i," he said in a deep, slow voice, hands on his hips. He walked over to the boy. "Yame. Stop it! Leavu Sandra alone. You look like Nakamoto boy-san, no? Better not to do this, sabe? I will tell-u your papa. No good-u you."

Frightened, the boy nodded his head and dropped the other stone in his hand. He ran off, kicking up the gravel behind him.

Two years into the war, there was mounting evidence of a subtle change in the hearts of people—of distrust and shame toward Sandra's family by some of their friends and neighbors. Once friendly, many of the families in the village no longer bothered to help or call on Sandra's mother. Somehow the people felt Sandra's father *must* have been guilty of something. What bothered Sandra even more was that people forgot Kenneth's role right after Pearl Harbor. In a reverse of allegiance, Kenneth gained popularity among the Japanese. It was as if his reputation rose as Sandra's father's plummeted. Now, even the children went after her.

Mr. Kawachi took Sandra's hand and walked her to the park as she cried, hiccuped, and stumbled along. He made her sit down beside him on a rock near the swan pond, gave her a handkerchief from his hind pocket and pulled out corn mash from another. The swans honked when they saw Mr. Kawachi. They climbed out of the water and waddled up to the fence where he and Sandra sat. He gave the birds some corn mash and Sandra watched them feed.

After the incident, Sandra went more often to the park. She didn't say much but followed Mr. Kawachi around. She had missed her father without realizing it. Not long after, she began going to the park every day after school, then later, on weekends. She started going there early in the mornings, too. She helped Mr. Kawachi pick up the fallen leaves, trim the plants, feed the fish. While she did her work, she confided in him.

"Kenneth is a bad man. He came with the FBI. He made my father say things—"

"Soo ne," Mr. Kawachi said.

"And we are poor, now. Mama has to work hard, my brother's always sick. My father doesn't know that Mama's having a hard time. She just says that everything is all right to him when it's not. She says she doesn't want him to worry."

"I think so your mama do rightzu thing."

"But, why doesn't she tell him the truth?"

"No can do nothing, eh? Only hurtzu your papa hea." He pointed to his heart.

"What about us? My sickly grandmother had to come all the way from Kohala to help because Mama has to work at Ako's Fish Market. And I don't know much about how my father is. First they took him to the volcanoes. Then they said he was dangerous so they put him on a boat. Mama says he's in Idaho."

"Idaho? Soo ka."

"Where my father lives is very cold. Do you think we can go there to visit him?"

"Saa," Mr. Kawachi said, sucking in his breath noisily, taking off his hat and scratching his head. He didn't know what to say to Sandra. "C'mon, we go. You come helepu me," he said, instead.

Over the next few weeks, Sandra learned from Mr. Kawachi how to catch fish with his two-stick cross nets in order to transfer them from pond to pond. He also let her help him shape the black pines into what looked like tabletops or clouds. With her help, he stunted the growth of some plants with wire, and reshaped them into lovely ornaments. In his shed on rainy days, she helped him cast the heavy cement stepping-stones and piled up the split rocks for his walls.

Mr. Kawachi even taught Sandra how to feed the swans. At first, Sandra was skeptical, afraid of the snapping beaks of the big brassy birds, their breath hot and moist on her hands. With Mr. Kawachi's encouragement, however, she learned to trust the birds enough to feed them. Soon, they were honking at her the same way they greeted Mr. Kawachi.

As time passed, it was as if she had always heard the *snip, snip* of Mr. Kawachi's garden shears, the sound moving in the breezes, the cut leaves drifting upon the open lawns. She had grown up with the sound, now more familiar to her than her own father's voice. As she grew older, Mr. Kawachi's face got mixed up in her dreams with her father's face. Once she dreamed that her father had died and her new father was Mr. Kawachi.

She couldn't imagine life without the soothing sounds of Mr. Kawachi's voice or his garden shears. In the morning the sound greeted her as soon as she woke up, and at night it was usually the last sound she heard before she went into the house. She could tell from the sounds where Mr. Kawachi was working in the park. If she didn't hear anything, she had but to peer from her bedroom window and see the top of his lau hala hat bobbing above the horizon of plants.

Sandra's father had been gone for what seemed like many years for she could barely remember what he looked like. She was six when he left, and she was already close to being ten. During this interval, her responsibilities at home had grown larger and she was permitted to go to the park only after she did all of her chores. Weekends, she'd rush through her work so she could go across the street.

One Saturday, only silence greeted her. Usually, while she did her chores, she could hear Mr. Kawachi's shears or his hand lawnmower grinding away. This Saturday seemed different. She looked out the kitchen window while drying the dishes to see if she could spot his hat among the bushes. She saw nothing.

After hurrying through her chores, she said to her grandmother, "I'm going to Kawachi-san's place."

"Don't stay too long," her grandmother reminded.

She looked in the most likely places—in the shed and under the arched bridge. Mr. Kawachi was not there, so Sandra searched a wider area: the rock garden, the bamboo grove, the swan pond. On top of it, to her surprise, the birds had not been fed. Seeing her, the birds honked and called, but Sandra ignored them and headed for Mr. Kawachi's cottage.

She had never been in the Kawachis' home. "You are never to bother Mr. Kawachi there, you hear? He does enough for you every day." But today was an exception. She wanted to know his whereabouts, if he had gone somewhere without telling her. She went to the front door and knocked politely.

"Yes?" Mrs. Kawachi said. "I'll be right there."

Sandra heard a shuffling of slippers making its way to the door. Mrs. Kawachi appeared, wiping her hands on her apron. "Oh, Sandra," the woman greeted. "Please come in. Mr. Kawachi is not around, but—"

"He's not around? I didn't see him in the park today. I looked everywhere. I thought he might be home."

"Mm-m-m, that's strange. I thought I heard him walking around the place not too long ago. You sure?"

"I'm sure."

"I wonder—Come to think of it, I haven't heard his scissors for a while, too."

Sandra and Mrs. Kawachi looked at each other. Without saying much, Mrs. Kawachi slipped on her geta and went running up a path by the house and began calling for her husband. "Too-san. Too-san! Sandra try the shed and the grove, again," she directed. Sandra retraced her steps and called for the old caretaker. She was having no luck.

After a while, Mrs. Kawachi said, "You start from this end. I'll start from the other.

"Too-saaaan."

"Mr. Kawachiiii."

Their calls ribboned the hedges, footpaths, and flowerbeds. After a time, while walking on the camellia path, Sandra came upon Mr. Kawachi. He had collapsed. Wedged tightly between a rock wall and the hedges, and an overhang of bamboo and palm fronds, he appeared to be scarcely breathing.

"Mrs. Kawachi, over here," Sandra shouted.

"What happened?" Mrs. Kawachi said, upon seeing her husband's twisted form. "Sandra, run over to Hirai-san's store. Ask the man if he would come over with his car to take us to the doctor."

"Okay, I'll be right back." Sandra ran to the store as fast as she could.

Mr. Kawachi had suffered a heart attack. He was taken to Hilo Memorial Hospital, where he stayed for a time. When he finally did come home, Sandra's mother made her promise not to bother him. "He is a very sick man," she said.

That was just before summer. Sandra had been so looking forward to working with Mr. Kawachi during her school vacation, but the summer began quietly for all of the children who frequented the park. And there was much to do. Sandra tried to help Mrs. Kawachi as much as she could between her own chores. She fed the birds, trimmed what she could of the plants, picked up the abundant leaves.

Toward summer's end, Sandra grew concerned for the birds. They were testing their wings. At twilight she could hear them crash into the fences as they tried to fly. Hearing the crashing at night, her mother said, "Like you, everyone's concerned about the birds. Kenneth Ichida, too. I smell trouble. He's sticking his nose, again, into other people's business."

Mrs. Kawachi came over one night to talk to Sandra's mother. She was disturbed by what she'd been hearing. "Kenneth is saying that he wants my husband replaced. 'Someone fit needs to take care of the park and the birds,' he said. If he gets his way, we'll have no place to live. I wouldn't know where to go."

By now Kenneth was a pillar of the community. Despite earlier suspicions about him, the years had reversed people's sympathies to the point where he, the person with questionable values, had been easily forgiven, even elevated. Although Kenneth later suggested that Mr. Kawachi could continue living in the park, Sandra felt wary of his motives.

Sandra soon learned that Kenneth was working to have the swans shipped to the zoo in Honolulu. It angered Sandra that he was still intent on destroying the park. After that, she saw several changes taking place. Because no one else knew how to cut the birds' flight feathers, some workmen came and reinforced the fence around the pond with barbed wire. They also draped a heavy net over the top of the fence in order to stop the birds from flying away.

But the crashing of the birds into the fences did not stop. In a matter of time, surely, one of the birds would be seriously injured by the barbed wire. The crude chain-link fencing sounded like shattering glass whenever the birds flew into it. Sandra could hear them scream.

Sandra went to visit Mr. Kawachi often but never troubled him with what was happening to the birds. She knew Mr. Kawachi suspected what was going on, but they never discussed it. After all, he could hear the birds' cries and had seen workmen walking about in the park from his bedside window.

Hope upon hope dissolved each time Sandra thought Mr. Kawachi would get better. She thought that if he could get well enough to take care of the birds, the birds would be saved. But Mr. Kawachi never improved. He remained in bed well into the beginning of fall.

One day, out of desperation because she learned that the town, swayed by Kenneth's influence, had finally decided to ship the birds to Honolulu, Sandra ran off to see Mr. Kawachi. She told him about the situation.

"You must do something," Sandra said.

"I try," he said, and nodded his head at everything that she said to him. "But me, Izu doan know what can do."

Mr. Kawachi, in his kind heart, probably felt nothing but pity for Kenneth who was ashamed of his Japanese ancestry, but the problem of Mr. Kawachi's own mortality far outweighed the problem of Kenneth or the birds. Sandra had to say something to show Mr. Kawachi that what was happening was truly a grave matter.

"The birds are like my father, aren't they?" she said, finally, pressing him. "Well, aren't they?"

"Soo ne."

A few more days passed and Mr. Kawachi and Sandra said little to each other about the birds. Each day, Mr. Kawachi merely directed her to feed the birds, to let them eat as much and as often as they wanted. While Sandra did not question Mr. Kawachi, she thought his action strange since the birds had always been well fed. When the shipment date for the birds neared, two huge crates appeared on the park grounds. That was the day Mr. Kawachi swung into action.

"You get me wire cutta, pick-u ax-u, bamboo stick-u," he said. By the time Sandra came back with the tools, he was dressed in his work clothes and ready to go out.

"But—you can't," she said. "You'll get tired. Your misssus and I can do whatever needs to be done."

"Too-san—" Mrs. Kawachi said in a tone of caution.

Mr. Kawachi shook his head and waved his wife and Sandra away with a resolve that Mrs. Kawachi and Sandra knew they could not go against. He used the bamboo pole as his walking stick while Mrs. Kawachi helped steady him from one side. Sandra dragged the tools along in a burlap bag. They marched slowly to the swan pond.

Both birds moved up in excitement, not having seen Mr. Kawachi since his collapse. He took out some mash, stuck his hand into the feed opening, and petted the birds for a long time. His hand stroked their long supple necks lovingly, as if he were playing a musical instrument. The birds honked and nuzzled his hands. But soon, he shooed the birds away. In confusion, they spread out their wings and flapped them vigorously as if to show their caretaker the strength in them.

Under his direction, Mrs. Kawachi and Sandra helped him cut a large hole in the fence. They also dug away some of the fence spikes in the ground. Mr. Kawachi then whistled to his birds to coax them out. The birds strutted toward him as if to play, but Mr. Kawachi shooed them away from him, flapping his own arms like a bird's.

"Ike, ike. Go 'way," he shouted. But the birds, happy to see him, continued to hang around.

"Too-san, please, you're tiring yourself. Let's go in," Mrs. Kawachi finally said. She braced her husband against her body and helped him home. Sandra followed them into the house. From a room that faced the park, Mr. Kawachi and Sandra watched the birds strutting on the lawn. They waddled about with their wings half spread, as if stunned by freedom. They didn't seem to know what to do.

"Will they be all right?"

"Eh," nodded Mr. Kawachi.

Sandra and the Kawachis watched the birds well into the evening. At twilight, the birds gracefully tested their wings. They flapped them slowly at first, their wings billowing like Saturday's sheets on a laundry line. Then the swans lifted themselves in ballerina steps on the tips of their red webbed feet and stretched their necks forward. They honked with excitement. They took short, running flights and in jerks lumbered through the park. They flapped, fluffed, and ruffled their wings.

At last the birds lifted off from the pond. In their flight they circled the park slowly, as if to find their bearing, and they flew north into the late afternoon sky, their dark silhouettes embossed as if on an ancient scroll.

People cheered all the soldiers who came home from the war. There were parades to welcome them home. But when Sandra's father came home, the occasion was quiet, without fanfare. People still whispered behind their backs about how Sandra's father had been sent to internment. Even after the war, suspicions about him remained and lingered. Socially, Sandra's parents withdrew from many of the people they once knew in town because the people acted as if Sandra's father had truly done something wrong. By this time she was eleven and sensitive to what she saw people doing.

"It's not true, is it, all the talk, about Papa?" she asked her mother.

"Of course not," her mother snapped.

"Then why don't we go to Kitano-san's house like before? We never go to visit Maeda lady, either. What happened?"

"It's not because of anything at all. It's just that people don't know what to say. They don't seem to understand and we don't want to make them uncomfortable. Makes Papa feel bad, too."

Sandra's mother continued to work at the fish market because her father seemed unable to work once he was home. One day when Sandra went to the fish market to wait from her mother, she heard her mother's co-worker say, "Mrs. Takahashi. You're singing a lot these days, aren't you?" She saw her mother blush with a rascal smile across her face. "Hey, your humor is back, too!"

Sandra's younger sister and brother also took to their father as if he had never left, but Sandra was shyer, not yet used to having him in their lives. She was having problems accepting him. He was not like he had been before; he was always sick, sometimes snapping at her, unjustly.

After his return, her father was much thinner. He sat for hours on the porch doing nothing and there was a silence in the house that Sandra could not understand. "Papa is always so cold," he explained, offering his white, cloud hands to have them warmed between her own. But Sandra had difficulty touching him. She avoided her father when she could, often running off to the Kawachis' house rather than talk to him. She felt more comfortable at the Kawachis.

"You are hurting your father's feelings," her mother said.

But Sandra couldn't help herself. She felt more and more drawn to the Kawachis. It got so that Mr. Kawachi began discouraging her from coming over. "Ne, Sandra," he said one day. "Okay for you come-u my house when your papa away. But no good for you come-u, now. Come-u see me when I betta."

Sandra was crushed, puzzled.

One day, Mrs. Kawachi stopped by the house to tell them that Mr. Kawachi had died in his sleep. "It was peaceful, so it was good," she said and turned to Sandra. "My husband wanted you to have this box of hanafuda. He enjoyed the moments you spent playing cards with him after working in the garden."

Without saying anything, Sandra snatched the box away, and ran into the house. She slammed the door to her bedroom and flung the cards across the bed. "Sandra—?" her mother said, coming after her. Sandra lay on the bed like a piece of flat senbei. "You apologize to Mrs. Kawachi."

"Why? Why do I have to apologize?"

"Because you just have to." Sandra made no move.

"I will talk to you later," Sandra's mother said and pressed her lips together.

Outside, Sandra heard her mother say to Mrs. Kawachi, "Children are difficult sometimes—"

"It's all right. She'll get over it."

"Too bad about your husband. You'll be lonely," she heard her father say.

After a time, her father walked into her bedroom. "Sandra-chan—"

"Don't call me Sandra-chan. Only Mr. Kawachi could call me that."

"But, he's no longer here."

"You can never replace him even if you tried."

"I'm sorry, but I'm still your father."

"I don't care. You weren't around to see us suffer. You weren't here when people did not talk to Mama or were unkind to us. Or when they threw rocks at me. You just weren't here." Sandra threw the dharma wheel at her father, the one he had given her when he left. "Here take this back. It never brought us luck."

Sandra saw the weariness, the hurt, the despair in her father's eyes. She immediately wished she hadn't hurled her hurtful words at him and could take the hard rock of them back. But to have been looked upon by her father with so much understanding at that moment truly frightened her.

Sandra ran across the street and down to the empty swan pond. A couple of pintail ducks bobbed in the water fishing for medaka to eat. She sat at the pond's edge. She missed the swans. She looked at the Kawachis' house and felt an inescapable sadness. Would she have to fight this sadness all her life? She didn't know.

She knew that Mr. Kawachi would have been appalled at the way she had reacted to her father. He would have been disappointed at her lack of control. She had to take her father back, somehow, otherwise nothing would come of her life with him. Her father was here. Not the swans. Not Mr. Kawachi.

Sandra looked back toward the house. Her mother and father were on the porch and waving at her to come in. It was getting late. By her father's gesture and the way he leaned into her mother, she knew that she had hurt him, but that he had already forgiven her.

Koi Pond

Even during his illness, Seijiro Kikuta said to his wife, Kame, "Land is everything. Hold on to it if you can." The land would save them. It always gave back what you put into it. "The land is for the children," he said. "They'll come back to it, you'll see."

But the children didn't want the land. They hated the place. In the first place they couldn't wait to get away, go to college and look for jobs elsewhere. Now, they were all professionals, living in big cities. "What can we do with the land?" the children said. "We don't want it, sell it. Come and live with us in Honolulu." Or "Come and live with us in L.A."

Disheartened by his children's audacity—for hadn't he worked hard for their sakes?—Seijiro decided to live out his life in the only place he knew. Children, he thought to himself, were thankless in the end.

"Hoooi," hollered Joseph Castro as he whacked the reins of his horse on a guava tree branch so the leather strip would curl around the wood and hold. He lumbered his massive, barrel-chested body down to where the Kikutas lived. A large, middle-aged Portuguese man, Joe owned land surrounding the Kikutas. The Kikutas owned a thirty-acre parcel—some of the most fertile cane land in the area—almost in the center of Joe's property.

Over the years he had known them, Joe admired the land's productivity and the way the Kikutas worked it. At one time, Joe wanted the Kikutas' land, which made him befriend them in the first place. Gradually, the friendship turned into something more. Joe grew to *like* the Japanese family in spite of himself and respected their industry and forthrightness.

On a half acre in one corner of his property, Seijiro had built a small but attractive single-wall frame house on stilts, a sizeable catchment tank, a chicken coop, a bathhouse, and an outhouse with two heart-shaped seats. Persimmon, orange, tangerine, papaya, and lemon trees shaded and cooled the area. Banana trees lined the stream, which began with a spring in the heart of the property. From this spring passed some of the clearest and coldest water in the area. All around grew the grasses. Nothing but tall grasses: kikuya, Wainaku, California.

"Kikuta-san, how are youuu," said Joe, greeting his friend. Joe touched the brim of his hat to acknowledge Mrs. Kikuta, who stood beside her husband.

"Ah, Mama-san," he said addressing Kame, "No look-see you long time. How you beeen?"

Mrs. Kikuta, unsmiling, nodded her head. She was always suspicious of the big Portuguese man.

"Hey, Seijirooo."

"Ichi, ni, san . . ." Seijiro continued counting as he measured a yellow, clear liquid weed killer and transferred it into a gallon drum. Despite his friend's greeting, he kept on working. Only after he had finished measuring the poison did he look up to greet his friend.

"Goood eh, the new poison?" Joe said as he watched. "Make the grass ma-ke fas, this one. The plantation boss, he akamai for use this. Some goood the poison. Fo' sure."

"Velly good. Real pololei. Numba one poison, dis-a-one." Seijiro tapped the drum with one hand and held up the index finger of the other. "But must-u take kea—bum-bye plenty pilikia, no?"

"Naaah, no pilikia. Me, I hapai the stuff on my back. And no need mask. Only humbug, the stuff. Rubber booots, he 'nough. Buuut, dat not what I hea fo'," he said, changing the subject. He then asked, "Where you going todaaay? Where you go hanahana?"

Seijiro looked up at his friend and pointed seaward.

"Oh yeah? You, dat side alreaaady? You working too haaard. Look see you bum-bye. When you pau, come drink whiskey with me. My boooy, you know which one, the one no mo leeeg—the one he lose in Guam—he get new baaaby."

"Oh?" exclaimed Kame, brightening. "Aka-chan? Most nice-u, ne."

She smiled for the first time since Joe had come, wrinkling her face like a crushed sack.

"Eh," nodded Seijiro in affirmation of his wife's delight and Joe's invitation. Children. Seijiro thought of his own and shook his head.

Seijiro paused to watch Joe climb back up the hillside to his horse. He then turned to Kame and smiled at her. Seijiro's teeth were yellowed by tobacco stains but set as straight as a row of hanafuda cards.

Kame liked it when her husband smiled. She felt warm inside, for straight-faced he looked stern, his overbite making his lips look thick and resistant, his jaws set. Prematurely gray since he was thirty-five, he always wore hats to conceal the growth of thinning white hair: pith helmets, Panamas, lau hala, and a blue-gray felt hat with a black ribbon trim to wear with his black suit.

Caught in the right light, his beard stubble sparkled in the sun. He smelled of burnt wood, must from the humidity, talc, and hair oil. Big-boned, he walked heavily, his toes pointing outward. Today, working in the sun, he looked healthy, silvery.

Kame was much shorter, a shadow of her husband. She worked for his comfort and well-being and the occasional nod of approval that he gave her.

"Kame, my work clothes," he said.

"Hai," Kame said. She immediately dropped the bamboo pole she'd been using to mix the poisonous concoction Seijiro had just measured into the gallon drum. She ran into the house to gather her husband's clothing.

Once outside again, she helped him into a long-sleeved palaka shirt and his "epulu" or apron pants, and wrapped long strips of protective rags around his arms and legs. Seijiro also wore a handkerchief—cowboy-bandit style—and a wire face mask like a catcher's, which, instead of stray baseballs, warded off the razor-sharp edges of the cane leaves to protect his eyes. Lastly, he squared a pith helmet on his head, knocked on it for security, and tied it under his chin.

After the plowing, the fertilizing with bonemeal, the planting of the cane shoots, it took another three years for the cane to grow before its burning for harvesting. As the cane grew, weeds had to be controlled. Otherwise, they choked the growth of the young cane. Hired women did the hoe-hana and pula-pula—the hoeing and planting of the seed cane—but the women were only good for getting rid of grass in the inner fields. For grass that grew along the irrigation ditches and the property lines, weed killers controlled the thick growth best.

After Seijiro was properly dressed, he poured the poison mixture with an old cooking pot and transferred it into a covered tank. "That should be just right," he said to Kame, peering into the tank.

"Yes, just right," agreed Kame.

The poison tank had a hand pump, spray nozzle, and a hose, the tank strapped on Seijiro's back like a backpack. He walked into the fields looking stiff as a mummy and worked the pump with his left hand. With his right hand, he held the nozzle to direct the spray. Whenever the pump was pulled, it made a sucking sound that alternated with the spray of poison. One only had to listen to the *shuck, shuck, sh-h-h-h-h-h* to know where Seijiro was at any time in the field.

Kame ran the household and tended the garden. While Seijiro worked in the cane, she sewed linseed oilcloth raincoats for the bachelor Filipino men who lived in the area, and bleached and boiled rice bags to sell—four for two bits. She used a large tarai in the yard to boil the bags, to bleach them. Later, she laid the cloths in the sun to whiten them further. She made extra money this way; earlier, it had helped to send her children through school. She knew very little about raising cane and left most of its care to her husband.

"Hoi. Give me some juice," Seijiro said when he came out of the fields. The hard work made him thirsty and he wanted some fruit juice to quench his thirst.

Kame dropped her work and fetched her husband something cold to drink. Seijiro lowered the tank from his back to the ground and went to sit on the steps, his legs apart, one hand on his thigh, the other mopping his forehead. He looked up to survey his land, taking long, breathless drafts of the juice that Kame had brought him.

Thirst satisfied, he filled his tank with more poison and went back into the fields. At the end of the day, he poured out the leftover weed killer and sprinkled it into the tall grass that bordered the property line between his field and Joe Castro's.

Wailuku River put an abrupt end to Hilo. The town was a backwater even in the decades after the war. A bridge spanned the river, and past the Pueo district a junction connected the old sugar mill road with Wainaku and Kaiwiki Roads.

The Kikutas lived six miles uphill from that junction. Off the main road, cane sagged into the roadway and wind rustled the leaves of sap-coated, ant-infested, molasses-smelling stalks. Honohono and California grasses lifted their tangled masses toward the sun. Vegetation everywhere. Grass grew taller than some of the trees and groups of gnats spun like carousels. How anyone could leave this place was beyond Seijiro's understanding.

Seijiro loved the smell of the dirt's sweet heat. Walking through the fields, he'd cup the soil of this land into his hands and let the dirt run through his fingers and inhale as if he were taking a breath of the earth. Every year he thanked the gods for the abundance given him. On an altar of stones, he dedicated food, an offering of dried squid, a strip of kelp, rice cakes, and tangerines, to the land.

At this time, the couple had only one indulgence—an elegant Japanese garden in which Seijiro maintained an elaborate pond. In this pond, he raised a school of elegant carp—a source of pride and joy in the void of children.

Seijiro had built his pond just before the war. During the war, afraid of being interned, he destroyed everything connected with Japan—all except the pond and its surrounding gardens, which were the only things he saved as symbols of his homeland.

He made the garden as authentic as he remembered, everything by hand, and scaled them to size. No detail escaped him. An entrance gate or torii towered on one side. Two stone lanterns decorated opposite ends of the pond and two overarching bridges spanned the pond's width as they joined each other on an island in the middle of the water. Seijiro forged the gate, the stone lanterns, along with the bridges out of a mixture of black sand, gravel, cement mix, and discarded barbed wire fencing. He shaped these items from memories of gardens past, those he had seen as a young man before coming to Hawai'i.

He hid flat cement pots of bonsai under a carpet of moss and Korean temple grass. Stunted and deliberately crippled arms of juniper and pomegranate ornamented the island. To the left of these plants, a bamboo spigot cycled clear water that was connected to the spring. Catty-corner to the spigot, a pole created a barrier to contain the water hyacinths and purple-colored pond lilies to one side. Just after the war started, Seijiro bought fish to put into the pond.

"Kame, come quick," he said one day. "Take a look at this. Nice, aren't they?"

"My, they look like—"

"Eh, imperial koi. From Matsunaga-san. He gave me the babies."

Kame stuck her face close to the rim of the bucket round as her face. "This must be the kind the Emperor of Japan raises in his ponds around the palace." She turned to her husband and asked him solemnly, "You think it's okay to have these here?"

"Saa, I don't see . . . why not?"

After a long pause she continued, her face grave. "There's a rumor that Joe Castro turned in the Kohashis—do you think that's true? Maybe he'll turn us in, too. People say you can't trust him."

"Turn us in—for fish? That's crazy. Hush, woman. Don't talk too much. No one knows for sure about Kohashi-san. Joe is pololei with us—a good man."

"Castro-san brag too much!"

"If he wants my land, he could turn me in and take it away. He could turn me in for something." Seijiro contemplated the thought, then gazed at the long stretch of cane before him. "But remember, he saw all the books and things we had from Japan. He never said anything about them to anyone. I'm sure of it."

"So you think it's all right to keep the fish?"

"We will keep the fish. Don't worry," reassured Seijiro, clumsily putting a rough hand on Kame's shoulder. "What can anyone do to two uneducated farmers? We are small fish in a big sea," he said, smiling.

The tiny fish were exquisite. They twisted like orange peels in the water. Kame slid her hands into the bucket of cold water to touch them, but the fish darted smartly away.

"Come. We must put them into the pond before they die." At the water's edge, Seijiro angled the bucket into the water and let the fingerlings flow out like gold confetti. The fish quickly found refuge under the duckweed and tangle of lily roots.

By the time the war ended, the couple had a grand-looking pond, and their children were all gone. Without the children, watching the fish had become a favorite pastime. After a long day in the fields, tending flowers, or doing other chores, Seijiro and Kame took some time out to feed the fish. They found much peace in doing this, their hands brushing lightly against each other's. Their verandah overlooked the pond and each evening they sat on their rockers and tossed crusty old bread that swelled like sea sponge after hitting the water. The koi chased after these bobbing morsels.

The koi grew easily—two, three, or more feet long. They smacked their thick lips to feed as they skimmed the surface, sweeping the water for tossed bread. Whenever Seijiro stuck his hand into the water or waded into the pond to clean it, the fish puckered and sucked on his fingers and toes. The fish—red, white, black, or tricolored—swam in lethargic circles. Others glimmered, gold or silver. Flashes of color emitted like neon from the pond on clear, full moon nights.

"Seijirooo, you come my house. Make one pond for me, tooo," Joe proposed to his friend. Other people had also asked Seijiro to help with their ponds. Many more came to buy the healthy fingerlings.

Joe liked to be around, days when Seijiro drained the pond. The prolific fish laid ribbons of sticky, translucent eggs on the water hyacinth roots and sperm turned the water murky.

"All-u time too much-i egg-u," Seijiro complained to his friend.

Joe laughed, slapping Seijiro on the back. "Like us—make plenny baaabe." The men laughed at their fecundity.

While Seijiro cleaned, Kame lifted the heavy lily plants with their long beardlike roots festooned with gelatinous eggs and let them dry on the banks. Later, she threw the plants back into the pond. The large fish attacked the dried eggs to feed on them.

The pain started in spurts. Sometimes it hit Seijiro like a mule kick. At other times it came as a slow, spidery crawl. The pain would stop him momentarily, but it was easily forgotten with the attention he focused on his work. Sometimes he doubled over with a moan, and if the pain persisted he'd stop working and walk out of the fields.

One day, he called out. "Hoi, get me some water, with some Alka-Seltzer."

Although surprised that he didn't want juice, Kame accommodated his wishes with a Welch's jelly jar of water, two fizzing Alka-Seltzer tablets on the bottom, air bubbles walking up the glass. "Yoroshī," he said after gulping the fizzy medicine and smacking his lips. He went back out to work.

At the time, Kame thought nothing of it, but in thinking back she should have taken it as a sign that something was wrong with him. "If only—" she sighed in retrospect.

That fall, several weeks before the rains hit, men worked strenuously in the fields to control the grass. All too soon the rains came. After the third day of a steady rain, Joe galloped over to the Kikutas on his horse and hollered to his friend. "Eh, Seijirooo. Come help. The flume—mauka side—look like going huli."

"Soo ka. We must-u fix-u, ne. Matte. I go witzu you."

The two men worked side by side far into the night to control the flume water. The long winding ribbon of the flume's frame threatened to topple over into the gulch. They hooted and whistled in getting the job done. After coming back home, they drank Seijiro's homemade sake. With much thigh slapping, they sang and toasted the land in its abundance.

"Kampai to the raaain."

"Heh, kampai to the flume-u."

"Kampai to the plantation booosses."

"Heh, to the cane-u, the grass-u. Kampai, kampai."

One morning after several days of constant rain, it let up a bit and the sun crept out from the clouds. In the afternoon, after Seijiro had worked all day, uprighting cane downed by the deluge, he went to the fishpond as he usually did. He came upon something strange. All the fish were swimming close to the surface and gasping for air.

"Kame, hurry, come take a look at this."

Kame put aside the laundry she'd been gathering from the line and ran to the pond. When she reached Seijiro's side, she cupped her face into her hands in dismay. "What do you think this could be?"

Seijiro shook his head. "I don't know. It could be anything."

He looked into the pond and tasted the water. Some of the smaller koi had already begun to turn on their sides and others had released their deep rich coloring only to display a sickly sheen.

"Go get me a fish net and bring me your wooden washtub. Fill it with fresh water from the spring." he said.

Kame obeyed and filled the large tub with clear water. As Kame stood by the spigot that ran the spring water into the tub, Seijiro called out to her: "Get me some Hawaiian salt, too."

Up to his waist in the cold water, Seijiro tried saving the larger fish in the pond. He'd corral a fish, hold it in his arms, and gently rub salt—on areas scales were slowly sloughing off. The fish looked puffy as if afflicted with dropsy.

Over the next few days, Seijiro did very little work. He devoted all of his time to nursing the fish. At night, he tossed in his sleep.

"Saa, I wonder what I can do," he said.

He dreamt nothing but fish dreams. In one of them, the strong carp swam a great river but could not ascend the rapids. They fell back, time and time again. He watched but could do nothing to help them.

One afternoon Seijiro went to talk to Matsunaga-san. "Maybe you would know. Many years ago—saa it must have been was during the war—I bought some fish from you and—"

"I remember. What's wrong?"

"Well, they grew to be very big, but now they're all sick. I wanted to know if anything like this has ever happened to you?"

"I can't say it has. It's very strange, isn't it? I'm so sorry about the fish."

"It's not your fault. I was just wondering if anybody else was having the same trouble." He walked away with his head down. Later he went into town and borrowed fish books from a friend. He searched for information and a remedy.

Kame stood by helplessly. She watched her husband take the sick fish, wrap his hands around their bellies, and guide them around and around the pond to help them swim. Each morning he was up early to cover the damaged skin of the fish with Mercurochrome or a salt poultice.

A tired, unshaven Seijiro took on a sickly look. He spat constantly. A sour mucus began backing up into his throat, causing him to gag. As the days went by, he watched every single fish belly up, slowly bloat, then die.

Seijiro performed his own unskilled autopsies on some of the fish. He didn't know what he was looking for, but he felt the answer lay in their stomachs. He never found anything. Finally, he resigned himself to their deaths and dug a shallow grave, lined it with lye, and dropped in the dead fish.

Joe came to console his friend in the best way he could. "Must be the poiiiison. What you thiiink? Maybe the waaater from my side, when go inside your spriiing, eh? What you saaay?" Joe's suspicion that the runoff from his fields may have seeped into the groundwater and into the Kikutas' spring appeared more and more plausible.

After all the fish had died, Seijiro drained the pond. Disgusted, he took his shovel and buried what was left of it. Fans of loose, black dirt flew violently into the air, and only a dark mound like a grave marked the spot where the pond had once been. Seijiro stripped the island of its plants and distributed the bonsai among his friends.

"Joe. Here. I give-u you this," Seijiro said as he offered Joe one of the ornamental plants, which had taken him years to grow.

"Naaah. That youuurs. I no can taaake—"

"Wassamalla you. You take-i."

"Okay, but no neeed—"

With a sledgehammer, Seijiro smashed the concrete bridges, the gates, the stone lanterns. In the following weeks, he neglected his work and his cane. Tormented, he and what was left of his garden took on a wild, uncompromising look. The smell of overgrowth, warm grass, decay, and death preened the air, and pain grew feathery, wild in Seijiro's body.

"I struggled all my life . . . for what?" he asked Kame.

Early in the spring, Seijiro was diagnosed with liver cancer. In the back of all their minds—Kame's, Joe's, the rest of the people in the camp—there was a strong suspicion that years of working with the potent chemicals everyone used in the fields may have contributed to his cancer.

When Joe went to visit him, Seijiro said, "This time-u I all-u pau. Me ma-ke, soon."

"Why you talk l'daat, you lolo Japaneee," Joe said as he tapped his head.

Seijiro smiled at Joe's crude encouragement.

Seijiro had few lucid moments toward the end. At times, he reminisced about his life, about his land, but he never mentioned the fishes, again. He died early that summer.

Right after the war, there had been talk about Seijiro's friendship with Joe. The Japanese community had shunned Joe because of their suspicions of him advanced by the rumor that he had turned people in during the internment. But Seijiro paid them no mind.

Kame, on the other hand, had a harder time accepting her husband's longtime friend. Her husband's friendship with Joe had been like a chronic toothache, where she never knew when the pain of knowing Joe would become more intense. Nevertheless, over the years she had maintained a veneer of politeness toward Joe for her husband's sake.

Several weeks after Seijiro had died, Joe came across Kame working in the fields. "Mama-san. How you beeen?" he asked from atop his horse. As he looked down at her, Kame looked up at him and nodded her head.

"I pololei," she said, half-heartedly.

She had taken over caring for the fields after Seijiro had died. Her children wanted her to quit this work, retire, live with them, but she had promised Seijiro she would take the cane to harvest, at least one more time.

"Pretty soon, I cut-chi, cut-chi cane," she said. "When pau, I give you all-u this."

She swept her hand across the breadth of what was now her land. The years and age, the leveler of all things, made this once mistrusted man her closest friend. She wanted him to have the first choice. "You buy, ne?"

Joe came around most when Seijiro was ill. The strong feelings of deep mistrust she felt before no longer bothered her. The old misperceptions were pierced and drained like the abcess of her thoughts that they were. Everyone was now too old to care about what mattered to them when they were younger.

Joe shook his head. "One time I like buy, but now, I too ooold."

"Your boy—no like-i? I give him—good-u price-u."

"Naaah. I no think so. Young folks nowadays—they no like work haaard. Too tough, cane work."

Kame understood what he meant about the children. She waved him on, picked up the nozzle, and continued to poison the grass in her fields.

Part II

A frog in a well does not know the ocean.
—Japanese proverb

Motonaga Women

"They were really something," people said of the Motonaga women. Beautiful, cordial, but cold, all of them. What happened to the girls after they left remains a mystery. Once, they lived with their mother in her plantation home on the Hāmākua Coast. All the village people knew was that one day the women disappeared, leaving their mother to fend for herself.

That was a long time ago. Now, the house is in disrepair, the porch termite eaten, the windows broken, the catchment sagging. The Motonaga lady is old, bent at the waist, and has no teeth. It's been said that not one of her daughters has come around since they left. Not even the granddaughter, the one the villagers said the old woman doted on. It's been said, too, that the girls moved far away—some speculate as far away as San Francisco, maybe Chicago.

None of the Japanese women in the small village where the girls had lived wanted to be in the same predicament—where children never come to visit. It was a fate to be avoided at all cost. For this terrible fate to be avoided, for it to serve as a lesson for the families, however, they would have had to know the story. But the Motonaga lady had been closemouthed about what happened to her daughters and why they left so quickly. What really happened to the girls the townspeople could only speculate; the circumstances were never made clear, except to me, her neighbor.

When the Motonaga girls were young, their father died suddenly. This left the Motonaga lady to raise her three daughters alone, the girls toshigo, born in a row. As Naruko, the oldest girl, once said to a friend, "It is lucky that our father died at an early age. Our parents might have had more children than they could afford, spouting them faster than sugarcane."

After Naruko came Yuri. Mie came last. They were all very tall, striking, slender, and elegant looking. Naruko was the only one who had been married. Although Yuri and Mie had dated, a creeping dissatisfaction with the unworldly men in their town destroyed any meaningful relationships for them. People called the girls "high kala," high-collared, behind their backs.

Naruko had a daughter called Tomi-chan who existed quietly among the ethereal-looking women in her family. As the years passed, she became more and more withdrawn, a brooder, living in a household that rattled like dried lima beans in their casings.

Tomi-chan's dad, Naruko's husband, had fought in the war and died in Anzio, Italy. The couple had been married just before he enlisted in 1943, and their daughter was born in the following year. Tomi-chan must have been but a few months old when her father died. Feeling sorry for Naruko who lived alone in Hilo at the time, the Motonaga lady took in her oldest daughter and new grandchild. The family of women were together, once more, under one roof.

Way before the war, when the Motonaga girls were still young and they went into Hilo with their mother, all heads turned in their direction. What the Motonaga girls wore and how they applied their makeup were hot topics for the day. Polite young girls admired the girls from afar. They hooded their eyes so as not to be obvious in their staring, held their breath, and straightened their backs to emulate the Motonaga girls' beauty, which they aspired to copy for their small-town looks and faces.

"High-toned," the Motonaga women dressed to the *nines*, the handsome, strong-willed mother in a day kimono, white tabi, and straw slippers; her willowy young daughters in pageboy bobs, American-style dresses, hats, two-toned pumps, matching purses, each with a white hanky tucked inside, a corner of linen showing.

The Motonaga lady and her daughters made up their faces skillfully. In the way that they showed up their faces cosmetically, the girls were something to behold. "They must use the best okeshō, ne, to have such beautiful and flawless complexions in such humid weather," the village women speculated.

In reality, the Motonaga women achieved their flawless looks suitable for the tropics by being crafty, looking *natural*, not giving in to having the white-faced looks the Japanese prized in the old country.

No one would have guessed the hours they spent making cosmetics. The mother collected rice talc for their faces from the bottom of the hundred-pound rice bags. The girls gathered lemons and guavas for astringents, ginger sap for shampoos, and they bought cheap witch hazel from the Japanese druggist in town.

With denim bags strapped on their sides, the girls climbed a tall winter avocado tree in a gulch by their home for a face pack to brighten their complexions and tighten their pores. They rubbed ice, dabbed cheap lipstick, or wild thimbleberry juice on their cheeks. They pinched, tweaked, and massaged their faces, and bit into their lips for more color.

The girls foraged for berries and selected plants from the rainforest nearby for their concoctions. They walked miles. But how grand the results, the girls looking so pretty, the rice talc giving a pearly sheen in the right light, and the berries accentuating their high cheekbones and full lips.

Outwardly, the Motonaga women appeared close-knit. "They get along so well, don't they?" people remarked. Often the women were used as examples of congeniality, their names frequently said to admonish errant children about family unity and harmony. They cultivated this reputation and perpetuated the notion for they were good at "keeping face" in front of people.

In actuality, the Motonaga women were vain and self-centered. Away from people's stares, they bickered among themselves, their talk filled with accusations and recriminations. Tomi-chan, who was born a happy baby, gradually grew sullen, becoming withdrawn in an atmosphere of fights and admonitions. At the time of the family breakup, Tomi-chan must have been around seven years old.

Very often, the women fought over money. "You're spending too much," Naruko said to Yuri, one day.

"You could share more of your husband's GI insurance with us, you know? We have so little. You can also work full time instead of working part-time at Kress Store so we can continue to volunteer for the church," Yuri said.

"Quit your volunteering. You girls should work full-time, too," Naruko said back.

"Then what would people think? Then they'll *know* we have no money. For one thing you can quit taking Sakamoto-san's taxi to work. Take the county bus. No one looks down on that."

While taking Sakamoto-san's black taxi to work was a considerable extravagance at the time Naruko must have felt it was worth showing others that her job was just a pastime for her. Yuri and Mie continued their volunteer work for the church for the same reason—in keeping with the illusion that they were comfortably situated financially. But there was always never enough and things got tighter after the war.

It was then that the Motonaga lady changed her outlook. She was tired of keeping up the pretense of being well-off and perfectly dressed. Although she had something small from her husband's pension from the plantation, she began supplementing her income, first by doing odd jobs for people, then later, working for the plantation as a cane cutter.

"Mama, it's shameful to have you working for the plantation," Naruko said one day. Her other daughters looked at her with narrow eyes, shook their heads, and agreed.

But times were difficult and changing and the Motonaga lady grew more practical as she grew older, releasing herself from particulars peculiar to Japanese judgment and tradition.

"You should do the same," she said, and while she was willing to accept her household's needy circumstances and forego frivolous luxuries, her daughters protested. They wanted to keep up their ever-thinning disguise of wealth in front of people by not working much. Too, they desperately hung on to the latest fashions.

Always desirous to be with the times, Naruko and her sisters announced to their mother one day that they had saved enough money to buy her some underwear. "From now on," Naruko said, "you're going to wear panties and bras like everyone else. Throw away your koshimaki." For once, and especially because they were going against their strong-willed mother, the girls held together like sticky rice.

"There's no need to buy me new things," the Motonaga lady said. "No one will see what I wear, so it doesn't make any difference. The Japanese underclothes work just fine."

"But what if you have to go to the hospital?" Yuri said, her nose flaring, a whine coming through her words. She had heard the hospital argument at the church where she volunteered and had used it to persuade her mother about the change.

"Yes, Mama. Do you want people to see your funny-looking underwear?" Naruko said, siding with her sister.

"People are going to laugh at you when they see your rice-bag panties and hip wraps. What if you fall in the cane field and get hurt and they have to take you to the hospital? You must keep up with the times, Mama. Nobody's wearing kimono and underclothing like yours. Before, it was okay but now, after the war, you have to wear more American-style clothes," Mie said, her voice more expressive than usual.

"Yes, you really should wear the proper underwear, Mama," Naruko said again, the girls nodding their heads.

"So what do you propose I do?" asked the Motonaga lady, her hands on her hips.

"We are going to buy you some new underwear, that's what we're going to do. From Sears. And you're going to learn to wear them. But first we have to measure you," Yuri said, her large dark eyes dancing over her mother's thin frame.

Of course, the Motonaga lady did not have her head buried in her sewing or in the red dirt of the fields like other Japanese women who would have had their wishes buried in their nonassertion, in deference to the young. She braced herself and prepared to go after her daughters, having picked up on their looks of disrespect. Blood rose to the Motonaga lady's head, which carried with it an unwillingness to back down. She narrowed her eyes like a cat's, stiffened her back, and readied herself for an attack.

This time, the daughters deferred to their mother, subsuming their own wishes. Just one ugly word between them would start them fighting, whereupon nothing would be accomplished. The girls understood this. They reined in their hard natures, temporarily, in order to get their way, a strategy they had come up with earlier.

"Come here," Naruko said with tact, overtaking the sensitive moment and concealing it behind her busy demeanor. "Let me measure you. I have to know your size."

"I don't want to," the Motonaga lady said, mildly protesting.

It had surprised her that her daughters had skillfully thwarted a fight that she had anticipated and looked forward to resolving. She would have to wait for another opportunity.

Mie handed her oldest sister a measuring tape taken from their mother's dresser. While Naruko and Yuri sat on their mother's sagging bed, Mie placed her hands on her mother's shoulders and spun her this way and that. "Measure under her breasts," Naruko said.

"Yes and measure her waist," directed Yuri. For the moment and although the Motonaga lady found the procedure distasteful, she went along, seeing no harm in getting herself measured.

Tomi-chan watched what went on as she sat on the floor nearby.

"Go get me the headpins and the bone marker. The blue chalk and pen and paper, too," Naruko said to her daughter. "And hurry. Don't tele-tele."

Whenever asked to fetch something, Tomi-chan dragged herself the same slow way she walked to school. Unlike her mother and aunts who were punctilious and excellent students, Tomi-chan was a poor student. She was not driven as her aunts and mother had been to do their best, to "show up" other people.

The Motonaga lady frequently lamented Tomi-chan's lack of spirit. "Funny child that one, always looking at the rain. Always hiding or climbing in the trees. Always running away."

As the years went by, the Motonaga lady grew more concerned about Tomi-chan's poor attitude—a persistence in her grandchild's tendencies to neither want to excel, nor to have any friends—wanting only to run away from her problems. "Not too good to be alone so much," the Motonaga lady scolded her granddaughter in rapid-fire Japanese.

Tomi-chan seemed happiest when she could disappear into the cane fields and belt out songs by Misora Hibari, Eddie Fisher, or Peggy Lee. People could hear her sing "Mañana" or "Oh My Papa" or

"Ringo no Hanabira," mixing the lyrics of several songs, giving them her own strange twist.

Paradoxically, even if the girls came across as aloof, they still prized cooperation and the ability to work in groups as something they needed in order to survive in their society. The women had instinctively mastered these behaviors well in front of outsiders, but they could not instill these behaviors in Tomi-chan. She was too independent. To the women, Tomi-chan seemed like a throwback, a feral child. When she came home with poor reports from school, she caused her grandmother and mother untold anxiety and guilt for their inability to change her.

As Tomi-chan sat at the foot of the bed, she watched her mother and aunts work over her grandmother. How efficiently her mother spread the tape, unwinding and rewinding it around her grandmother's irregular body as she wrote cryptic figures on paper.

"Honestly Mama," Naruko was saying, "I don't know how we're going to fit you. Look. Look at you, your breasts. They're hanging down to your waist. Your stomach too, looks fat and flabby, everything sagging." Naruko shuddered. The others confirmed what their sister said with their eyes. "That's because you don't wear a bra. Am I not right girls? Mama needs to wear American-style clothes."

"Someday you'll be sorry for what you say to me. Everything sags because of *you*." She looked at each daughter, piercingly.

The day the box from Sears arrived, everyone assembled once more around the Motonaga lady's bed to take a look at the contents of the package. Yuri opened it in haste, while her mother folded the tissue paper the new underwear was wrapped in, for use in the outhouse. In their home nothing went to waste. This was how the women scrimped and saved. As long as the girls could remember, their mother collected all the wrappings shipped apples came in—green, purple, orange tissue paper—from the vegetable man. That was one way they saved to wear the latest fashions, a faint smell of apples about them.

The Motonaga lady unbound her body wrappings and tried on the new garments. "I like these nai-lon-u pantaloon, but I hate this," she said, pointing to the bra. "Why do I have to put on these funny things that I must struggle to wear?"

"Because it's the right thing for women," Naruko said.

But the Motonaga lady felt it strangling, too tight to support her sagging breasts adequately. "I don't want them," she said and tossed the bra aside and wrapped herself in her old rice-bag cloth.

"Oh, Mama!" cried out Naruko, beside herself, as she retrieved the bra off the floor. "I never saw such a hardhead."

"Mama, please use them," Mie said.

But no amount of coaxing by her daughters could change the Motonaga lady's mind. "You girls like cumbersome things," the Motonaga lady said. "You use them."

"I spent good money for them," Naruko said. She waved the bra in the air. Her voice grew shrill. "And you're not going to wear it?"

"Throw away!"

"You got your nerve!" Naruko said.

"Yeah, you have the nerve," Yuri said.

Not to be left behind, "You're certainly boneheaded, like Papa used to say," Mie said, acting surprised.

"How you girls behave! How shameful! You have no respect." Furious, the Motonaga lady grabbed the bra from Naruko, flung it on the bed, and stormed out.

Naruko gave a long sigh. She had never seen her mother so angry. "Oh, well," she said, letting out a breath of resignation.

"It's your fault, Naruko," Mie said.

"No, it's not," said Naruko.

"Yes, it is," said Yuri. "You started it."

Tomi-chan covered her ears.

Suddenly, their mother came flying back into the room. This time she carried a pair of large scissors in her hand. It looked as if she wasn't about to let her daughters off so easily, or her grandchild, without a lesson. She snatched the bra off the bed and punched out the cups of the bra with her fist to the bra's ample cup size. She then snipped the bra in half and tossed one cup to one side of the bed, the other to the opposite side.

Seething, she glared at her daughters. She pointed first to one bra cup then the other. She said: "This is Japan. It is a land where men constantly tell you what to do. And this is Hawai'i, another ogre island. I left one ogre island for another. I thought I was free of ogres when your father died. But, you girls are worse. Oh, my brazen, ungrateful, beautiful daughters. What have I done?"

Shamed, the girls cowered under their mother's tongue-lashing and cast their eyes on the floor. Naruko tried placating her red-faced mother. "Mother, you're being a bit melodramatic, don't you think," she said with forced lightness in her voice.

What Naruko said, however, was a bit too snide for her mother's liking. It was the last cane stalk, the last stick of wood for the bath fire. The Motonaga lady, furious at her daughters' disrespect, wheeled around and said, "Get out, all of you. You're no longer welcome here."

"Go, go," she screamed. She took the scissors and ran after each of them. The girls flew out of the house like scared chickens from a coop. "You too, Tomi-chan," she said and pointed to the door. "Go with your mother."

The Motonaga lady tied her kimono sleeves with her sash. She gathered the bottom of her kimono, hitched up the cloth between her legs, and tucked part of it into her front waistband. She then began to overturn each of her daughters' dressers, threw their purses and clothing and wicker suitcases out the window and into the yard. Such a spectacle of delicate underwear, silk blouses, and beautiful dresses floating out of the windows and settling upon the grass, the hedges, and the trees had never been seen before. But no one around saw the display or heard the commotion, the houses in the village too far apart.

"Mama, why?" Naruko asked.

Each time one of the girls approached the house to talk with her mother, the Motonaga lady went after that daughter and chased her out. This went on throughout the afternoon. Later, when things quieted down, the girls tried calling out sweetly to their mother.

"Mama please, be reasonable," Naruko said, her tone cajoling. She paced the grass and occasionally gave it a sweep with her feet.

Once when Naruko inched up to the door, she found that all the doors and windows to the house had been locked. She walked down the steps and said to her sisters, "Mama's locked all of the doors. What are we going to do?"

The girls, astonished by their mother's actions, began blaming each other. "It's your fault, Naruko," Mie said.

"I would shut my mouth if I were you," Yuri said.

"Shut up, both of you! I'm tired of all this. I'm still your oldest sister."

They tore at each other and hissed like fighting chickens. Later, exhausted, everyone remained quiet for the rest of the day—the day open as a wound—raw in its confusion. They sat on the lawn. They circled the trees.

As night approached, the women grew apprehensive. "I guess Mama's not going to let us in," Naruko said. "How much money do we have?"

"Not much," said Yuri.

They finally decided to catch a taxi into town. While gathering their belongings, they realized that Tomi-chan was nowhere to be found. The women had forgotten all about her during the fight with their mother.

Just before sunset, the sisters went from door to door. "We're looking for a tall ladder," Naruko said. In their search, the girls smiled pleasantly at their neighbors and thanked them politely. "We need to help our mother to pick some avocado tomorrow," Naruko said.

People suspected nothing. No one noticed the high color of the girls' faces or their cry-swollen eyes. The young Motonaga girl, it was learned later, had climbed the tallest rose-apple tree in the area and couldn't be coaxed down.

Soup

I dragged our old green, painted-over, fanned wicker chair up to the front window and pulled myself into the basketlike seat. From the high back of the chair's rim, I peered across Kīlauea Avenue, then down the gravel dirt lane directly across our house. Mr. Sato's cherry tree at the head of the lane blocked my view, but I noted that some of the cherries were ripe and ready to eat. In the future, I would watch to see when Mr. Sato left the house so I could go and pick some.

Then I saw *her* again. This time she had on a pair of thigh-high, black rubber boots. In one arm she held what looked like an old and small Easter basket woven in rainbow colors. She had a red kerchief tied around her head Indian fashion and walked down some steps, which stuck out from the side of their unpainted house like a tongue. I lost sight of her as she rounded the corner toward the back of her house.

"Come on, Mari, it's time to set the table," my mother said.

"A-w-w-w man, tell Rei do it. I *always* gotta do it." I really didn't want to stop watching the girl across the street.

"Your sister's doing the dishes tonight. It's your turn to set the table. You remember—every other night, taking turns?"

"I know, I know, but it's Rei's turn."

"Mari, you *know* it's your turn, so don't lie!"

"Okay, okay, you don't have to yell at me."

I walked over to the table. Mother was at the kitchen sink scraping a burdock root, slicing it thin, to eat with slices of Portuguese sausage.

"What you making?" I asked, looking into the sink at the white slivers of the root. "Oh, that. Ugh, I hate that stuff."

"You eat what we have, Mari. Don't be ungrateful. And don't make a face," she said and sliced the root more furiously. "Another thing. I don't want you staring at the people across the street from the window, you hear? We don't do things like that."

"Can't do this, can't do that. Can't do anything around here," I said under my breath as though I were rolling marbles in my mouth.

"Mari!"

"All right, all right," I said and moved my head from side to side.

How did my mother know I was staring at *her*? The next-door neighbor girl said that Japanese mothers had eyes behind their backs. I was beginning to believe it.

The girl across the street was new to the neighborhood. The principal in our school put her in my third grade class at Kapi'olani Elementary School. She didn't say much, and kept to herself her first days in school. She was bigger than most of us, even the boys. Without much experience in these matters, we could still tell that she was going to be a beautiful girl when she grew up. "A looker," as my uncle said whenever he saw a good-looking girl in town. The rest of the girls were envious of her in school. She had big, light-colored eyes; deep dimples; and thick, straight black hair that she wore in braids. A small circular scar on her right cheek served as a diversion to her good looks. I later learned from her younger sister that she had once put the car lighter on her face and burned herself.

Slim and tall for her age, she had good posture. Her pixie nose was high but not held in a snobbish manner. And something else. Many of us wished to be what she looked like: *hapa*-looking. Half-breed, even if she wasn't.

After setting the table, I took an armful of Classic Comics—*A Tale of Two Cities, The Rime of the Ancient Mariner, Uncle Tom's Cabin*— from a stack we had in our parlor and sat on the wicker chair to read them. I was just getting involved in one of the stories when my mother called me, again, right in the middle of a hanging!

"Mari, you listening?"

"Uh, huh, I'm listening."

"Pretty soon, dinnertime, so call Daddy. He's outside. I think he's fixing one of his fishing poles."

"Okay," I said without moving. "Daddyyy come hooome. Kaukau-uu," I said from where I sat, partly because I was lazy, but most of all because I didn't want anyone, especially *her*, to see me outside and calling my father.

"Mari, I tell you. Where you came from I'll never know. Next time, don't yell out like that, you hear? Now go outside, go find your father. Tell him to come in. And do it nicely." Mother towered over me. She had her hands on her hips and stared me down. I averted my eyes from her scalding look. Yes, I thought to myself, Japanese mothers saw everything. They had incredible sight—from the back as well as the front.

"Daddy heard me," I said to excuse myself. "He's coming, I heard him putting his stuff away. I hear him coming."

"Yes, but next time don't yell, okay?" I nodded. My mother didn't withdraw her look even then.

Karen Kaneshiro, the new girl in my class, sounded very smart. She didn't speak pidgin and the teacher placed her in the first reading group. In addition to all of her academic skills, she could play the meanest dodgeball game any of us had ever seen, and the boys kept on asking her to join their teams. I wanted to be popular like Karen so I latched myself onto her, professing to be her best friend. *Cross my heart, hope to die* kind of best friend. Very soon, she and I were walking home from school every day as if I were the key to her popularity.

"What school did you come from before this?" I asked one day at the beginning of our friendship.

"'Amauulu Elementary."

"Whoa, 'Amauulu—such a small school. Good, that you came to Kapi'olani—we can be best friends. From now on, forever and ever. I bet you didn't have a best friend in 'Amauulu."

"I did."

"Well, I'm different. I'm gonna be better than any of your other best friends."

"Okay, if you want to, I suppose so."

"So tell me, how come you folks moved to Hilo?"

"Oh, I don't know. We used to live with my grandmother, and my parents were planning to move to Honolulu to open a restaurant. But I really don't know *why*."

"Me too," I said. "Lots of things I don't know *why*. I don't know why my Aunt Bea not talking to her sister. I don't know why my mother never went to school. Sometimes I ask but they don't say anything. They look at me like I stupid."

"Yeah, I know what you mean."

Adults lived in a very different world back then. To me it was fun to watch the adults when they didn't want us, their children, to know something. They talked in Japanese or with a lot of innuendo. They hedged a lot or simply ignored us. I learned many Japanese words that way.

Karen and I *did* become best friends. We spent most of our time together. We crossed Kīlauea Avenue between the houses to play in each other's yards. We shared all of our little girl secrets.

I liked going over to her house better than staying on my side of the street. It was much more fun there because her family had all kinds of ducks in a pond situated on the side of their home. I loved to watch Karen feed the ducklings and pick up the eggs as she walked among the nests in her rubber boots. When Easter time rolled around, I figured she would have the strongest eggs. No one would beat her duck eggs in an egg fight, not even the boys who cheated by covering the top of their eggs with wax. It was worth being her best friend just for that—seeing her win.

"You come with us any time," Mrs. Kaneshiro said, when I went on an outing with Karen's family. They were warm and made me feel welcome. I rode the backseat on the left, behind Mr. Kaneshiro, because the right side was Karen's favorite seat. I got the left seat because I was the guest and Karen's sister had to sit in middle, on the bump, where the driveshaft housing ran down the length of the car. Karen gave her sister a solid whack on her shoulder when she started to protest about my having the second best seat.

"Guests come first," Karen said in a low rumble.

I went on their picnics, too, and got to eat things not prepared at our home: Okinawa dango, steamed duck, sweet and sour pork, braised oxtail, pig's feet soup.

"What did you folks eat today?" my mother asked after one of my outings with the Kaneshiros, curious about the food they cooked.

"Champuri or something."

"What's that?"

"I don't know, but what we had was real ono—something with pork, I think. Ask Mrs. Kaneshiro yourself," I said. My mother never responded.

If I mentioned we had something like innards, or tails, or feet, my mother would say: "They eat those kinds of food because Okinawans were always very poor. They always had to eat things like that. We never had to." And there was pride attached to her words.

"But taste so *ono*, Mama."

"Just don't make a pig out of yourself when you go over."

One day I asked my mother, "Can Karen come over to play today?"

"Sure she can come. I told you anyone can come over as long as you all play outside."

"Can she come inside to play? How come we have to play outside? They always let me inside their house."

"Never mind. Just play outside like I'm telling you to. I just cleaned the house. I don't want you coming in barefooted after you play outside. Bad manners to go in the house hadashi."

"Yeah, but—"

"Don't 'but' me," my mother said.

I didn't understand my mother, especially since we had the run of the house at Karen's place. When Anne, another neighborhood girl came over, my mother allowed her to play in the house. Although my mother never let me serve snacks to the Kaneshiro children, Karen's mother never forgot to give me something to munch on. Whenever they were over at my house, as if by unspoken cue, the Kaneshiro girls ran home—with me following—to eat their snacks before returning to our yard to play. We never questioned this difference.

One day, I went with Karen and her family to 'Amauulu Camp to visit her grandmother. To my surprise, Karen's grandmother looked nothing like my grandmother. She was squat and husky and very jovial. We came upon her on a low rise filled with cucumber vines on both sides of the road. There she was, carrying two buckets of slop on a pole across her shoulders to take to the pigs.

"Oh-h-h, so stink." I said, pinching my nose and grabbing Karen's arm in revulsion, "Pee-yeeew, how can you stand the smell?"

"I know it stinks, but wait till you see the babies. Come. Follow me. You'll like the piglets. They're the cutest and smart."

The grandmother had a kerchief around her head that moved when she smiled, her face broad and open. Her dress was very colorful, too, with a lot of reds, blues, and yellows in the print. These colors startled me, because all the older Japanese women I knew in town, mostly my mother's acquaintances, wore only subdued colors—grays, blacks, browns. Nothing but dull colors, like their personalities, I thought to myself. The women I knew seemed somber after I saw Mrs. Kaneshiro, who was so lively. To my further surprise, she was adorned with blue tattoos that looked like wristlets and anklets of flowers. I wanted to turn her around like a vase and trace my small fingers across the blue designs. I must have been staring at the woman, because her eyes caught mine several times. She smiled; I smiled back.

"So cute," I exclaimed, looking at the babies when we reached the sty.

"But don't touch them—the mother is very possessive," Karen said.

"What's *possessive*?"

"Oh Mari. That was one of our vocabulary words. Don't you remember?"

"That's not mine. I not in the A-group like you, you know."

That evening at home while having dinner, I recounted the pleasant day I spent in 'Amauulu. "Ma, funny you know, old Mrs. Kaneshiro—she had blue tattoos all over her body. And they talk funny kind Japanese. Dum tada, dum tada, dum—dat's how they sound. Her words come tumbling out the mouth."

"That's because they're Okinawans."

"Okinawans? What's that?"

Having had too much fun in a long, full day, I was not looking for an answer or explanation. "Boy, was some fun, today. I wanna go back. Karen said I can sleep over at her grandma's house. I can, o' what?" I asked.

Ignoring me, my mother and father started talking about more pressing matters, especially about a letter that had just arrived from my mother's younger sister, Sachiko. Unlike children, adults could do this ignoring without consequence. Sometimes they talked with their eyes, a few words sprinkled in between. There was always an undercurrent of something going on in the house that children were not aware of.

Sachiko lived in Honolulu. I knew that Sachiko left Hilo some years back and was studying at a business school to become a secretary. Once, her goal had been to become a clothing designer, having had a flair for drawing, but her father, my grandfather, stifled her ambitions by insisting that she go to business college, instead. "Designing? What kind of job is that? Useless. Get good government job," I remember my grandfather saying.

"Sachiko wrote and said she's going to get married next month to a guy she met at vocational school," my mother said

"Honolulu boy?" my father asked.

"He comes from Mānoa, Sachiko says in the letter."

"As long as not saila-boy—then, that's okay."

"But, worse than that," Mother said lowering her voice and eyes.

"Why?"

"*Uchinanchu dayo*," mother said. "Mama and Papa are going to be real mad at Sachiko for marrying an Okinawan boy."

"Is that like Karen folks?" I asked.

"Shush, Mari."

"Well, is it, or what?"

I followed the conversation as if it were a ping-pong match. "What's Uchinanchu?" I asked.

"Never mind, Mari," my mother said, dismissing my questions. Turning to my father, she said, "The wedding's going to be in Honolulu. Got to hurry up, though . . . I think she's papaya."

"Can I go, Daddy? Huh?" I asked.

"Where? Oh, there, I don't know," he said and looked at my mother.

I also looked at her and said, "What's 'papaya' mean, Mama?"
"Papaya?—something you don't want to be."
"If you going, Mama, I want to go."
"Go where, Mari?"
"To Aunt Sachi's wedding."
"We'll see."

Soon after, Karen and I were walking home one day from school when Wayne Matsuda caught up with us and began pulling at our pigtails on the run.

"Stop pulling our pigtails, Wayne," Karen said as she spun around on her heels.

"Yeah, stop pulling our pigtails," I said, brave in Karen's shadow. A big girl, she was a match for any boy.

"You guys think you smart or what? Buta ken-ken! Buta ken-ken!" Wayne said.

"Shut up, Wayne," Karen said and lunged at him in fury. But Wayne quickly slipped from her grip on his shirt as he whirled himself around.

Wayne continued to tease us. "Buta ken-ken, buta ken-ken."

"C'mon Karen, let's get um." I said. As I ran up to Wayne, he directed his teasing toward me.

"Buta ken-ken lover. Mari's a 'big rope' lover."

"Shut up, Wayne. Shut up!" I said.

"Big rope lover. Big rope lover."

I swung my bag at him. "Goddammit Wayne, I going tell my mother."

"Ahana kokolele. You broke my okolele. You saying bad words. Go, go tell your mother. See if I care. Your mother, she not going do anything."

Wayne was right. I wasn't sure what my mother would say. My mother was not going to get involved.

When Wayne ran down Kumu Street from Kīlauea Avenue where we had been, Karen and I gave up chasing him. It was there that I turned to Karen and asked, "What's buta ken-ken?"

"You're so stupid! Just so stupid," Karen said. She faced me and began shouting. "Why do you think your mother doesn't let me in your house to play and we cannot eat at your house? Why do you think we don't go to the same church? Why do you think my father has a hard time finding a job?"

"I don't know."

"Then you're *really* stupid, Mari. A birdbrain."

"A what?"

"A birdbrain! And I don't want to be your friend anymore. Don't bother me." Looking as if she had been carrying the burden of a hundred centuries, she turned her back on me and walked away.

From that day, a cold feeling fell over our relationship, settling down on us like something wet that we couldn't dry off. While something stopped me from playing with her, I continued to spy on her from behind our green wicker chair. I'd been rebuffed but didn't understand why I felt drawn to her. Somehow, I wanted her to come to *me*, to sing out to me in her high, clear voice and ask me to come out and play with her. But she never did and I never went over to her house.

Since I no longer had Karen to play with, I spent more time at home and weekends at my grandparents' house. As Sachiko's wedding loomed closer, a certain anticipation hung over the family. One day, a letter came from Sachiko, begging my grandparents to come to Honolulu to participate in her wedding.

"I want Papa to give me away," Sachiko said in her letter.

"Tell her I'm not coming," my grandfather said to my grandmother.

The day the letter had arrived, my grandfather, grandmother, and I had been sitting on the porch making lau hala rope handles for purses they were weaving for their business. My grandfather was cutting strips of lau hala leaves into long ribbons along a row of sharp razor blades. *Swish*, went the leaves with every one of his strokes.

"Papa, enough already. Poho to get angry. You're going to be the loser," my grandmother said.

"Bakatare. Sachiko is crazy," my grandfather said, swishing the leaves more vigorously.

"I don't care what you say. I'm going to Honolulu. You're the one who's crazy. I want to see our daughter get married. I want to meet her new husband. I want to see what kind of family Sachiko is marrying into."

"You're going without me? Then go. But Sachiko is no longer my daughter! Tell her not to set foot in this house!"

"Don't be so foolish and hardheaded. How can you say she's not your daughter?"

"If she's going to marry an Okinawan boy, I don't want anything to do with her," he said.

He shifted himself and faced his back toward my grandmother. I watched, not daring to say anything. I tried to make myself as small as possible. I didn't understand how adults could be so misunderstanding of one another.

"Your own daughter. I don't care what you say, I'm going to Honolulu," Grandmother said and went back to weaving.

No one spoke after that. What was unsaid from then on could only be felt in the air. Even Grandfather appeared surprised by Grandmother's sudden, adamant reaction. She had never defied him before. Bristling like a cat, my grandmother stormed from the porch into the kitchen and banged the cast-iron pots and pans. Even my grandfather knew when to stop.

I whistled for our dog and ran down the steps. I disappeared into the American guava trees.

A week or so later, Mother and I picked up Grandmother from her home in Wainaku and drove her to Hilo Airport, so she could fly to Honolulu. Grandfather was on the porch. He stood by, sullen as a child. I didn't want to step out of the car. I felt that if I did, I would fall off the earth.

"How come you not going, Ma?" I asked.

"We can't afford it," she said simply, but I couldn't decipher Mother's *real* feelings. Did she secretly take her father's side?

A week later Grandmother returned. She seemed uncommonly happy and chatted away about the big wedding reception held for the new couple. "Sachiko looked so pretty," she said. "She had a nice gown and a large wedding cake. The food was delicious, too. So many wedding presents, and everyone gave Sachiko a nice send-off on her honeymoon. The Higas are nice people."

Not long after that, pictures of the wedding arrived at my grandparents' home. "I like see," I said. One picture showed Grandmother in the reception line, receiving guests who must have noticed Grandfather's absence. But my grandmother in a small blue-gray hat with a wisp of a veil looked gracious and unconcerned. I noticed that Grandfather craned his neck to look at some of the pictures as Grandmother passed them around for my mother and me to see.

Later, Sachiko gave birth to a fine, healthy boy with none of the curses that people said attended a child when a Naichi married an Okinawan; the baby did not look like a monkey, nor was he as hairy as someone told us he was going to be.

Once, when one of Grandmother's friends came over with the obligatory baby gift, beginning with her sympathies she said, "It must be hard to accept such a grandchild." Grandmother would have none of it.

"The baby is no different from a Naichi baby!" Grandmother said to this *friend*. "I'm very proud of my grandchild. He's a beautiful child."

Easter came around and went. Karen won the Easter egg fight and she was the most popular girl in the class. She beat the boys with her duck eggs, even if they waxed their eggs so they would be thicker than usual.

Karen and I never played with each other all the rest of the year, and after that summer I would never see her again. She and her family packed up and left for Honolulu as planned. The last I saw of Karen was in the backseat of their car looking across the street at our house, while I peered back from my window. We stared at each other, but neither of us waved good-bye.

I had missed her.

Later that year, during the Christmas holidays, I accompanied my grandparents to Honolulu on business. They went to talk to a wholesaler about selling more of their lau hala products in Waikīkī. And every time we passed a restaurant, I wondered if it were Karen's family's restaurant and how they were doing. I looked through the phone book for a telephone number but there were dozens of Kaneshiros and I didn't know Karen's father's name.

Sachiko's husband took my grandparents all around Honolulu

during their stay, and we went around the island to Lāʻie one day where we saw the Mormon Temple. At the end of our trip, New Uncle, as I called him, took me up to his parents' house for a visit while he drove my grandparents to the jobbers. New Uncle had his nieces and nephews over at the house in Mānoa to meet and play with me. My new friends and I caught guppies and explored a small stream in the back of the white, prim home in the valley.

At lunchtime, we were called into the house for some pig's feet soup. I relished it, having forgotten how good it used to taste at Karen's, especially on a cold and rainy Hilo day. Mrs. Higa, Sachiko's mother-in-law, had cooked the feet just right, soft and to my liking. The skin melted in my mouth.

Just then, New Uncle arrived with my grandparents. I didn't want to go home yet, but I was prepared to leave immediately, sensing that my grandparents wouldn't be coming into the house. But, much to my surprise, just as I was about to pick up my jacket and walk toward the door, my grandparents came striding up the walkway with New Uncle. The elder Mr. and Mrs. Higa went out to greet them. Mrs. Higa had the baby in her arms and everyone stood around her, admiring the new grandchild. To my surprise, even Grandfather. He smiled a smile that I hadn't seen for a long time.

For several minutes longer, they all exchanged greetings. They bowed to each other repeatedly. "Please excuse us," my grandmother said. "We're such a bother."

"Oh no, it's no problem. We're very happy to have you here."

"Thank you very much for taking good care of my daughter and my grandchild," someone said, softly. It was my grandfather. Everyone looked up in surprise. My grandmother had a large grin on her face as she looked at my grandfather. After that, only words of respect and politeness passed in conversation, which made me feel good inside.

Grandmother and Grandfather soon settled themselves inside the Higas' home. Grandmother went up to the altar where the butsudan stood and paid her respects. The Higas weren't that much different; they even worshipped the same way.

They then served my grandparents some pig's feet soup, made of a savory broth, a good mixture of seaweed, white radish, green onions, and ginger to warm our insides.

The Cardinal

Even during hurricane seasons, the storms were mild. Long bursts of wind whooshed across the land. They often toppled the outhouse, which was easily set upright by my grandfather, Uncle Joei, or Uncle Joe as we called him, and a disgruntled mule. "Whoa, whoa," my grandfather said, guiding the mule, using his heels as brakes, digging them deep into the rich, soft dirt.

A few months of warm rains marked the winters and springs. Summers started early in the islands and dragged into late October; long but mild tradewinds helped to ease the heat and humidity. Cane haul mules flicked their tails, swayed, and dipped their muzzles into the talcum-fine red dust; wilted and lethargic chickens roosted in the coops; fish circled without relief in the warm ponds. As they slept in the middle of the long winding roads, disheartened dogs "woofed" forlornly into the distance when aroused from naps in the hot sun by pestering flies and honking cars.

Besides cane, my grandparents grew oranges, persimmons, avocados, guavas, lima beans, long eggplants, won-bok, and tomatoes on their land. Heavy fruits ripened and cracked the overburdened branches, and vegetables sagged on their plants. To save them, Grandfather and Uncle Joe hauled long bamboo poles from the gulch to prop the fruit-laden trees and firm the plants that drooped.

Fruit flies, gnats, mosquitoes, and other insects swarmed into this lushness and decay. A host of feeding birds followed the insects. Mountain doves and mynahs flew in first, but they were soon chased out of the area by brazen sparrow flocks that undulated in broad, brown masses. Brash, noisy, they dominated the area. Other more timid birds whiffled secretly past in the trees, looking for opportunities to feed.

Although the sparrows came in abundance, they left without nesting. Chinese thrush, mejiro, cardinals, and other birds were soon darting among tree branches near the house or the bathhouse or outhouse, busily building their delicate nests. Successful nesting pairs showed up year after year.

Frequently, I'd climb one of the trees and chase birds off their nests to count their fragile eggs.

I spent whole summers at my grandparents' home, usually staying there until school started again in the fall. Together with Uncle Joe, their youngest child and only son, my grandparents lived a quiet, frugal existence in a small plantation community, a life marked by routine but laborious work.

The year I was eight, Uncle Joe was going to be a senior at Hilo High School. My mother, the eldest in the family, never graduated from high school so she was always after Uncle Joe to do well. The age difference between my mother and uncle was such that Uncle Joe could have passed for her son; in many ways she threatened him like one, her feeling being that the old folks could not make a lasting impression on her brother.

"You better study harder next year. Don't be so moloā, give Mama and Papa a bad time. Maybe you think they're old and don't understand much but don't try to fool them. You're going to have to answer to me," my mother said.

"Yeah, yeah," Uncle Joe said back with a twist of his mouth.

Uncle Joe, in turn, taunted my mother for not having graduated from high school. "Class of 1950," he'd say, strutting in front of her like a bird, his hands flapping like wings from his armpits.

"That's because I had to help put all of you through school," she said.

My immigrant grandparents indulged their only son, who had been born after six girls. To his sisters, he was a study in undisciplined willfulness, and in their opinion, terribly spoiled. When he turned sixteen, to everyone's consternation my grandparents bought Uncle Joe a brand new '48 Plymouth. They bought the car with the idea that Uncle Joe would take them into town once a week to shop.

My grandparents' wishes, of course, were seldom fulfilled. Nights before this duty, Uncle came home drunk, his eyes bloodshot with the lines of slightly cracked eggs. He couldn't get up the next morning.

Early on, my grandfather got after my uncle to keep up his end of the bargain. "Hoi-i-i. Wake up!" he said to no avail.

"Go away," my uncle moaned and turned over, and my grandfather ended up calling the taxi to take him and my grandmother to town.

After acquiring his car, Uncle Joe became intolerable to live with. Haughty as a rooster, he gained a reputation in school for being slick as oil with the girls. While not particularly handsome, with a slight overbite and eyelids drooping like a tired bird's, what he lacked in looks he made up for in sheer personality. Friendly on the outside, he called out to his friends and gave them his "hi" sign. Always immaculately dressed in board-stiff khaki pants and fancy aloha shirts, he was the envy of all of his classmates.

My grandmother starched his clothes, Chinese starch simmering on an old kerosene stove *plop, plop*, and she slaved over a hot iron to press them for him. He had a long row of Kabe-silk shirts hanging from a bamboo post above his bed that my grandmother had sewn for him on her old White. His small closet held his pants, his dress shirts, and his BB gun. Before going out on a date, Uncle filled the house with a series of commands to my grandmother as he prepared to dress: "Ma, iron the blue shirt for me—I need um tonight," or "Go iron my pants, again, the crease, crooked," he said, his voice on the verge of a tantrum.

"Hai, gomen nasai," Grandmother said, scuttling off like a bird to straighten his things.

"Stop ordering Mama around," my mother said to Uncle Joe, and to my grandmother, my mother said, "Mama, stop doing everything for Uncle Joe. You're spoiling him." Of course, my grandmother never listened to my mother, her life revolving around spoiling her only son.

Uncle Joe's shirts sported magnificent roaring red tigers, green, flame-throwing dragons, sweeping-in-the-sky eagles. The animals writhed across the bodice. Bamboo and other intricately woven designs on his silk shirts swayed on his back. How all this colorful display must have dazzled the girls, the shirts flagging the girls' attention in their brightness. And above the sports collar of these aloha shirts, Uncle Joe dropped a slicked ducktail down to the nape of his neck. Carefully sculpting the groove, he oiled his hair with VO5 and dipped his comb into a jar of water.

On one of several occasions, after much primping, he brought a girl to the house.

"Are you going marry my Uncle Joe?" I asked, clinging to the girl's arm. "Are you going be my new auntie? I wish you would be my new auntie."

"Beat it kid, 'kay? Get lost!"

Uncle Joe directed and thumbed me away but with a grin on his face. Not embarrassed, he rather enjoyed my posing these questions—the asking like a game between us, making it seem to the girls that Uncle had a lively, even marriageable interest in them. They seemed flattered. I liked the role I played in his games.

My mother and her sisters also possessed a real interest in Uncle Joe. Besides talking about his girlfriends, they were intrigued by the circumstances of his birth. "Imagine," my mother said, "Mama having a baby at forty-five. Remember how she tried to hide the fact from us and how she got bigger and bigger? How she blushed when Katsura ba-san folks used to come over and tease her after finding out she was pregnant: 'Your Papa, got plenty power' they would say, and how they'd laugh, slapping their thighs and covering their black teeth with their hands. Remember? Poor Mama was so embarrassed—another baby after all those years."

While my mother and aunts laughed at my grandmother's expense, I never thought there was anything unusual or special about Uncle Joe's situation. I liked having him as my young uncle. I didn't care about these conversations, only wanting to follow him around, hang out with him, be *like* him. Since I couldn't go everywhere with him, I waited around the house by hanging on the gate or climbing the trees, disappearing for long hours in the branches of the orange, sugi, or peach trees. Or just plain lay around like a cat on the chicken coop roof until Uncle Joe came home from some baseball game, or fishing, or joyriding with his friends.

Once home, he usually brushed me aside. "Get lost, kid. Stop being a pest. Go. Go play with your dolls." But I stuck around, hanging back, following him wherever he went. I wanted him to see that I was mean, tough. Gruff like him.

One day, I followed him into the peach tree in the back garden. Although he was already in high school, Uncle Joe still liked to climb this tree from where he could see the view.

"I want some," I said and ambled toward his nestlike sitting place.

"Go and pick yo' own. Get plenny on the tree."

"But I like the kind you get in your pocket. You get the good ones."

"Awww, why you gotta follow me every place I go? You think I yo' slave or what? Go pick what you like by yo'self. You not one kid."

"But you wen pick all the good ones, already, see? No more good kind."

"Damn brat. You mo' worse than me. And they call *me* spoiled."

Uncle Joe straightened one leg and dug out a couple of half-ripened peaches from his pocket. The peaches were oval and flushed like bird eggs. We ate in silence, the only sounds the crunching of the fruit against our teeth.

After a while, I asked, "Uncle Joe, when you get out of high school next year, where you going?"

"Doan know. Why, botha you where I go?"

"I just wanna know what you going do, das all. No need get mad."

"All I know, I not going to be like them, that's for damn sure," he said, nodding toward his parents who worked below us in the cane.

"They work so damn hard for jes a few bucks."

Grandfather was hoeing a row of weeds while Grandmother followed from behind. In backbreaking motion, Grandmother picked up the weeds that Grandfather had scattered on the ground. She hit the dirt off the clumps of grass on her thighs and placed them into a burlap bag.

I then asked, "If you not going no place, you going getting married?"

"Now, who said anything 'bout getting married? Why you kea if I get married or not?"

"I no kea. I jes like know."

"Eh, by the way, stop fooling aroun' my stuff in the drawer before I wring your neck!"

"I never touch nothing. What I wen touch that's sooo precious, anyway?"

"Just no touch my stuff. I warning you."

"You mean the white balloons in the drawer—the one I pop? Dey so junk. Small too. I like the box, but—the one you squeeze the two sides fo' open with the peacock on top. Re-so-var ends. What that—*re-so-var*?"

"None of your beeswax, 'kay? Stay outa my stuff. Trouble with you is, yo' mother let you do anything you like, you know dat?" he said, smacking his lips, taking a bite of his peach, his teeth flashing as it dug into the firm flesh.

"All I know, I not getting married," Uncle Joe continued. "I goin' join up the Air Force, I think. I not waiting till I get drafted. I gonna sign up—get outta hea. Papa folks gonna get mad at me, but I no kea. Let them get mad." He flared his nostrils at the thought of a confrontation with his parents. "I know Papa like me stay hea, cut cane, but I doan wanna be stuck in this place. I wanna go—California, maybe. Everything so backwards, hea."

"Then you gotta go war." My idea was that boys got drafted or volunteered for the army and went to war. I had seen it in the movies.

"Who said dat? Nobody's *gotta* go war."

"I see it all the time in the movies—Saturday Mickey Mouse Club—down Palace Theater. In the movies, if you go army, you gotta go war, for fight."

"You see? Your mother let you see too many junk kine movies. No good for you—you know dat?"

"Well, you too. You get too many girlfriends and you drink too much bee-ya. Anyway, if you so smart, how you know you not goin' war? How you know you not going ma-ke?"

"I'm not going ma-ke cuz no mo war—dat's why, stoopid."

"If I so stoopid and if you so smart, tell me how people ma-ke den?" The association, one of war and dying, had been fixed in my mind.

"Wat you wanna know fo'?"

"I jes like know, dat's why."

"Eh, now you really talking stoopid. Why no ask dem?" he said, nodding toward my grandparents. "They should know. They going ma-ke, right hea, in this god-damn place." Uncle Joe said in a grumble as he slid off the tree, "Sheez. How I know how people ma-ke? Nobody know dat. Who talking about dying anyway?"

Of course it was useless to ask my grandparents anything. Whenever I asked my grandmother something, all she ever did was to grin and nod her head. "Eh," or "Soo, soo," was about all I could get out of her.

Among my uncle's many possessions was a mail-order Daisy BB gun. It was something Grandfather, I remember, did not want Uncle to have but eventually bought for him because my uncle wore everyone down by his nagging and pouting. Uncle Joe took this gun out very rarely now, the novelty of owning it having worn off. Once in a while he went with his friends to hunt doves, or to shoot at targets from the verandah in the cane fields or at fruits hanging from the trees. More often than not, however, the gun stayed in his closet. I coveted his gun.

Like all of his possessions, Uncle kept his gun in mint condition. The blue-barreled gun had a crank action and a walnut stock. Uncle shined the barrel, usually with a swipe of grease from his hair and a shot of spit from a rolled tongue and pursed lips. He rubbed the moisture between his palm and gave the stock a firm going over, polishing the gun off with a clean rag before putting it away.

This immaculate gun was the gun of my dreams. I always wanted to be like one of the soldiers I saw in the movies. I wanted to shoot like them: "Bud-da, bud-da, bud-da, bud-da." Dressing up in jeans and an aloha shirt, I made believe it was a uniform with all kinds of safety-pin medals I made up to put on my chest. To complete my outfit, I needed a bayonet and rifle. A small pocketknife sufficed as my bayonet, but I needed Uncle Joe's rifle. All I wanted was to be tough like the army war guys; I didn't want to be like any of the silly girls who giggled and covered their mouths whenever they laughed—like the ones Uncle Joe brought home to make goo-goo eyes with.

Uncle Joe took out his rifle one day and I danced around him, trying to get at it as he raised it above his head. "Stop botherin' me, squirt. Cut it out—you no shame or what, fo' act l'dat?"

"C'mon Uncle Joe, lemme try," I nagged. "I wanna learn how fo' shoot." I jumped up and down and around him to get at the rifle. Watching him, I had learned about persistence in getting one's way.

"No fool around. Dis not one toy."

"Dis not real. Use only BBs."

Grandmother silently eyed us over the rim of her glasses as she embroidered a pillowcase on her lap. Her eyes had an admonition in them that told me to mind myself.

I wished everyone dead. I stomped my feet and filled my cheeks with air. Grandma went back to her sewing and Uncle Joe shrugged his shoulders. He walked into his room, and I heard him put his rifle away in the closet as I whined into my shirtsleeve.

"Junk, dis kine!" I said.

After that incident, my obsession over Uncle Joe's gun only increased. I watched my uncle carefully whenever he used it, and I had learned its use in my mind. Soon, I knew all the steps by heart: the dropping of the BBs in the barrel; the cranking of the gun; putting the cheek up to the gunstock, closing the left eye, and aligning the right eye down the barrel to the sight with the target; finally, rounding the finger around the trigger and squeezing it slowly. I couldn't wait to get my hands on the gun.

The opportunity appeared one day when the ratoon crop had budded and the weeds needed to be cleared. "Boy-ya," I heard my grandmother say to Uncle Joe, "We go hoe-hana mauka side—tsumorrow, ne?"

"Why tomorrow? I like go movie."

"Joei, bum-bye you go."

"Gonfunit."

With this, I knew everyone would be out of the house the following morning.

Early the next day, before sunrise, I heard everyone get up and prepare for work. I imagined my grandfather and Uncle Joe walking up front with the hoes, Uncle dragging his face and feet and muttering under his breath about his bad fortune, while Grandmother followed from behind, carrying the heavy bags and water can.

The house was caught in sudden quiet. The drip from the catchment tank on the side of the house resonated loudly on the hardened earth and dogs barked in the distance. The smell of coffee and burnt toast filled the air; it enlarged the silence.

I jumped up, dashed myself into my jeans and shirt, and wore a GI peaked hat made out of a sheet of old Japanese newspaper. I sliced some bread, spread poha jam on it, took huge bites, and downed it with some lukewarm tea left on the stove.

I then ran into Uncle Joe's room and searched his closet for the gun. Tucked behind his saila-moku pants and his aloha shirts stood the gun on its stock, buried deep in one corner.

At last. I stroked the barrel upon pulling it out. Next I took a pillbox of shot from the shelf, and with one hand dropped the pellets down the muzzle. From Uncle's room I went out to the porch. I cradled the gun on my shoulder and looked through the sight. Aligning my eyes down the long, straight barrel, a new world emerged: binocular, singular, chosen.

Once in the yard, I plinked at some cans on the fence posts. Next, I aimed at the waiwi and tangerines on the trees. After several tries, I finally dropped an orange, which crashed with a thud onto the ground. "Bull's-eye," I yelled.

After a time, I found shooting at stationary objects no longer fun; I wanted a moving target. I tried shooting at the sparrows, but they were flying too high and fast for me to hit them. Then I caught a glimpse of red. That was it! Why not the cardinal pair in the persimmon tree? They were flitting back and forth, building their nest. I crouched down and staked them out like a real army trooper.

I observed that the male swooped out to this branch or that branch with the female following him. The male was deep red, the color of a blood clot. His hood flared like a warrior's helmet in the gusts of wind, and his dark, beadlike eyes shifted across the land with the soft feathers on his throat lifting in the wind. Black rings around his eyes made him look as if he were wearing a harlequin mask. The female, on the other hand, looked faded in her color, like red chintz left out in the sun too long. She was not as interesting as the male bird.

Wherever the male bird flew, the female followed; this was the pattern. They flew from the persimmon tree, swooped down into the garden for twigs and grass, then up into the peach tree that stood in the farthest corner of the garden. They idled on the tree and then flew back to their nest with some regularity.

The male bird called out. *Stweet, stweet, stwit, stwit, stwit, stwit.*

Stweet, stweet, the female bird answered. She flew to his side. They were in a hurry to build their nest.

Looking around for a good place to ambush the birds, I decided to shoot them in the peach tree from behind the banana plants. I crawled from under the persimmon tree on my belly and snaked my way toward the banana patch. The male cardinal, attentive to every move in the area, called to his mate at every strange movement.

My shirt clung to my body. I grew hot and sticky, crawling in the thick grass. I itched all over, my nose twitching, close to sneezing. Acting like a good soldier, I moved only what was necessary. But as I approached the banana trees, I could no longer see the birds and wondered if they were still in the grass. Sensing danger, they could have flown somewhere else, I thought. Standing up, I would have given myself away were it not for a small and indiscreet call the male made to his mate. With this call, I knew that the birds were still searching for twigs.

Upon reaching the banana trees, I huddled under the wide leaves for protection and rested the gun on a cut stump while I caught my breath. Minutes passed as I waited and wiped my perspiring hands across my jeans. It must have been only ten in the morning, but the sun was already high and grasshoppers buzzed steadily near my ears.

A sudden flutter. A red ribbon of color streaked into the air with a settling of red on a high branch of the peach tree. It was the male cardinal. He whistled for his mate. No answer. At that moment, I tried to place him in my sight but, agitated, the bird hopped about in a twitter and I couldn't pin him down. The female cardinal, labored by a body rounded with eggs, finally gave a weak whistle and lumbered up into the tree with a small twig in her mouth. Upon seeing her, the male glided down to her side. They stayed on the branch for a long while, as if to rest. There, the birds gripped the branch tightly; they swayed in the light breeze.

In that instant, as they rested, I raised the gun butt to my shoulder. I placed my cheek on the cold, hard barrel with the sight up to my eye, but my view of the male cardinal was obstructed by a branch. Wrapping a nervous finger around the trigger, I focused on the smaller and lesser red blur up ahead.

I squeezed my finger. There was a loud "pop" in my ear. *Stweeeet, stweeeet*! Sharp bird cries of alarm filled the air. I leaped up. I had hit it. I danced my way up to the bird at the bottom of the tree.

As I approached, I saw the stunned female bird on her side. Her small head lolled off toward a small incline in the dirt. Blood spurted with each beat of her heart from the wound in her chest. Suddenly, the bird's tiny body went into a series of fierce contractions. The bird laid two eggs in succession. I clamped my hand to my mouth. "Oh, my!"

I picked up the bird, realizing the awful thing I had done. Holding her, I thought I could retrieve her life somehow. I blew softly on her beak, still thinking that dying didn't happen to *real* things. But her heartbeat was already diminishing in my palm.

Above me the male cardinal screeched and battered the air with his wings. He screamed as he flew up, then down. He plummeted toward me in a dive as if to knife me. He made pass after pass—in attack—first above my one ear, then the other. All the while he called for his mate.

Cheep, cheep, the female bird cried feebly in my hands.

I cradled the bird, near death, on my chest. I tried to keep the heat from leaving her body. The bird gave some weak chirps as it tried to lift its head toward the open sky. Her wings twitched in a last attempt to fly. Opening her eyes, she looked up at me until her eyes went vacant. She gave one last *cheep* before dying.

I quickly dug a hole under the peach tree and buried the bird and her eggs. I packed the earth solidly, like brown sugar, with my hands. The earth made a deep, hollow sound. A sound of mourning.

Swinging the gun at my side, I ran back to the house. I wiped down the gun, now sticky with bird blood, and shoved it deep into the corner of the closet under my uncle's clothing. I ran into the room I slept in, changed my shirt, and stuffed the bloody one into my suitcase. Going back out to the porch, I looked out and watched the crazed cardinal.

"I didn't mean to do this. I really didn't," I said.

When Uncle Joe and my grandparents finally came home I acted as if nothing happened. I read comic book after comic book—*Archie, Tales from the Crypt, Superman*—from Uncle Joe's stack to keep my mind off what I had done.

But the bird kept reminding me. He did not let up. For the rest of the day, he cried as he flew around the house. I couldn't block out his calls. His whistling was incessant. He flew from tree to tree, wire to wire, rooftop to rooftop, over the fields and back again. He took his cries far into the night.

Early that evening Grandmother beckoned to me. "Come, come," she said, motioning with her hand for me to come to the window, our faces pressed to the pane with just enough twilight for us to see the bird against the sky. "Look at that. Strange, isn't it. The bird seems to have gone crazy. I wonder what happened to it?" she said in Japanese.

Later, I could hardly bear to eat my dinner. "You okay, or what?" Uncle Joe said. "How come you not eating?"

"I not hungry," I said and splayed my hair with my fingers.

"Is your stomach sore? How's about some rice gruel?" my grandmother asked.

"I all right, Baban. I not hungry, 'kay." That night, I cried myself to sleep.

The next morning I woke to the cry of the cardinal and remembered what had happened the day before. "Stop it. Just stop it," I said but couldn't muffle the bird's loud calls under my thick futon.

In the meantime, Uncle Joe tried to cheer me up by tapping my head or giving me a deliberate bump whenever he passed me. He got no reaction. "Hey, whassa matta wit you? You wen lose your mouth o' wat?"

The cardinal persisted in calling for its dead mate, another two days. At intervals, between sewing Uncle Joe's school clothing, my grandmother went to the window, trying to figure out what was wrong with the bird.

"Sad, isn't it?" she said. She made clucking sounds and shook her head.

On the third day, the male bird's maniacal calls diminished, the cries taking on a deeper, more mournful sound. Equally mournful, I watched the exhausted bird from the porch as he hopped on the branches of the old persimmon tree and circled his half-built nest. He then flew up, circled the house, circled the quilted countryside, and soared away.

"Eh sis, I think you betta come pick up Tami, take her home. She not herself. She no even laugh, nowadays. Maybe she sick," Uncle Joe said.

I overheard snatches of their phone conversation as my Uncle Joe talked to my mother. Soon after, Mother came to pick me up to take me home. I don't exactly know what Uncle Joe told Mother, but from then on, I was forbidden to go to the Mickey Mouse Club at the Palace Theater on Saturday mornings.

The strange cardinal was quickly forgotten by most of us. Summer ended and we all went back to school. The rains swept over the land to fall heavily on the iron roofs of our houses in yet another cycle. That school year, however, I didn't see much of my grandparents, or Uncle Joe, or any of his girlfriends.

All too soon, the school year ended. By this time, Uncle Joe had graduated high school. It was summer once more, with the fruits and vegetables ripening, the birds and insects flying in, and the winds swooshing through the cane.

That summer I did not go to my grandparents' house to stay as usual. Change had come to our family: Mother was stricter with me, my grandparents did not want to watch me, and Uncle Joe went off to war.

Boys' Style

A viva, a vivo, a viva vivo vum
A viva, a vivo, a viva vivo vum.

Annette Kushida forgot the words to the rest of the cheer. It went *something, something, sis boom bah! Spartans, Spartans, rah, rah, rah!* Unlike her classmates, she could only remember the catchy parts.

Below her, in blue and white uniforms, the smug, preppy-looking cheerleaders bounced up and down the gym floor in their routines and waved their pom-poms to the cheers of the Hilo Intermediate School crowd. Because the school gymnasium was so small, junior varsity games were held in the National Guard Armory gym a few blocks down the hill from the school, down Waiānuenue Avenue, next to the Wailuku River.

Annette sat on the opposite side of her school's team, on the high risers, just under the ceiling. Too shy to participate in the cheering, she and her best friend, Naomi Seki, who was shyer still, sat on the hard benches way above the crowd, where only a sprinkling of students stayed, mostly the really serious couples—those who wanted to make "uji," according to Naomi. That day, their school team was playing the Seasiders of Laupāhoehoe School.

On the floor, the boys whipped their basketballs about in a pregame warm-up, running in a circle, shooting the balls. Just before the game started, the Spartans went back to their bench to sit, towel-dry themselves, and wait for last-minute instructions from their coach. Cheerleaders, as if on cue, gave one last cheer and skipped off the floor with Alan, the mahu cheerleader of the school, swishing by, holding up the rear like a trail sweep.

As the girls passed the players seated on the long benches, Annette saw Louise Bergen, the cute hapa-haole, the head cheerleader, tap her boyfriend Kealoha Castro on the shoulder. Kealoha looked behind him, jerked his head in acknowledgment and followed Louise with his eyes as she made her way up the bleachers behind the players.

The head coach, Gus Amarillo, clapped his hands and the boys surrounded him as he squatted in the huddle. A buzzer sounded in a low grinding noise. The boys rose, made a circle, and slapped their hands, one over the other, then lifted and dropped them all at once in a "Rah!"

In his pep talk, Coach Amarillo's voice rose in volume. Annette could hear him from where she and Naomi sat. "Okay you guys, let's go, go, go!" he was saying. But Annette was really watching Louise, who stood in the aisle near the band. As soon as the music began and the school team rushed out on the court, Louise ran down to the sidelines. She leaped up and split her legs in the air, her pom-poms touching her toes. Annette was always surprised at how Louise could do a split in the air.

Kealoha, the team's star, loped his lanky body into the center ring for the jump ball. He leaped, straight as a spear, and tapped the ball firmly to a teammate. The guard who caught the ball ran it down to the Spartan's side of the court and made a shot. The ball hit the rim. Kealoha caught the rebound, took to the air, then aimed the ball in a jump. Swish. It went in. It was the beginning of the end, a sign of things to come. Laupāhoehoe in the dust.

Throughout the game, Annette riveted her eyes on Kealoha and his every move. Even at halftime, when Louise put a towel around Kealoha's shoulders, Annette watched without taking her eyes off his figure.

Annette was in love. She wished she had a boyfriend like Kealoha. Tall and handsome, he was the best-looking ball player this side of the Pacific Ocean. Portuguese, Chinese, Hawaiian, he was the boy every girl dreamed of dating. He was super good-looking. But he belonged to Louise. Inseparable, Kealoha and Louise were the golden couple. Annette knew that no one like Kealoha would ever look at girls like her and Naomi, unsophisticated eighth graders, unlike Louise and her friends who all had nice titties and "sway" hips. Kealoha didn't even know Annette existed. He looked right through her whenever they passed each other in the school hallway. She could well have been on Mars.

Every day after school, using an old rubber ball she found under the house, Annette palmed the ball and bounced it up and down the length of the block in front of her house. Saturdays, when her mother went to work overtime at the Waiākea Kai School cafeteria, Annette went to the nearby gym to shoot baskets. In the gym, she would set the ball with two hands and shoot it, the same way she had seen Kealoha set and shoot.

She shot the ball from various positions around the court. Imitating the boys, she dribbled and side-banked the ball on the backboard. She made overhand and underhand passes to Kealoha, her invisible player. Up, then down the gym floor she dribbled. Sometimes Kealoha was her opponent, using his body as an obstacle to prevent her from shooting, and she would, in the imagined full-court press with the score tied, overcome the obstruction of his tall figure by giving him the body and head fake, using her "body English" to pass by him and score. He'd try to catch up with her and steal the ball by reaching out with his long hands, but she'd be too fast for him. Then she'd make a pretty lay-up. Sink two in a beautiful arch.

Annette loved the game. She played relentlessly by herself or with the younger boys who came into the gym. She didn't play with the older boys who were too tall and swift in their ball handling, and the other girls were too timid, never playing full-on basketball like her. If the girls who showed up at the gym played with Annette, they always wanted to play silly games like Horse or Twenty-One, and Annette had to retrieve the ball too often.

Annette's school's physical education curriculum followed the national sports schedule in general. In the seventh grade, they had health classes, so that didn't count; in the eighth grade, they could play sports. When school started in September, the girls played baseball. Later in the year, they would play basketball, which was supposed to cover the winter months because it was an indoor sport. In the spring, it would be swimming, along with tennis.

In the autumn, however, the girls did not play football like the boys but took a short hiatus in order to learn how to be *ladies*—how to sit, how to balance books on their heads to walk properly, how to walk with one foot before the other, how to put on makeup. Miss Sugimoto, their gym teacher, set up mirrors on long tables in the gym.

"Dip you hands into the cold cream and massage," Miss Sugimoto said.

"Like this, Annette?" Naomi asked her friend.

"Beats me. Feel sticky on the face, like get cobwebs on top. What I don't understand is that if this is supposed to clean the skin, how come it feels dirty? Stupid yeah, what girls gotta do."

Next they learned how to do their eyebrows. "Place the pencil alongside your noses and inner eyes to mark the start of your eyebrows. Then situate the pencil along the outer edge of the irises of your eyes to mark the highest point. That is your arch. The pencil, when placed on the corner of the nose and eye, diagonally, marks the end of the brow. Now fill in the brow with your pencils. Get it?" Miss Sugimoto said.

Naomi laughed at Annette. "You look like one Kabuki actor. No, you get eyebrows like Stink Ann of Moʻoheau Park."

"Shutcho face," Annette said.

The girls learned how to care for their pimples, too. Noxema cream was popular. So was Clearasil.

"Don't pick on them," Miss Sugimoto said.

"Yeah, Annette. No pick on your pimples, eh?" Naomi said and popped a blackhead by squeezing it with her fingers.

"Ho, you so ete," Annette said.

While she didn't say anything at the time, when Naomi admonished Annette for picking on her zits, her best friend was right. Annette did pick on her pimples when she got excited, especially times when she watched Kealoha play ball.

Later, the girls learned how to brush on a light-colored lipstick and use a touch of foundation. "Not too much, not too little. You don't want to clog your pores," Miss Sugimoto said. "You want a 'natural' look that's more becoming for young women," she added.

Clumsy in their attempts, Annette and Naomi looked as if they had buds for her lips. Mascara smeared into rings around their eyes and made them look like raccoon sisters. Annette and Naomi giggled their way through these makeup lessons. And no matter how hard they tried, they just weren't *with it*, the other girls snickering at them.

When basketball season rolled around, Annette felt relieved, happy. No more cold tea bags on the eyes to reduce puffiness. No more lemon water astringents to bleach the skin. No more how to be ladylike. Basketball had begun. Basketball was her game. She could shine. In this sport, she was sure to be first pick—for hadn't she practiced all summer? She felt confident enough that she could vie for captain.

The only thing Annette hated about going to gym class was having to change in the girls' locker room. The lockers and showers were situated in a detached building on the side of the boys' gym. This meant that after changing into their blue gym uniforms, the girls had to parade past the boys' gym.

Whenever the girls passed by, the boys lined up to look at the girls. They whistled or gave the Filipino love call. "Psst," they hissed with their mush-mouths. Everyday, without fail, bold Barney Kam called out to Sandra Hara, the prettiest girl in Annette's class: "Eh, ova hea Sandra. Wayne—he love you." Or to May Rodriques, another pretty girl he said, "Hey May. Look, hea Calvin. He like chance." If Sandra or May looked the boys' way, the boys swooned or chased each other. Annette wouldn't have minded being singled out like that if the calls had come from Kealoha. But the boys she knew were crass, not suave like him. "Wow, check out the legs," the boys teased as they watched the girls stream past.

On the first day of basketball practice, Miss Sugimoto, who was also the girls' gym teacher and coach, made several teams of six girls each to play each other in a scrimmage, plus their substitutes. Annette was puzzled. Wasn't basketball supposed to have *five* players? she thought. She didn't understand it. "Ah, Miss Sugimoto, this is not how the game is played," she said, raising her hand.

Miss Sugimoto ignored her. She went ahead to explain the rules of *girls'* basketball.

"But, but—" Annette cried out.

Miss Sugimoto paced the floor in her white uniform as she talked.

"We will have three girls to guard the back court. They cannot enter the front court. Three front court girls will keep the ball in play. For the other team, three players will act as defense in the back court, and three for the front."

Annette couldn't believe her ears. What were they playing anyway? What once felt and seemed so natural, no longer felt that way. According to the rules, the ball handlers could only dribble twice before shooting or passing. They were also warned not to use both hands to set the ball in order to shoot it. It was a violation, unladylike to do so.

"Shit," Annette said to herself. "What is this? I don't believe it!"

In the days that followed, Annette took extra steps and extra dribbles out of habit. Miss Sugimoto constantly called her on these violations. She wasn't used to this kind of basketball. She just could not get the hang of this so-called *girls'* basketball. She couldn't discipline herself enough to slow the tempo. She fought it all the way. All she wanted to do was to play boys' style.

"No, no, no, no!" Miss Sugimoto scolded and blew her whistle. "This is like a dance, okay? Don't misstep. You'll throw everything off."

"Okay, I'm trying," Annette said.

"Hold it. Annette, how many times do I have to tell you? You can only bounce the ball two times before you set and shoot. And don't use two hands to shoot the ball. One hand lay-up, only."

"Yeah, yeah. Bounce the ball two times. Don't snatch the ball away. It's unladylike. Don't use two hands to set and shoot," she chanted to herself.

"Steady, steady. Pivot, before passing the ball to the other rover. Don't you understand? This is girls' basketball. G-I-R-L-S basketball!" Miss Sugimoto ran from the back court to the front court as she shouted.

What was there not to understand? Annette caught the drift.

At the end of one of these practice sessions, Miss Sugimoto called Annette to the side and said, "You're a good player, Annette, but you need more control. Don't forget, dribble two times, then pass or shoot. Dribble, pass. Dribble, pass. Got the rhythm? That's the way to take it down court. You have great skill, a gift for the game. Apply it." Despite her bad attitude, Annette was the best player.

At the end of the basketball season, as part of their semester's grade, the girls were to hold an exhibition game during the lunch period. Coach Sugimoto invited the school's varsity basketball team, cheerleaders, teachers, and principal, and all of the eighth grade class.

The day of the game, Annette suited up, reluctantly. Miss Sugimoto assigned her as the B-team captain. "Big deal," Annette said to Naomi. "Everyone's going to be so bored. They're not even going to watch the game."

"I no kea," Naomi said. "I no like people watch us play dis stupid kine game, anyway."

In center court, Annette won the toss for her team. In the first play, her back-court defensive team threw the ball to her in front court. She dribbled the ball and threw it to Naomi, her teammate. Naomi faked her opponent who tried to block her. She dribbled twice and passed the ball back to Annette. Close to the basket, Annette heard calls of "shoot, shoot." She gave it a try. The ball hit the rim of the basket and rebounded into Naomi's hands. "Awww," the crowd cried. Cautious, Naomi dribbled once more and bounce-passed the ball to Annette who bounced the ball and shot it into the air. Good. Two points.

The game plodded along. But close to the ending of the game, the teams ended in a tie. Miss Sugimoto called for a time out, her right palm quickly tapping over the fingers of her left hand in a T. She huddled with the girls in Annette's B-team. The assistant coach huddled on the opposite side of the court with the A-team. Squatting low, Miss Sugimoto sat in the center of the girls gathered and proposed her strategy.

"Move down cautiously—get close to the hoop, all right? And give the ball to Annette so she can shoot it in," she said to Naomi and the other player in front court. "Do your part girls, this is a team game. Hustle. Don't care about how you look. Let's go, let's go!" The girls joined hands like Annette had seen boys do, and dropped them in a "Rah!"

The once lethargic crowd, indifferent up to this time, perked up and began shouting for their favorite side. Everyone felt the tension in the air. At that moment, while bringing the ball up court, Annette saw Kealoha's tall figure in the crowd. She noticed that he was watching the game intently now. Before this, his attention had been on Louise, who was going around, trying to get the students to cheer. Now, even Louise had the crowd's support. Annette saw Kealoha look up at the score board.

> *A vivo, a viva, a vivo, viva vum*
> *Boom, boom, sis boom bah,*
> *Spartans, Spartans, rah, rah, rah!*

The crowd chanted the cheer. Annette heard a united stomp of feet on the floor with the words "Boom! Boom!" She felt it in herself like a strong heartbeat.

At the whistle, Annette nervously threw in the ball from the half-court line to Naomi, who dribbled twice and looked up to see what she could do. The clock was running out. Most of the students and teachers were on their feet. Naomi dribbled, then passed the ball back to Annette. Annette bounced the ball forward but was heavily blocked, three on one. She glanced around her. "Shoot, shoot!" the crowd shouted.

Annette gave a quick glance to where Kealoha stood. He was also shouting at her to shoot. But in this small moment of inattention, she lost the ball to dainty Sandra Hara who stole it from under Annette's arm. She heard a plaintive cry of disappointment from somewhere in the audience. It sounded like Kealoha's deep voice. Annette could have kicked herself. She would have to redeem herself in the next play.

Annette blocked Sandra and tried to get the ball back. Instead, the whistle blew to indicate that she had fouled the girl. She saw Kealoha shake his head in disgust.

Fortunately, Sandra missed both of the personal foul free throws, the ball ricocheting off the rim. But Sandra's team still controlled the ball on the rebound. If the A-team made the next basket, it would be aloha ball for Annette and her side. She just could not let that happen. Also, if she didn't retrieve the ball here, now, Kealoha would never know her from Jane or May or Janice or Karen for the rest of her life. She didn't want him to think of her only as a loser.

Annette raised her hands in front of Sandra to block her at midcourt. In just the luck of an opening, Annette stole the ball away. She caught a glimpse of surprise on Sandra's face as she ran off with the ball.

And it was as if Annette had fallen into another dimension. Her feet felt light when she moved, as though across meadows and fields and flowers. She leaped like sheep over fences.

She dribbled the ball down to her side of the court—boys' style. She handled and maneuvered the ball—boys' style. There was no stopping her from playing—boys' style. The shackles around her ankles had been removed, and she was running on air, fueled by the power, support and freedom of her calves and thighs.

When she arrived at the basket, she stopped, set the ball with two hands, aimed, and shot it through the hoop. A roar blossomed from the crowd. There was a whoosh from rising bodies just before the buzzer sounded to end the game.

Pandemonium. Whistles blew. The coaches swiped their hands over each other in front of their bodies like windshield wipers to nix the play. But Annette didn't care. Her teammates ran out and rapped her on her shoulders. Students clapped, stomped their feet, and whistled crazily. Boos and shouts all over.

Annette had a flying feeling. Naomi came over and congratulated her. "Nice job. What a shot!" she said, giving her a full slap that sent Annette flying.

Naomi, extended her hand to pull her friend up from the floor. "We did it," she said, the two girls grinning broadly at each other. Other students spilled down from the bleachers to talk to Annette and pat her back.

Miss Sugimoto, red-faced, blew and blew on her whistle, but no one seemed to care. Best of all, Kealoha was on his feet and making shrill whistles with his long fingers in his mouth. Catching Annette's attention, he smiled and gave her the "e-zay" sign.

Ho'olulu Park and the Pepsodent Smile

In our small town, Ho'olulu Park was built as a racetrack for amateur horse racing. When the townspeople realized that pari-mutuel gambling for racing would never be legalized, they turned the in-field of the race park into an all-purpose field and used it for baseball and football games. While all gambling and betting in the Territory of Hawai'i was illegal, the practice was widespread on the island, and, as my father put it, "unda da table."

With his old cronies, my father placed small bets on whatever sport was being played. Time after time. And with hope inextinguishable. He kept on going to these games, hopeful of winning the jackpot with his "anty-panty" betting, his version of penny-ante betting. "Nex' time," he'd say each time he lost, spitting into his hands and rubbing them together.

Being that he had only daughters—an unmentioned failure, boys prized in the Japanese culture to carry on the family name—my father took my sister and me on outings he would have made only with sons had he had them—basketball, track racing, fishing, football, baseball, boxing—many of these events at Ho'olulu Park. My sister quickly excused herself from these excursions. "I have a way," she'd say, her friends swinging by the house to pick her up.

But I was introverted, had few friends. I was timid about learning to drive at fifteen; I had to rely on my father to go places. I became his right-hand man in a life where many things needed to be fixed—the old car, the secondhand washer, Uncle Taru's bike. I was my father's efficient sidekick. "Eh, pass me the wrench," or "Gimmie the ply-ya . . . no, no not dat one . . . da one ova dea. The long-nose ply-ya."

I was the son he never had. I wore pigtails and tucked them under a baseball cap, wore jeans, aloha shirts, cross slippers, and carried a pocketknife in my back pocket like the boys in town.

While growing up, I didn't know very much about the father I rode around town with in his red-primered World War II surplus truck, which he had bought at an auction soon after the war. The truck had a nasty red coating that stained everything that touched it—unsuspecting hands, the brush of a white blouse, the seat of a pair of jeans. If you scraped away the red coat, the dull brown, red, and green colors of combat camouflage emerged like somber fall colors.

My father was gruff and always had a scowl on his face when around the house. He had a long body and short legs that he covered up with a short-sleeved white shirt and khaki pants. His face was round with high cheekbones and his hairline receding. "I was one round-face bugga," he said in describing what he looked like, the few times he talked about himself as a young boy, living in 'Ōla'a. Although he sat tall in the cab of his truck, when he stepped out, only then did one realize that he was of middling size, not strapping and large as his image in the cab belied.

Recently, I learned that my father quit school in the sixth grade because he was mysteriously paralyzed and not able to walk for a year or so. According to the aunt, my father's sister, who disclosed this information, the doctor at the time suggested that my father was afflicted with a mild case of polio, which he eventually overcame. Cruel, the other kids in the plantation camp teased him about his early attempts to walk, which made him hate school.

"Damn buggas make fun of me. Afta dat I neva like go school. So I wen quit."

When he got better, with the family so poor, no one cared that he did not continue his education. He went to work in the cane fields.

I learned from others, too, that my father was a quiet man, which I can't envision, really, for he was talkative at home, especially at the dinner table where he dictated how things should be done in our family. We often choked on our food and ate with tears streaming into our mouths. How he scolded us! And everything was a scold: "Why you no cut your hay-ya?" "No sit l'dat!" "How come you had one B, not one A?"

Uneducated, his philosophy was simple: children should be seen but not heard; good Japanese children obeyed their parents and never got into trouble; grow up with good Japanese values and you'll never go wrong in life.

But I was a misfit. I dug my nose, went barefooted, wore Aunt Sue's burgundy Cutex nail polish, shaved my legs, never wore house slippers, and wore lipstick. I was disobedient and improper in my bearing. I hated to go to Japanese language school in the afternoons and to the Buddhist temple on Sundays. I was not smart, filial, or radiant in school like other Japanese children whose parents doted on them. "The Shigeta girl wen graduate college. All the kids their family wen graduate college. You guys gotta be like dem," he said to my sister and me. He heaped his expectations on us through his scoldings. How was I to ever meet them?

I feared my father more than I respected him, for underneath his philosophy ran an immovable, frightening streak. Once his mind was made up about where we should go, how my mother should wear her hair, how the children should dress, there was no changing his mind. He was the one who had my mother braid our hair. He was the one who approved of jeans.

"Why must I wear these brown Buster Browns? Why can't I have oxfords like everyone else?"

"Because your father wants you to wear these shoes," my mother said, and my poor mother, caught between us, mediated the rough path between her husband and her daughters.

"I'm not going to wear them."

"You'd better. He's going to scold you."

"Yeah, yeah, I know. You don't have to tell me."

While growing up, I wanted to be that typical Japanese obedient good girl from a typical Japanese family. But I was a failure; I never listened to anyone.

I was born during the war on a humid day in the middle of the blackout. Children like me were called blackout babies. But more than a blackout baby, my mother said I was a terrible crybaby. "I didn't know where you came from!" she said.

I cried at everything: at the drop of a hat, a coin, a book; a slammed door; someone singing; the sweep of searchlights across the windows; a barking dog. Everything startled me, and this made my mother angst ridden. "How are you going to grow up calm and good?" she said.

Later, I was morose, given to quick tears and periods of intense emotional swings—at times overwrought, then driven to self-pity and silence. When the neighbor girl would call for me to come out and play, I remember days my mother would say to her, "She can't come out to play. She's not feeling well." But it was not because I was sick. I was just blue.

There was a time I remember wishing I would contract polio—not because my father had it, for I didn't know it then, but because I wanted to be paraded in an iron lung like the haole children I saw in the "March of Times" newsreel that played before the main feature at the Palace Theater in town. Thinking of it, I wanted to be different, I wanted to be famous. The cameras would roll in and I would be the first Japanese polio victim to be put in an iron lung and photographed. People would come and see me. Pity me. "Oh, look at her. Isn't she darling? It's such a pity that she has polio," they'd say.

When I was a child, I was the busiest thing you can imagine between what my mother called my "blue" days. Busy, busy, busy—that's what I was. I'd do all kinds of things, like sell ice-box or ranger cookies to all the neighbors in order to buy a pair of red shoes, or sell dried sour lemons to the younger children for a Chihuahua in a cup that I had seen in a comic book advertisement.

Once, when I was about nine or ten, I entered the national Pepsodent Smile contest. Before this, people had praised my teeth as beautiful, white, almost perfect.

"Oh, your daughter has such nice teeth," friends complimented my mother in those years before braces. The perfection was unusual for Japanese, they said, for most children had crooked or "buck" or "milk" teeth in small, crowded jaws.

I first learned about the Pepsodent Smile contest when walking home from school one day and seeing the larger-than-life-sized posters of some haole children—regional winners—in the Standard Drug Store window. Although our family used another brand of toothpaste, I begged my mother to buy some Pepsodent for the rules and entry form.

"Please, I promise to use all the paste. I won't waste it."

"Make sure you don't. I don't want you to hide and throw it into the wastebasket."

"I'm not going to do that."

One rule stated that the picture sent with the entry form and the box top had to be a studio, wallet-sized photograph. "Please Mama," I begged again—my hands together and up to my forehead in prayer—this time for an advance on my allowance so I could have my picture taken at the Modern Camera Shop. "Mr. Kanemori takes the best pictures."

The photo studio was on Front Street next to a doctor's office and two doors down from Sun Sun Lau Restaurant. Mr. Kanemori put me on a stool in front of a velvet curtain backdrop and had me angle my head, first to one side, then the other, and smile. He snapped pictures over and over again.

"The proofs should be ready by next week. But since I know your father, I'll make it early for you. Come see me in about three days, and tell your father not to forget the softball game this weekend."

"Thank you Mr. Kanemori," I said, politely. "I'll let my father know."

After what seemed like an interminable wait, I received the photographs, chose one, and sent the picture of myself—a tanned Japanese girl with a wide, perfect-teeth smile whose thick hair was slicked down with green pomade and shiny as black patent leather shoes—to the smile contest. I was sure to be a winner. I was sure to have my picture blown up into a gigantic poster which would be placed in every drugstore window across the landscape of America.

For days after sending my entry, I waited for my father, who picked up the mail from the post office box in town, awaiting word that I had placed in the regionals.

"How come she wait for me get the mail everyday?" he asked my mother.

"She entered the Pepsodent Smile Contest."

"Oh yeah? What dat?"

My mother had to explain it all to him. At the end he was as excited as I was about the contest and elated that I had taken the initiative to enter it. He gloated over the prospect: his daughter could be a winner!

Later, he looked at me proudly and said, "So, I hea you wen send your pickcha mainland, eh? Ho, good fo' you."

He joined me in my enthusiasm and was as hopeful as I felt. It must have been as though he were placing another bet; it was the holding of the purest kind of hope—in one's child—unadulterated and, like Ivory, ninety-nine and forty-four one-hundredths percent pure. The praise he gave was of the highest order given to anyone in our family, like a pat on the head, and this was as good as it would get.

But it was my sister who took me aside in her own inimical fashion and said, "Don't be stupid. Do you think you can win? You just wasted all your money, kid. Do you know who we are? No fool of a judge is going to pick you, a Japanese girl, no matter how beautiful your teeth. He probably looked at your picture and laughed."

"That's not true!" I lashed back. "You're just jealous." It never occurred to me that I didn't have a chance to win because I was a Jap. It never crossed my mind. But after what my sister said, deep down inside I knew that what she said was probably true.

As soon as I had a chance, I ran from home into town, down Kīlauea Avenue, then down Hālaʻi Street, which was not very far away. I stood in front of the drugstore window, which was elevated like an altar, and stared at the oversized pictures of three smiling children with their perfect teeth. The latest winners in large captions: Kathleen Taylor from Kalamazoo, Michigan; Stuart Finley from Norfolk, Nebraska; Charlotte Kilgore from Boulder, Colorado.

I sobbed in anguish in front of the tow-headed children with their light-colored eyes and perfect white teeth. People stopped at the window to see what I was looking at and crying about. They turned to look at me, then back at the pictures. They shook their heads or looked over their shoulders as they walked away, unable to comprehend what I was crying about, for all they could see were pictures of those beautiful haole children.

Feeling drained after crying so hard and long, I went back home and hid in my bedroom. For days, I did not go out, even for meals. This was unheard of in our family. My father could not understand my behavior. He expected that we all eat together, no matter what. He went around and around about the situation. "Forget already. Tell her all *pau*!" he said.

"Let her go, she'll get over it," my mother said.

"No good, the way she ack."

"It's okay. She was disappointed."

"Dat's why no good, you spoil the damn kids."

He wanted everyone to be like him, where everything was easy—simple and without fuss—if one did the right Japanese thing, which was to face one's disappointments, stoically. Little did he care if I felt dashed like a wave against the Kau coastline. Little did he care that I felt like cane fallen in a hailstorm. He just couldn't understand my moping and, I believe, he was pretty close to getting me out—bodily. He never thought for a minute that I had been presumptuous, and that I had been chastened by the episode. But my sister was right. Who was I to send my picture to some place as far off as Chicago, Illinois, in 1952?

I was not the kind of daughter who sat quietly with her father whenever on an outing with him. At a very young age, going out with him meant getting *away* from him and going off by myself. That was the purpose.

"I'm going, okay?"

"Whea?"

"To play in the park."

"Go. Lousy kid, I tell you," he would say under his breath.

At Hoʻolulu Park, I balanced myself on the whitewashed two-by-four outer fence that circled the racetrack. I went way out, to the back of the park, and from there walked the circle, my hands outstretched as if in flight. The trick was never to have my father see me fall off the beam.

Besides the occasional horse race, Hilo High School used the park for baseball in the spring and football during the fall. The horse race viewing stand was a tall, ugly red building with hard, uncomfortable wooden risers that overlooked the whole place. "The old people sitting place," the students called it.

The top portion served as a viewing stand, which also functioned as the announcer's stand where the broadcaster spoke into heavy mikes that looked like mini versions of a knight's helmet. Chicken wire fencing shielded everyone sitting in the stands from foul balls, sparrows, or myna birds during the games. I felt as if my vision were cut into hexagonal-shaped pieces every time I sat up there. Try as I might to look beyond the wire screen, the foreground was occasionally thrown into focus, making it seem as if I were looking out of a beehive. At various times our high school used the bottom part of this building as a dugout for baseball, a dressing room for the football players, a shelter for the school band.

The times I sat in the viewing stand I hated it, trapped between my father's coarse friends—a baseball cap, club T-shirt wearing bunch who chomped on boiled peanuts that they ate with their gold teeth and open mouths—men who looked and acted like my father. Even their conversations were predictable. There was one that I remember disliking with a passion.

"Eh, Asa. Dat your daughta?"

"Yeah. Dis my numba two daughta."

"What—you only get two girls? No mo boys?"

"Yeah, no mo, I only get two cock-a-looch."

Everyone laughed and slapped their thighs. I felt my face getting hot, demeaned at being called a "cock-a-looch."

As I grew older, I managed to slip away before the men started talking. I hated when they scrutinized me and said things like, "Big girl, eh now? Wat grade you?"

Once, when I was younger, I just wanted to get away from them. *Him.* As I grew older, I didn't want to be seen with him, even if I did depend on him to take me around. He didn't understand my attitude; he had a disgruntled look on his face whenever I fled his side and disappeared. He didn't seem to like it when I went to sit with my classmates on the field bleachers.

Usually, he and I arrived early for a school game to beat the crowd. I sat with my father for a few gratuitous minutes, and as soon as the audience thickened, I ran off. "Bye, I going," I said. I went on to find a seat among the other students. Rain or shine, I stayed outside. Only occasionally did I turn to see if my father was still around. An empty seat in the bleachers where he'd been sitting meant he was in the car and waiting for me.

I was a junior in high school. I learned about it the Sunday morning after it happened. Alice, a classmate and my closest friend, had called me with the "do you know what happened?" news as soon as she heard about it.

"What? You must be kidding," I said. I couldn't believe it, let alone say the word to myself comfortably: *Rape.* Yes, rape. Who would have thought, in Hilo, our small town?

Most of us did not know what the word really *meant.* We were all so naive. Years before, even when Alice first explained what happens, I sat dumbfounded, unable to comprehend what it was all about. In dramatizing the action, Alice's eyes grew larger and larger. She threw her arms around her body and held it and spun in a circle. "He might do it to you in the car," she said. "Or he would drag you into the cane fields, then tear off your clothes. He going whip out his you-know-what, put his lips on your mouth and lie down on top of you—poke you and poke you and make you do things you don't want to—slam his body against yours." Alice scrunched her face and covered it, dramatically.

On the phone that Sunday morning as she was telling me the news, Alice sounded breathy and wide-eyed as the day she told me all about what could happen to girls. "I heard it was pretty bad," she said. "The boys dropped her off at home, her clothes all ripped. The boys couldn't get away because the father knew who they were. Stupid, yeah them." The story spread like cane fire.

That gloomy Sunday afternoon there was a football game scheduled at Hoʻolulu Park. The air felt charged with an inexplicable electricity. While I did go with my father to the game—Hilo High versus Honokaʻa High—I didn't go up with him to the grandstand or sit the obligatory time, but stayed downstairs and hung around the stairwell near the dugout.

The school band played under the stand's wide eaves during the games. The song leaders with their blue-and-yellow flared skirts and the cheerleaders with their two-colored crepe paper pom-poms did their number. The bass drum kept time. The stomping and clapping *Vikings, Vikings, rah, rah, rah* could be heard across the field.

Blue cummerbund-waisted band students with white pants and yellow shirts trickled in, took their seats, adjusted the heights of their music stands, put their instruments together, lapped their reeds, and did trills and scales to warm up. I knew the girl who'd been involved played for the band. I had half expected not to see her there. But she *did* come, and she bravely acted as though nothing had happened to her.

After some team and school announcements were made, the band played the "Star Spangled Banner." The students then played the school alma mater. Everyone sang: *Beneath the tropic skies of Hilo—* The crowd sang the alma mater even louder than they did the national anthem, so strong were the ties everyone in our town had with the high school. *And loyalty and honor shall forever be thine.*

With the coin toss, the Honoka'a team winning over the Hilo Vikings, the band played a spirited "El Capitan" by Sousa. "Tap, tap, tap," the bandmaster signaled. He stood before the band members on a small step stool and pumped his baton and hand fiercely as if to overcome the roar of the fans at kickoff, pointing with his chin to the brass, percussion, or woodwind sections. An occasional squeak marred the air.

I watched the bandmaster, his glasses sliding down his nose in the humidity. A light wind lifted his uniform, a yellow satin shirt, and exposed his midriff circled with a brown belt that held up a pair of sharkskin, white choke bottoms that brushed the tops of his white bucks with red rubber soles thick as flank steaks. The sight of his yellowish flesh made me shudder.

But I was not there to watch the band, nor the bandmaster, nor to listen to the music. I had come to watch *her*—the girl the boys had spoiled, had made secondhand, had made imperfect. Who would want to touch her now? Who would want to marry *her*? Although I didn't know what to expect, I felt disappointed. I had expected something more. Perhaps I expected more shame and guilt to be written all over the girl's face. Perhaps I expected her to be bruised and hurt. Perhaps, too, I expected her to break down and cry in her humiliation. Maybe carry on.

But she simply played the musical piece before her and smiled her usual smile and never looked around to see if others, like me, were watching her or talking about her. Was she stunned? Was she in shock that she could act as if nothing happened?

I wasn't prepared to see *nothing*, absolutely nothing. I did not have the words to shape my understanding. Instead of rallying around her, I could only look and stare like everyone else who knew her, our hearts and minds too small. Seeing her so strong broke my heart. I couldn't have been so bold.

The next day, Monday, the boys charged with the offense had their pictures splashed on the front page of the paper. They were boys I had grown up with, had gone to kindergarten with, and had been friends with all my life. I supposed it was possible to know people and not know them. Who could know what dark thoughts we harbored in our minds? It gave something of an understanding to what the radio show *The Inner Sanctum* portrayed. It was hard to reconcile what the boys did with the smiling girl in the band.

With my sister in college and my mother working part-time at a neighborhood grocery store, it was just my father and me on weekdays, spending most of the late afternoons together until my mother got home.

When my father read the paper that day, I saw him tense his body. I could see his neck tighten, the strain of its thick cords. He hands gripped the edge of the paper tightly and he straightened his back, which made him look large on the chair, as if he were sitting in the cab of his truck. I felt a lecture coming on and wondered what he was going to say.

"This one hea—dat's the Miyata family's young boy, eh?" he asked, while looking at me above his glasses and tapping the paper with one hand.

"Yeah, that's him," I said.

"You better not go out with this kine boy, you hea? No good this kine Japanee!"

How could one tell? "Yeah, yeah," I said, not understanding my father's reasoning as to how I was to know a good Japanese from a bad one.

"Dea motha and fatha neva teach 'em right, dat's why dey like this."

"Hard to tell if they good or bad—till they do something wrong," I said in a mumble.

I had aroused my father's anger. "Just no go 'round boys l'dis, dat's all. You hea? They no good! I catch you hanging around this kine boys, you watch out."

"But Dad—"

"No 'but' me."

"But you don't understand. It could have happened to anyone, including me."

"What you mean, you too?'"

By this time he had taken off his glasses and put the newspaper down. He looked straight at me. "No get smart. Noting like this can happen to good girls. You come from one good family. Undastan?"

"I know, but the girl came from a good family," I said. *Maybe even better than us.* The tone in my voice begged for understanding, but as I said this to him, I could see that he was furious. More than I'd ever seen before.

"No talk like that!" he said, raising his voice, gnashing his teeth. He pushed his chair back, suddenly, and stood up, his face red and inflated like one of his truck tires' inner tubing.

Frightened, and without saying anything, I also got up. I kept my eyes on him and his hands. I headed for my room.

"It can happen to you, too, eh? What kine answer, dat? Come back hea, no walk away from me," he demanded.

As he rushed toward me, he reached out and barely missed grabbing my arm. He had never hit me before, but I felt that he might this time. I thought I would never make it to my room, my body moving too slowly for the rush I felt inside.

I slammed my bedroom door and locked it, *click*, and sank the door hook into its eye just before my father's fist came crashing down on the face of my door. Each of us breathing hard, we stood on opposite sides of that barrier.

I later heard my father turn away in frustration like a heavy, wounded animal, and, like acquiring polio, or gambling that went "unda da table," or winning a national smile contest, or rape, he did not consider that there were times in life, in our human condition, that things would not work out, that they were completely out of our hands.

For a long while after that incident, I stayed close to my room and clear of my father.

The girl who had been raped stayed pretty much to herself. Everyone was polite, but we really didn't have much to say to her. Her mother came every day after school to pick her up in a large and dark old Packard that swallowed her whole whenever she dropped herself into the backseat. In school, she walked by herself through the corridors when we changed classes. She looked lonely, but she never let on. Never let her head go down. The boys had more visitors at the prison than she had friends.

The girl involved graduated with honors at the end of the school year and later testified at the trial. That summer, I followed the rape trial closely in the *Hilo Tribune Herald*. The unpleasantness of it dragged on like the heat. While the girl was the only one who came forward to charge the boys, it was learned that as many as twenty other girls had been gang-raped on cane field backroads.

The jury convicted all of the boys, and they were sent away to serve time in jail. At the end of summer, the good Japanese girl left the islands and went off to school, but she had buried her secret deep in our psyches.

I did not go anywhere with my father again. Often, in the months before leaving home after graduation, I saw him drive off, alone. There was something terribly lonely about the way he sat in the high cab and went off by himself.

Occasionally, when I did get to go to a game with a generous friend or two who gave me a ride to the park, I'd turn toward the risers and see my father perched in the grandstand. I wondered if he ever looked for me, or even missed me, as I looked to see if he was there. The space between us, from the bleachers to the fields, was like sadness and what we were as father and daughter. As Japanese.

The Wall

Bad words on the wall. I had seen them often where the old TB hospital, Puʻumaile once stood. Years before, because the weather was good there—with clean air and sunshine for the patients—the County of Hawaiʻi on the Big Island built a TB sanitarium on that spot. One day, a winter storm from the North Pacific barreled in and damaged the place. Later, a tidal wave washed away the buildings and crumbled sections of the tall, lava-rock retaining wall. The wall sat like a row of jagged teeth at the end of Five-mile Half.

I remember a neighbor woman, Mrs. Kuraiya, who was TB-conscious during that time, leaning over the broken fence between our yards and saying to my mother, "If you have TB or if anyone in your family has TB, people will look down on you. So, it's better not to catch TB. You can end up at Puʻumaile and be an outcast." Turning to me, she said, "And you, you can't play with normal children if you get TB." But, as I was to learn later, in our town the disease was not the only condition by which people accepted or didn't accept you. At least the stigma of illness stood out in the open.

When I was quite young, I used to go with my father to the end of the road near the wall, near the wreck of the hospital, to watch the water for fish. It was said that if you listened carefully, you could hear the cries of the dead in the wind. If the water surrounding the area was not rough, whitecapped, and choppy, my father cast his bamboo rods and stuck them between the rocks, the lines baited with ʻōpelu strips to hook the elusive ulua. People prized this fish for its white meat and vigorous fight. For my father, more often than not, it was the fish that got away.

I wasn't interested in fishing. Most Saturdays I went with my father so that my mother could do her chores without me underfoot. My older sister behaved well and needed little supervision. I was the one my mother complained about, the one who "got her goat" or was "in her hair." Although my father gave her time to be away from me, it was time he didn't look forward to. He was short with me, never nice.

While my father fished, I explored the tide pools for gobies, mamo babies, black wana, false stars, sea cucumbers. Or I'd find a special stick of guava or Christmas berry to poke and prod the sheltered tide pools thick with algae, brown and slimy, the rocks encrusted with barnacles and shellfish.

But the best fun I had was to balance my way across the top of the tumbledown wall. I could cup my hands and yell for the longest time without anyone scolding me. The crashing waves on the nearby rocks swallowed my screams as if into its bowels and regurgitated them in their wild pound and hiss against the rocks. I collected opaque sea-ground beer and green soda glass around the wall and jingled my pockets with this private collection of jewelry. But, secretly, I went to the wall to look at the words: "Kilroy was here!" "Jap." "Fock." I went up to the words and traced the letters of the different handwritings with my fingers. People used coral or chalk to write on the wall; pocketknives to carve words and hearts on the trees; or chisels to make grooves into the large, gray surrounding boulders. Near the word "Kilroy" that was on the wall, someone had drawn a skull wrapped in a pirate's bandana with a patch over one eye, superimposed on cross bones. There were also swastikas and other symbols I wasn't sure about. An inspired artist drew a naked woman with breasts that looked like eyes.

"Who's Kilroy?" was something I could ask my father who shrugged his shoulders. As for the rest of the words? I knew that even at my age—six or seven at the time—the words were not to be asked about, especially used. But I mouthed the words and noted them in my mind.

In the late fifties, Hilo was a conservative backwater. We were two to three years behind in fashion compared to the rest of the country. Two small supermarkets, one set of traffic lights, one high school, and back-door milk delivery served the county. The yasai or vegetable man came to the house twice a week. With the advent of television and statehood, we were catching up; but TV programs were still being broadcast one week late. Although Dick Clark's show, *American Bandstand*, which was featured on Saturday mornings, kept the teenagers on our island abreast of the latest in music and fashion across the country, no matter how hard we tried, we looked dumpy in our poodle skirts, Sandra Dee haircuts, and crinolines. We sounded strange in the "hip" talk we imitated.

"Don't try to copy people on the mainland," my mother said. "We're too different."

"Different—how?"

"We have an accent."

And we did sound odd when we tried to imitate how people spoke on TV, our accents sing-song, we being of Asian ancestry and all that. We said *cool man* and *daddy-o* and *skin it*—expressions we picked up from the movies—and sprinkled the words into our pidgin, which made us sound "different" in town and gave us the mild air of delinquency we wanted to achieve. We cracked our Spearmint gum and snapped our fingers with every expression we mimicked. We thought we were hip. In reality, we were hick-town.

Two gangs, the Rebels and Crashers, dominated our high school. Cora Nishi, Susan Akita, Martha Valesco, and I hung around with the Crasher boys. All through junior year, one of the Crashers, Steven or Steve "Cash" Kutsunai, wanted a chance with Martha, who was the prettiest girl in our bunch. She had put him off all year long.

"I don't want to go steady with you," she said. Nevertheless, Martha was flattered. I could see it in how she flicked her long hair back.

"C'mon, give me chance," he said back.

Come-on words oozed out of him like hot 'ōhelo syrup. And because Steve, one of the more popular guys in the Crashers, liked Martha, who was a gorgeous, Filipino-Japanese hapa girl, and because we associated with Martha, the rest of us became part of the *gang*. We became the Crasher girls. And because she had the car, Cora was our unofficial leader.

Weekends, Cora made the arrangements with the Crashers to go either to the beach, theater, or our favorite place to hang out—a cane haul road in upper Kaūmana we called "Happy Valley." In Hilo, weekends were usually spent hanging out on some cane haul road smoking cigarettes and drinking beer. At other times, we went to Pu'umaile with colored chalk to draw hearts with their pierced arrows or swear words on the wall in the blaze of the cars' headlights.

Vivacious, Cora was on the shorter side. She pranced around, elf-like, from boy to boy and talked risqué. "I know you *like*," she'd say.

"C'mon, no just talk cause I ready fo' go, anytime," the boy she was teasing would say.

She also offered unsolicited advice to boys who were having trouble with their girlfriends. "Just quit her. Get a better girlfriend!"

Susan was the tall one in our bunch. She loved to flirt with the boyfriends of other girls in our school—Joyce Kobayashi and her gang of girls, Sally Santos and her bunch. Predatory, Susan teased the boys and made their girlfriends feel insecure.

"Come here. I wanna tell you something," she'd coo to some guy and take him behind a car to let him French-kiss her and touch her rice-cake breasts. The girls in school hated her. They called her "easy fish" or "cockteaser" behind her back. But she didn't care. "They just jealous," she said and brushed off their anger as petty. Susan also loved to drink, although I always thought her drunkenness was exaggerated.

Like Susan, I didn't have a boyfriend. No one was interested in me. Boys I had crushes on never shared the same interest. I had too many pimples. I was chubby, homely, bookish.

Because there were very few summer jobs for high school students on the Big Island, many of us went to Honolulu, Maui, or Lāna'i to work in the pineapple fields or at one of the pineapple canneries in Honolulu. Girls landed jobs as packers or trimmers at Dole Pineapple, or Del Monte canneries; boys landed jobs as Ginaca machine attendants or tray boys.

In Honolulu, the girls stayed with relatives. Or, if you were one of the luckier ones, you rented an apartment in Mō'ili'ili with other girls for the summer. You shared the rent, utilities, and food, and still went home with money saved. When not working, we spent time in Waikīkī or at Ala Moana Beach, or downtown Honolulu where we walked up and down Fort Street and peered into the store windows of McInerny and Liberty House, which had the "good" clothing we hoped to buy before returning to Hilo.

One of our preoccupations at the time had been to get to know as many boys as possible from the different high schools in town—boys from McKinley or "Tokyo High," Kaimukī, Farrington, Roosevelt. "What school you from?" was the first question girls asked boys when they first met. Exchanging and collecting class pictures became a major pastime. Silver friendship rings on the right ring finger or on a chain deep in the cleavage, or wallet full of photographs that fell out like a Slinky testified to a person's popularity.

My girlfriends and I met a cool bunch of boys from Honolulu while working at the cannery. They were polite, clean-cut boys from McKinley. "They good guys," a girl from Honolulu testified. Popular and nice. This gave the guys a stamp of approval, but it also gave us a *rep*. Byron "Fly" Kuroda, Dennis "Mongi" Uchida, Michael "Mushiman" Kano, all came from good middle-class families. They belonged to the best school and church clubs—the ROTC, Key Club, Slide Rule Club, and Young Buddhist Association. They planned to go to college. They had futures.

They drove their own souped-up cars and during the school year worked part-time for their neighborhood service stations. Their fancy cars sported the popular tuck-and-roll Naugahyde upholstered seats of white and red or turquoise or black, the cars cut low to the ground in "Pologee dago." Three-cigarette-packs high. Girls riding around with these boys looked like ornaments, their hair teased and wrapped in chiffon kerchiefs tied under their chins, Elizabeth Taylor style, and topped with straw hats and dark cat-eye glasses. They wore toreador pants and aloha shirts with collars whipped up in waves.

We paraded with the guys in a long line of hotrods up and down Ala Moana Boulevard or Kalākaua, the strip of Waikīkī. Nights, we went from Kapiʻolani Drive-Inn to KC Drive-Inn, back to Chunky's Drive Inn, looking for drag races and hiding from the Honolulu Metro Squad—the burly, black-booted Hawaiian cops on motorcycles who patrolled the city. Most races went from stoplight to stoplight in short bursts of speed, the cars involved burning rubber and fishtailing to the next light.

Rebel Without a Cause. The boys played their own version of Chicken, pushing for ever higher speeds in the quarter mile, and the girls wanted to be loved by someone like James Dean and wished they could be Natalie Wood. Heady in the excitement and oblivious to danger, we raced the freeways. If the word got around for a big race, cars made their way from all parts of the island to a remote area in Mokulēʻia. Flags came out of cars and starters waved off the competitors on a long strip of road closed off to everyone except local traffic. Everyone watched for cops.

"On your mark, get set, ready . . . GO!" The flagman between two cars shouted, and dropped the flags for the race. For the runs, Cora, Martha, Susan, and I stayed on the sidelines and cheered Byron's car. In an earlier race, Byron had blazed his '60 Chevy Impala with its 327 block, dual carbs with blower, chromed headers, slicks, and shortened rearend against a '57 Bel Air big block turbo-trans. It was an uneven race with cars of different power. On the line, the large, smooth back tires gripped the road. The cars dropped their rear ends only to leap out like cougars. Byron, the Japanese James Dean, easily won the race. "He won! He won!" Martha screamed and jumped, clapping her hands like Natalie Wood in the movie.

Byron won several races that evening. Even after the races, passing cars revved their engines and bucked their cars in challenge. Martha rode in the front with Byron and Michael, the rest of us huddled in the back seat. She was the queen of the races.

Byron and Martha soon became a pair. Dennis had his eye on Cora. No one liked Susan or me at the moment and we felt no strong attraction to any of the other guys in the bunch. We liked to think of ourselves as *playing the field.* Although we ached for attention, our excuse was that we just wanted to be friends with all the guys.

It ended up being a whole summer of wanting to get laid, working for clothes money, saving up for college tuition, and listening to tinny music on cheap made-in-Japan transistor radios, the latest songs on the Hit Parade. Songs like "Venus," "Bird Dog," "Sleepwalk."

Soon summer was over. We quit our cannery jobs to go back to school in Hilo, which began the week after Labor Day. "See You in September" was the big hit and we were going home. At the Honolulu Airport gate, we said our good-byes to the boys we had hung around with all summer. "Don't forget to write, okay?" Byron said, his eyes on Martha.

"Don't forget to write, too!" responded Martha. "You'll probably forget all about us as soon as we leave."

"Not true," said Byron.

"You mean it?" asked Martha.

The boys had leis for us. They placed them around our necks and awkwardly said their good-byes. Byron promised that they would come to visit, and we could show them around our island.

"My uncle lives there. He said to come stay at his house," Byron said.

"Deal," Cora said. "Don't make yourselves scarce." In our hearts we never expected them to come. Not really.

"See you lahtas alligatahs," purred Susan.

"Yeah. Aftah while croca-d-i-a-l," Dennis said. "Skin it." We rolled our hands in the palms of the boys' hands. We waved good-bye to them until the interisland jet-prop lifted off the ground.

Hilo seemed even more of a hick town after our summer in Honolulu. We were part of the class of 1960 but began our senior year on a downbeat. We couldn't wait to graduate. Move on. At this time, many relationships in our school were being made or broken. Everyone seemed more serious, thinking in terms of marriage and settling down.

"You heard," Cora said. "Clifford and Sandra—they engaged to be engaged. Sandra accepted a promise ring from Clifford."

"How long they went?" Susan asked.

"Since elementary," I said.

"Suckers!" Susan said.

Howard and Ronald, the school's kolohe boys, began hitting the books, becoming super serious in their studies. Gladys Yamada brought a *True Confessions* magazine to school and stuffed it between the pages of her history text to read in study hall. Jeanne Arruda brought *The Bride* to prepare herself as Clyde Asari's wife when she finished high school. For others, college loomed on the horizon.

The time was frightening for those unattached. It could feel as if you were being passed over and left behind. Everyone wanted assurance that they would be married in the near future. After graduating from college, these steady couples would get married. If you graduated college and you weren't married or planning to, people considered you *old* at twenty-four.

November. Even in a seasonless tropical climate, small changes occurred during the winter months. Thanksgiving rolled in with the dampness that overcame the town. My father went fishing less, the seas too rough, the rains running off the chalk-written graffiti in streaks on the Pu'umaile Hospital wall. And Martha got more and more involved with Steve. It seemed she had forgotten all about Byron. Frequently, she wore scarves to hide the hickies on her Audrey Hepburn neck, while Steve walked around—moony, his eyes arrow-shot—escorting Martha by her elbow through the hallways of our school.

One day, even before the first bell had rung, Cora came rushing to our hangout between the bathroom and the stretch of lockers where we smoked. She said that the guys from Honolulu had written and planned to come to Hilo. Languid as a cat, Susan disengaged herself from the balcony she had wrapped her long legs around. "You sure?" she asked.

"Yup," Cora said. "Byron, Dennis, and Michael them."

"When?" Martha asked, her eyes brightening at the mention of Byron's name.

"They coming on the day before Thanksgiving. Think of where we can take them."

I chewed on my pencil, thinking. Susan gave me a disgusted look as she flicked yellow Mirado pencil flecks of paint off my face and the collar of my blouse.

"No give me back my pencil. Get your gala-gala on," she said, happy that the boys were coming.

The boys arrived, and we picked them up at Hilo airport. We

hardly recognized them. They were dressed in their best clothing—heavy gray woolen drape pants, long-sleeved dress shirts in pink or white, crossed-leather slippers, and satin baseball jackets with tigers embroidered on the backs. Michael carried a Martin uke and Dennis gave us a pineapple from his mother.

"C'mon we go," said Cora. "We take you guys Banyan Drive, Baker's Beach, down Five-mile Half. Downtown too."

"Shoots," Byron said.

Later we took the boys over to Byron's uncle's home in Waiākea Uka where they were staying. Byron's uncle offered his nephew his hopped-up, two-toned '56 Chevy to cruise. That night, we arranged to eat at Sun Sun Lau Restaurant and, later, catch a movie at the Palace Theater where *Summer Place* with Sandra Dee and Troy Donahue was playing.

At five, while dressing to go out, the phone rang. "Gonfunit kids. I going rip the damn phone off the hook," my father said, irritated because of the many phone calls I'd been receiving since the boys were in town. "Why you no help your madda around the house once in a while? Only go out, spend money. Das all you good for."

"Yeah sure," I said in disrespect. My father's eyebrows shot up and he curled his lips. He was right on the verge of saying something nasty, but when I answered the phone, he simply glared and went into the bedroom.

It was Cora. She was calling to let me know that she was going to be late. Martha was having trouble going out with us. "Steve's giving her a bad time," Cora said. "He doesn't like the idea."

"Like the idea of *what*?"

"Her hanging out with other guys. He think he own Martha."

"Oh," I said, surprised. It was good to be liked by someone, and I wished I was liked by a boy. But being held back from having fun?

"He's so uncool," I said.

"Yeah, real uncool," Cora said. "I going be late for pick you up. I'm going to Martha's house first. Susan said she'll call up Bryon guys to tell them to meet us later."

"I'll wait," I said, but was anxious. I felt stranded and beached like one of my father's fish.

Martha didn't go out with us that night. "Where's Martha?" was the first thing out of Byron's mouth, and we had not yet cleared his uncle's driveway.

"Her mother's sore at her."

"What happened?" The tone in his voice was suspicious.

"Oh, you know how it is with parents," Cora said, covering up, telling him how Martha's mom was angry with her and how she'd been grounded. We congratulated each other with our eyes at the story.

We had dinner and went to the movie as planned. Later, we drove to Puʻumaile. We showed the guys the wall. We picked out chunks of white coral from the ground and wrote the boys' names, and they wrote our names on the wall in the light of the car's high beams.

The following day, which was Thanksgiving, a defiant Martha, having fought with Steve, came with us to show the boys around. I could almost feel Byron swoon. I saw him holding his breath in what seemed the passing of strong feelings, careening through his body.

In a moment away from the boys, Cora asked Martha, "So how did you manage this with Steve?"

Martha shrugged her shoulders. She said, "I'm tired of Steve's possessiveness. I want to have fun, too. This is my senior year, the last time to be free."

Nonetheless, she appeared restrained, troubled, preoccupied throughout the day. She was not aware of Byron's attention. We heard him ask Martha, "How's school these days?" more than once.

We went to several scenic spots along the Hāmākua Coast and ended up at Kolekole Park where we had a picnic. We had brought sushi, okazu, sodas, the bento from Kawamoto Store in town. With musubi and spam in our hands, we walked over to the water's edge and watched the waterfall cascade into the river where it met the sea. But it began to drizzle, so we moved on to the park pavillion with Martha, who wanted to show Byron the graffiti board. Byron took out his knife and he and Martha carved their names into the soft wood. "I don't think you'd better put our names together," I heard Martha caution Byron. "This is a small town."

"Take a chance, why not?"

"I don't think so—" Martha said.

After that, Byron and Martha walked up the driveway along the river and walked back down again. On several occasions, I saw Martha burst into laughter, thoughts of Steve, from what I could gather, far away. With the waterfall crashing nearby, I couldn't hear much except to notice how warm they appeared toward each other. Susan and I nudged elbows. "Jes like old times," Susan said.

The sun appeared once more after a light shower. Martha perched herself on the hood of the car next to Susan and me. Byron and the rest of the guys went in for a swim. Watching everyone, Martha grew suddenly maudlin. Tearful, she wanted to be taken home.

"I wanted to have fun, but I just can't. I don't want to be a killjoy, but I think I better go,'" she said, her words not heartfelt.

"Why do you let your boyfriend do this?" I heard Byron ask Martha as we prepared to head home. "He doesn't own you. Stay with us."

"I can't. You don't understand. I'm sorry, really sorry," she said, between sobs. "I can't help it."

When she reached over for some Kleenex in the car, her blouse sleeve crept up her arm, and the other girls and I could not help but notice the black-and-blue marks. We knew then why Martha couldn't help herself. Steve. Still Steve. *What a dumb shit*, I thought to myself.

Late that afternoon, Cora took the boys to her home for Thanksgiving dinner. The rest of us went home. At about ten-thirty, while getting ready for bed, the telephone rang. "Who's calling dis late?" my father said. "Tell your damn friends not to call so late."

"Yeah, yeah, I'll tell them," I said. By nine, streetlights flashed their yellow caution signals in our town. Restaurants all closed for the night. A call from nine o'clock on was considered late. I rushed from my bedroom to the phone in the parlor.

"I tell you, deese kids nowadays," I heard my father say to my mother.

I answered the phone and moved my body into the corner, where the wall phone was hooked up, to muffle the sound of my talking. It was Cora. "Can you come out?" she asked.

"Sure. If I sneak out," I whispered. "What's going on?"

"Tell you latah. Meet me across the street. At eleven."

"Okay, but—" Cora hung up the phone.

I dressed quietly, wore a pair of jeans under the old muʻumuʻu I slept in. "Nite," I said and made believe I was going to bed. My parents were listening to a Japanese radio program, and I waited for the station to sign off with *Dream when you're feeling blue*— After the song, and once the national anthem played, my parents would turn off their lights and go to sleep.

I snuck out the back door. I ran down the steps barefooted. Carrying my slippers in one hand, I leaped across Kumu Street. I was safe. It was as if I were the only person alive as I crossed the rain-slicked asphalt that gleamed like a silver stream of water in the blue-black night.

I waited in the shadow of Mrs. Tabara's wī tree until I saw Cora coming down the road in her blue Ford. She stopped the car. I jumped in. Cora had a deep scowl on her face.

"So, what's happening?" I asked.

"Byron guys got beat up tonight," she said. "They called me from a pay phone. They want to meet at Puʻumaile."

We drove to the wall where the boys said to meet them. We drove up to where they were parked and saw that Byron's uncle's car was smeared with white paint and obscenities.

"Take a look at this!" Michael said in despair and threw out his smashed uke as we pulled up alongside.

"You guys call the police?" asked Cora.

I saw the boys shake their heads, dark looking in the night shadows. "Nah. What for?" Byron said, his voice shaky. "We don't want to make trouble. Besides, who going pay for the damage on my uncle's car?"

"About seven guys jumped the three of us when when we were parked on Banyan Drive," Michael said.

"Seven to three? What chicken shits," I said.

"It was still early so we went for a ride in Byron's uncle's car," Michael said.

"Later, we parked under the trees. We couldn't see much in the dark. All I know is that these guys jumped us and said something about not liking the idea of their broads hanging around us guys from Honolulu," said Byron.

"Damn Steve," said Cora. Somehow, the Crashers had the notion that we *belonged* to them.

"We're leaving first thing in the morning," Byron said. "I don't think I can stay at my uncle's house. The car is pretty badly damaged."

"We'll take you guys to the airport," offered Cora.

"Nah, we'd better catch the taxi. We don't want to get you guys into more trouble," said Byron, looking like a beat-up Marlon Brando from *On the Waterfront*. Dennis sat up higher in the car. In the light he wiped off some blood from his cut lip with a wet towel as we sorted out what happened. He also nursed a swollen hand. Michael's jaw puffed up lopsidedly and one eye bulged as if a bee had stung it. Byron had a gash on his left temple.

"You guys okay, but?" Cora asked.

"I think so. My stomach hurts, from a punch in a gut, but I'm okay," Dennis said.

"Maybe you better go to the hospital," I said.

"Not *that* sore," Dennis said, testy about his situation.

This was the last time we saw or heard from them.

"Hey, I feel like telling the guys off," Cora said the next day. "What'd you say?"

"Yeah, me too," I said.

"Dumb asses," Susan said.

After telling Martha what had happened, she too was on our side. "I really want to break up with Steve," she said, shaken at how the Crashers had hurt our innocent friends. That night, Cora arranged a meeting at Puʻumaile with the boys involved, the rendezvous set for the large clearing behind the wall.

The unpaved road to Puʻumaile was bumpy and Cora swerved her car this way and that to avoid the large potholes. Indicating that it would rain soon, black clouds passed swiftly over the moon when we arrived at the clearing. Sea spray misted the area.

We waited for a long while. We tried singing. We listened for the patients' screams and cries but that only frightened us. We turned to making out some of the slogans and initials on the wall.

"What's that, over there?" asked Cora.

"Can't see," said Susan. "It's too dark even with the headlights on." She continued to crane her neck. "I get it. I think it's B.K. loves S.H. Barry Kohashi loves Sharon Harada. Look, check this out. Diane loves Arnold. Can you beat that? I didn't know they liked each other. The nerve. I just made out with him." Checking her watch, she said, "I wonder if the guys coming."

"Maybe they know they wrong, so they not coming," Cora said.

"If I know Steve," Martha said, "he'll come. You can bet on it."

"Maybe they too chicken," Susan said.

But the boys did come. They came in a large group, many cars in a caravan, and certainly more boys than were involved in the affray with our friends. The cars formed a loose circle—headlights turned in as if they had come to support another fight. I didn't know what they expected. It was as if they thought we would have a whole gang of boys to help us and jump *them*.

Steve's truck, with several boys seated in the back, was the last to bounce into the circle. Rodney, a friend of Steve's, jumped out of the truck bed and walked to Steve's side of the cab to talk to him. He lumbered his pudgy body over to our car and shielded his eyes from the headlights.

"Stooge," said Susan under her breath when Rodney walked over. He placed his arm on the door and leaned over to see who was in the car with us. Satisfied that it was only us, he said, "So what?"

"So shit!" Cora said. She faced Rodney squarely. After giving him the eye, she told him what was troubling us. "Tell Steve it was a dirty fight. We don't want any part of you guys. You guys think you *own* us, or what?"

"That all?" asked Rodney, a curve on his lips.

Susan, disgusted with Rodney's and Cora's benign conversation, stuck her head out of the car window, and began shouting: "You guys got your fricken nerve to beat up our friends."

"Shallup Susan, you cockteaser," Steve shouted back, leaning bodily out the car window. "You think the otha guys betta than us? Think again. They nothing but panties."

"You guys, the panties. Not them. Was seven 'gainst three! Damn cowards."

Steve hurtled terrible words back at Susan, like "slut" and "cunt"—words I had only seen on the wall. At his verbal attack, Susan, as if stunned by how far he was pushing it, stuck her head back in.

Steve continued his verbal assault. "The guys deserved it. They in the wrong territory." He stopped his tirade for a moment and said, "Martha, you there? Come on out, you coming with me!"

"What can I do?" Martha asked, a baffled look on her face. "Don't tell him I'm here."

"He can count heads," Cora said. "Don't be stupid. He knows you're here."

"Martha?" Steve said. "I know you in the car. I wanna talk to you."

"Don't go, Martha," I said. "You'll be sorry." I stuck my head out of the car and said, "Steve, Martha doesn't want to talk to you. She doesn't want to go with you, anymore." I pushed my voice forcefully into the rain.

"Let her tell me that herself."

"Fock you," Rodney who was still by our car, said to me.

"Fock you too," I said.

Soon Steve's other friends began yelling obscenities. Everyone began shouting at once. The f-word had more syllables, combinations, and permutations then ever imagined. "FOOooOOooCK" came out like a loud-soft, loud-soft melody out of one of the guys' mouths. Nothing was left to the imagination. The boys called us every expletive connected to the female body.

The words debased and cursed us. The boys' voices grew louder and louder in the verbal affray, the authority of deep voices in profanity—of men, of fathers, of boyfriends—prevailing. In the end they drowned out our voices.

I thought then of my father, how he put down my mother from time to time with words, not in the same manner or these same words, of course, but with the feeling of power and might in the tone of his voice. The constant orders, the constant accusations. This night was there in my parents' confrontations with each other and my father with me. It was in the language, the mean, harsh, and ugly words, the intimidation brought about by deep, angry voices. How they were said, more than anything else.

Finally, in a quiet spell, when everyone seemed to have run out of bad words and energy, Cora walked out of the car to meet with Steve. She suddenly glared at me and stormed off.

"What—?" I asked.

Susan and I stayed back in the car where Susan opened a can of beer she found on the floor. She began singing, "Rum and Coca-Cola." She was not drunk but swayed as if she were. She drank some beer and swished it in her mouth like mouthwash. After a while she walked over to where Cora talked with Steve and the others. I stayed in the car with Martha, who sat sobbing. To console her, I patted her back. She shrugged off my hand.

Cora and Susan soon walked back from Steve's car. "Don't worry. Everything's cool," Cora said. "The guys want to remain friends . . . except they don't want you around." She was looking at me. "The guys don't want you hanging around us."

"Who me? But why?"

"They . . . we . . . can't have you around, that's all."

I didn't understand it. It didn't make sense. I didn't think that someone could just tell me who I could or couldn't hang around with. "We all said bad things—why pick on me?" I said, surprised at the rejection. "All of you said the same things too, right?" I looked over at Susan. She looked down.

"We just telling you what the guys said. Don't blame us when everybody ice you come Monday morning," Susan said, pushing one side of her face toward me. "We still like be friends with the guys, but well, you gotta go. You can't hang around us guys anymore. Those are the rules, 'kay?"

"I still don't get it. What did you say, Susan—to the guys I mean—about me? You must have said something. Or you, Cora?"

"It was because you were against Martha's going back to Steve. Rodney heard you encouraging Martha to stay away, and he told Steve. You also called him a prick."

"You guys called Steve the same thing. What's the dif?" Cora and Susan could not answer me.

We had all been nasty, but if there was something more, I was never to know. It could have been something as simple as needing to pick on someone. I only knew that, come Monday, I would be alone, isolated, like someone with TB. I didn't understand what brought this change, but the gang, perhaps, needed someone to pick on. All I knew was that the profanity that the boys shouted made us feel unworthy of ourselves and, ultimately, unworthy as friends. The name-calling had power. It intimidated my girlfriends and overcame their resistance. It was enough to change things. Break up our friendship.

Martha screamed. "Shut up, everybody. Enough already!" She gave me a quick hug. "I'm sorry," she said and ran from the car to Steve. In the circle of the cars, she screamed once more, "Shut up, everybody. Just shut up."

She held her hands over her ears and howled as if in pain. My mother never screamed or moaned in pain, but like Martha, she had moved in the same agitated way when my father said something wounding.

Looking about her, she left Steve's car and ran back to Cora's car. "I forgot my purse," she said. She retrieved it from the front seat of the car, and I watched her slink away, looking beaten. Her head down, she moved toward Steve's truck, her purse clutched in her arms like a baby—the baby she didn't know she was carrying.

> *To know, know, know him,*
> *is to love, love, love him,*
> *and I do, and I do, and I do.*

The song played lazily on someone's radio and drifted into the night air and its sweetness collided with the sound of cars starting up and gunning their engines. Shielding her eyes, Martha looked back toward our car as if for one last look at what she was leaving behind. She seemed to take a deep breath and swallowed hard before turning her back to us and walking away. Steve opened his car door and gave her his hand so she could step into the cab.

"C'mon. I'll take you home," said Cora. I learned something about sadness that day and leaned into the cold air of the open window.

Car doors slammed, engines started, and we all watched Martha go off with Steve beside her in his truck, the headlights cutting a wide swath of light across the wall and into the drizzle.

Part III

By inquiring into the past, one understands the present.
  —Japanese proverb

Small Rebellions

I go home once a year, to Hilo, to visit my parents. I go in August because it seems to rain less—anyway, that's when I've had luck with Hilo's finicky weather. There were times when it wasn't August and I was housebound for two or three days, waiting for the rain to let up. I know my parents mean well, but they, together with the rain pounding on the roof, can be very trying. Tiring under these circumstances. And even if you're already forty-two, you can feel like a child again under the old umbrella of your parents' constant bickering and boredom, which turns into telling you what to do. The part I dislike most is their asking the very questions they had asked while I was growing up: "Where you going?" "What time you coming home?" They can't get away from the old habit of concern.

Arriving in Hilo is usually the same. I'm picked up by my mother at the airport terminal where she avoids paying for parking and parks her car on an isolated, grassy knoll in a no parking anytime, tow-away zone. It is far removed from the arrival area so she is usually late to greet me. She has a long walk but doesn't take that into account.

"Hello," she says, breathless and hurried. She helps me drag my boxy Samsonite and a bashed carton of omiyage to the car.

"Aren't you afraid they're going to tow your car away?" I ask, when we reach her car. I lean against it as she rummages through her handbag for the car keys, which jingle like loose change somewhere at the bottom.

"Oh, I don't know. They never towed it away before," she says, finally retrieving her keys and moving toward the back to open the car's trunk. "I don't think they ever do. Here not like Honolulu."

"You sure about that?"

She shrugs her shoulders. I put my things in, and she slams the trunk down with unmeasured force. Swinging the car door open, she gracefully hops into the driver's seat.

"Why don't you move over this way," I say as I move to get out of the right side of her '80 Plymouth. "I'll drive."

"No, no. I hate to drive, but only short, the way. I can do it."

Nevertheless, I feel disconcerted because my mother doesn't drive as well as she used to. Her driving is elaborate and jerky, her turns overly deliberate. She speeds up and slows down without apparent reason. I notice her reaction is slow, speeding or crawling when she shouldn't. Some burly local in a four-wheel-drive with roll bars yells and flips the bird at us. "Hey, wea you wen get your license, man—Woolworth's?" Mother waves at him in dismissal.

"How come Dad's not here with you to pick me up?"

"Oh, you know him. He went golfing this morning and he didn't come home in time so I came by myself. Every time the same thing."

"He always does whatever he wants to, doesn't he?" I say. "I hope he's helping you around the house."

"Oh, no more than usual. He only get in the way." She leans into a turn. "Men funny kine, when they retire. Some days he only hang around me; some days he don't want me around."

I glance over at my mother behind the wheel. She is seventy years old, sharp as a chopstick, and has all her teeth. We don't have to take her into the mountains of Narayama to die like they did in old Japan when a parent's usefulness seemed gone. Today, however, I do see that she's looking frailer than before. She looks shrunken, her breasts flaccid. A potbelly hidden under an old loose-fitting floral blouse is the most substantial thing about her. She doesn't buy herself anything new anymore.

"Look, tomorrow, why don't we go shopping to buy you some new blouses?"

"No need. When makule like us," she says, "waste time to buy anything new. I don't want to spend the money."

"And why not? Why not enjoy it?"

"I'll give it to you and the kids."

"You don't need to sacrifice for me and the kids, you know—"

"What you said?"

"I said don't make sacrifices for us."

Her shiny black hair curls stiffly under thick hair spray and back-combed control. It's dyed and teased almost to the point of being comic when contrasted to her lined face and droopy white eyebrows. "I should never have started dyeing my hair," I'd heard her lament.

"Why don't you stop dyeing it and let your hair grow out for a change?" I'd suggested.

"Oh, no. Daddy would never hear of it."

"And when are you going to stop Dad from telling you what to do and running everything in your life?" She never answers me when the conversation reaches this point. She knows it exasperates me to think that my father dictates almost everything in her life.

"Oh look, Daddy home already. His car is hea. Must be he hungry. Oh, try look at the roof—the canec sagging in the garage again." My mother downshifts to go up the driveway, and I see my father puttering in the yard, swinging his golf club.

"Hi, Dad. You gotta help me with my bags," I say as I roll down the window and call out to him from the car. My mother brakes hard and suddenly for the final stop. Our heads nod like a pair of kokeshi dolls.

"I tol' you, Mommy. How many times I gotta tell you not to brake the car l'dat," my father says as he walks over. Until his retirement, my father ran Hira's Service Station on Waiānuenue Avenue. He approaches us now, as he had approached so many of his customers.

"Oh shush, useless man," my mother says under her breath. I raise an eyebrow as she slips out of the car fluidly and straightens herself out. My father does not hear her brisk, condescending remark. She never answers back or says anything sharp to him directly.

I get out of the car and walk over to my father to kiss him hello. He sees me coming, so he hurries to get my bags, his body already halfway in the car trunk when I reach him. This time he manages to dodge my peck and I catch him on the ear instead. He doesn't like my displays of affection.

When I go into the house, everything is exactly the way it was the last time I was there. Familiar smells greet me—a fragile but distinct mixture of senkō, lemons, bananas, and Pine-Sol disinfectant. My throat catches in nostalgia. I walk to my old room and change my clothes.

"Mommy, go get me some ice cream," I hear my father say. "I pau eat, already. I went with Sato guys, Cafe 100."

There he goes again, I think to myself, ordering my mother around. "I'll get it for him, Ma," I yell out, going from the bedroom to the kitchen, pulling a T-shirt over my head. "You just relax," I say to her. Nevertheless, she comes bustling into the kitchen to retrieve a spoon and the ice cream from the freezer.

"Why don't you go and sit down. I'll do it. Besides, why don't you let him get it by himself?" I say.

"Oh, no," she insists, shaking her head and furrowing the space between her eyes. "It's much easier for me to just do it. One time, he sulk for two weeks. I didn't do something or other for him—I forget the reason now—but not the big face."

"Here. Go give the ice cream to Daddy," she says. "Save me the trip."

"I *said* I was going to do it."

"So good you hea."

All our lives, my father gave the orders and my mother obeyed. And whether she felt up to it or not, Mother always had the house spotless, the meals cooked on time, and the children tended to. On top of this, until her retirement, she held two jobs. Because she was so efficient, because she was so obedient, my father had the best of lives—"Just like one taishō," we said behind his back.

Although my father has ruled my mother's life ever since they've been married, I do realize that he has been fairly kind and circumspect toward her, when ordering her around. He doesn't rant or rave, and has been only mildly insulting, unlike other Japanese men I have known or heard about throughout the years. My parents seem to have led a fairly good life, so who was I to try and change it?

The next day, my mother and I drive up to the Volcanoes National Park. To my mother's relief, my father decides not to go. He'd rather hang around with his buddies, serious senior citizen "mallies" who congregate at the Kaikoʻo Mall in town. They are all retired and play golf with him between bouts of different ailments and trips to Vegas.

"They like a bunch of teenagers, sit around the mall all day. They talk too much," my mother says of them. "Nothing to brag about in our family. I wonder what Daddy talks about? Don't you wonder?"

I shrug my shoulders.

Free from my father, we spend a carefree but quiet day at the park. We browse and admire the paintings and jewelry at the art center. Later, after circling the steaming bluffs, we go over to the Volcano House, a small quaint hotel overlooking Kīlauea caldera. Not up to walking any of the trails, our sightseeing had been idle and from the car.

We linger over a light buffet lunch of salads, mahimahi sandwiches, and slices of ʻōhelo pie, mesmerized by the majestic view from the dining room. Clinks of glass and silverware hover in the background. It's a clear day and high clouds stipple the blue sky. The air is San Francisco brisk.

"I like this kind of weather," my mother says, "Reminds me of Jim."

"Who's Jim?" I ask.

"Oh, he's a boy I knew once in San Francisco, when I was living with my uncle in Sebastopol. He died recently. Mmm, maybe it was best I didn't get married to him, I might be a widow today."

"And I wouldn't have been born, or my father would have been different at least. Is he the guy holding the large trout in the photo album?"

"How you know? And what's wrong with Daddy? Shame on you. He has his faults, but he's not that bad. He never meant anybody any harm."

"That's true," I concede and leave it at that.

When we arrive home, my father is fast asleep and snoring steadily on his recliner. The television blares and the picture rolls forward in waves. I walk over and turn it off.

"No turn um off," my father says, sleepily. "I still watching."

I walk into the kitchen. "He has it so loud. Is he getting deaf? I swear there's something about people who fall asleep in front of the TV. Dad always seems to know when somebody's going to turn it off—like he's got antennas glued on his head or something."

"That's why I never turn it off," says my mother.

"Mom, I gotta give you credit, the way you put up with everything. He's such a big baby."

"Oh, he's not that bad. Besides, I have my ways."

"What ways? That's news to me."

"Oh, you know—" she says.

"Really? Now, that's something I have to see."

It is close to dinnertime when Mother and I get home from the park. Too lazy to cook, we rustle up what my mother calls a "cowboy" dinner of canned pork and beans, French bread lathered with margarine, and a tossed green salad.

"Dad, dinner's ready. Come and eat," I say when we finish preparing the meal.

"Okay. Pretty soon I come. You folks eat. I wanna see sports firs'," he says from the living room.

My mother and I begin dinner without my father. These days I look at her in a more tender light. I must be getting older, becoming more tolerant and understanding, I think and laugh to myself. I find my mother a remarkable woman.

"Das all we goin' eat?" asks my father as he looks at the meager spread of food before him when he comes to the table. "Whea the rice? You know I like rice. How come you neva cook da rice?"

"I was too tired to cook rice," my mother says. She then ignores him and proceeds to serve my father some salad.

He continues to grumble. "Hey, you know I no like parsley, Mommy. Why you put parsley on my plate when you know I no like dat?" Looking to me, he spins his forefinger around his ear and says, "So lōlō Mari, your motha. She get more crazy when she get old." My father smiles at me and gives me a wink.

I turn to my mother, who doesn't seem indignant but appears absolutely radiant. Her cheeks glow and she bustles to clear our plates to contain her mirth. Once over the sink, she washes the dishes vigorously. I go over to join her.

"And what was that all about?" I ask, puzzled. My mother hums along and smiles at me with a twinkle in her eye but doesn't elaborate. She ignores me. That night she decides to retire early, so I don't get to talk to her in any serious way about what went on.

The next morning, I wake to a house that is floor-creaking quiet. I can hear the wood shift and expand in the day's rising heat. The iron roof pings in the sun. The air is humid and I feel sticky all over and can smell the lemons drying in their gallon jars on the lawn. Mother donates them to the Hilo Hongwanji Buddhist Church bazaar every year, and she sews towels, crochets dolls, and bakes cookies for the annual event. Her hands get swollen from all the lemons she has to lomi.

"I don't know about Mommy. I don't know why she gotta do all this stuff," says my father. He grumbles about her generosity, so she hides the dolls and stacks of towels from him in the closets.

"He wants me to pay attention only to him. Just like one baby nowadays," she says.

I go into the kitchen and fix myself some sliced bananas on rice and fried eggs and smother the whole thing in shoyu. No one can stand seeing me eat bananas in this manner so I'm glad no one is around to make a fuss. I lean on the counter as I eat and inspect all the magnets my mother has collected on the refrigerator door facing me. There are miniature sushi, kamaboko, fruits, animals, and buttons with little sayings on them. This collection is just like my mother, I muse. I like best the button that says: "Life is a series of activities."

It's my mother's painting class day and my father is probably out golfing. My mother's car is in the garage, so I guess that she's left the car for me to take. I change, take my camera, and think of places I want to see. Today, I have no desire to visit old friends. There's a timelessness certain places have that people do not; people change too fast and grow older.

Sometimes it's good to be alone, so I plan a solitary day. There are places in and around Hilo town that I never tire of and must visit: Lili'uokalani Park, Banyan Drive, Five Miles, Rainbow Falls, and 'Akaka Falls. If I don't visit these places, I feel as if I haven't gone back to Hilo at all—like trying to recapture a lost childhood through familiar places which, on the surface at least, seem changeless.

Early that evening, I return from my visiting and walk in on my parents watching television. They look as if they belong in an old-fashioned parlor, surrounded by their accumulations—a mishmash of old pictures, books, my father's softball trophies, my mother's paintings, and her crocheted Miss Piggy dolls—old and timeless, like all those places I need to visit when I go there.

"I'm hungry," I say. "Mom, don't bother to cook tonight. I'm taking you folks out to dinner."

"So good of you. I so tired today. Nice change for me," my mother says appreciatively. "Let's not go any place fancy, though. How's 'bout Chinese food?"

"Sure. And we can go just like this. Don't bother to change," I tell them. "We look decent enough."

We go to Tou-In Restaurant on Kinoʻole Avenue. Next to the restaurant stands a waterfrontlike bar. Stale beer, a blue-gray haze of cigarette smoke around the lights, and strains of piano music combing the air. As we approach the restaurant, a black vehicle with two small children playing inside blocks the entrance. The children look restless and shift their eyes back and forth into the bar and back. They don't bother to look at us.

"Must be they're waiting for someone in the bar," I say. "So sad to see kids like that."

"At least your father never went bar to drink. He drank some, at home, but not too much," my mother says as we skirt the car to enter the restaurant.

"Speaking of drinking, how is old Mrs. Takahashi doing, anyway?"

"She's fine. She looks real good."

"You remember how her husband loved to drink?"

"He wen ma-ke because he drink too much," answers my father as he moves up and joins us in the conversation. We find a booth to sit in. "Nice man and drink okay, but not too good when he come home and bus' up the old lady. You can hear late at night—kotonk, kotonk—him bussing her up. Next day, everybody shame. We gotta look away. Us all neighbas but cannot look her in the eye. Too much pilikia when drink l'dat."

"I don't remember that at all," I say. "How awful it must have been for her."

My mother looks smug. My father has never been brutal with her like some other husbands. Some women we knew endured this treatment all their lives yet could never leave their husbands. "Cannot help—whatever happens, happens," I remember one woman, with yellow-blue bruises on her arm and face, saying to my mother a long time ago. My mother shook her head so sadly that I always remembered it.

I order some abalone soup and my mother decides on beef tomato and sweet-sour shrimp Canton. My father wants kau yuk.

"No good that," my mother says.

"Only lilibit," my father says. It's always about food.

We chatter about inconsequential things while the food is being served. When the soup comes, my mother rises to serve my father.

"No give me too much soup. I'm going to be too full for the rest of the food, bum-bye," my father says, as my mother serves him. "I tol' you not too much," he protests again. "You always give me too much," he says, reverting to a small pout.

I see that special gleam I had seen the night before in my mother's face, joy playing on her face that I see but don't understand. I remain baffled, but my mother is happy, and she chats lightly, pattering along as if down some easy lane. I don't question her mood. I let it go. We are all very genial, and I'm happy that we get along.

Early the next morning, my mother and I catch the auction at the fish broker's and we buy flat, round fish cakes for me to take back to Honolulu. She lectures me about being good to Sam, my husband, and I nod quietly. I do not contradict whatever she says as I would have when younger. She's feistier than she's ever been before, and I like that.

I have only an inkling about what goes on with her, but I think I'm beginning to understand what she meant earlier, about her "ways." I'm only guessing that she has survived all these years by sabotaging my father's wishes, relishing her small rebellions. Perhaps this is the way she has made herself happy and made life more bearable under my father's demands.

I drive home. I pat her thinning hand affectionately from across the car seat.

Late afternoon. It's time for me to leave Hilo. It starts to rain. The sound created on the small, wood frame house makes me feel melancholy. I want to remember the smells, the busy noises, the coziness, until the next time.

My parents drive me to the airport. We settle back in our seats and concentrate in collective effort on getting into the right lane to the right cut-off in a heavy downpour. As we approach the terminal the rain stops.

"Park where I always park," my mother directs. "Daddy, you see the fork in the road? Over there," she signals with her chin, "by the sign."

"Right, the No Parking Anytime sign," I say. "Dad, maybe you better not—"

"Park over there," my mother insists. "Nobody going bother the car." My father pulls over. I'm surprised that, for once, he does what my mother tells him to do.

"You'll be sorry, Mom, for telling Dad that," I mutter to myself.

"Huh? You said someting, Mari?" my father asks. I don't answer him.

We get out of the car. My father and I carry the luggage toward the airport. He mumbles under his breath about the distance. My mother looks guilty. There has to be some repercussion, I suppose, about the parking space she has chosen.

"You don't have to stay with me," I say after checking in. "I'll be boarding soon and it may start to rain again—in fact, I think it's drizzling."

But they stay. And the wait is long. After making a lot of small talk, my father finally says, "Mo' betta go, eh Mommy, what you tink?"

My mother nods her head, but she is slow to rise. I go over to her and give her a hug. She hugs me back. I then walk over to my father and grab him around the waist. "Be good, now," I say and give him a hug. It's hard for him to do this, but I pull him close to me as he shrivels in my embrace.

"I always good," he says, grinning.

I watch them walk away from me.

I wait for my plane and board. From my window, I mentally pick out places I know as I look out toward Puna. The tarmac is slick and the plane starts up. Rain bears down on us heavily and leaves a gray, bleak, and dreary blanket over the town. I worry about my parents, who have a way to walk. I wonder if they have their umbrellas with them.

The plane lifts off. As it rises over the airport and the grassy knoll where my parents had parked, I see my father with his arm looped casually around my mother's shoulder. Both of them are looking up toward my plane. They are waving, slowly, like trees. Suddenly, my mother stops waving and points down the road. I swear she is laughing. My father looks resigned in the way his shoulders sag. In the distance, I see her green Plymouth being trundled off by a tow truck.

The plane rises higher. The gap between the car, my parents, and me widens, and the rain diminishes us all.

Ahukini Landing

We make an error, my wife and I. Instead of taking the left turn, which would have taken us into Līhuʻe Town, we go straight ahead, from Kauaʻi's airport terminal, and end up at a place called Ahukini Landing. Before we know it, we are facing a breakwater, which adjoins the parking area, and a long, broken-down wooden pier with a small house perched at the end. The pier juts into the harbor. Tied to some couplings, two or three small wooden boats with open bailwells swing like lazy hammocks and slap the water in the movement of the tide.

Sometimes I get into trouble with my wife, Merle, by making mistakes like this wrong turn, resulting in a lecture or a Japanese big face, the habuteru as they call it. But much to my relief, I find that she doesn't mind this wrong turn since she has immediately spotted some fishermen on the docks.

A weekend fisherman's daughter, no matter where she goes, she wants to see what the shore-casters have in their buckets. I always thought that this was an unusual pastime, but, as it amuses her, I have indulged my wife's activity wherever it has happened, following her from behind, politely looking into people's buckets for fish, making enthusiastic, husbandly comments.

It doesn't matter what island we're on. It doesn't matter that she doesn't know these people. If Merle sees people fishing, she just has to know what they're catching. It's a habit, a long line of Japanese fishermen strong in her blood. The salt of it.

So it doesn't matter, either, that the pier at the landing is falling apart and dangerous, the planks washed away or broken. With some of the planks gone, the boardwalk looks like a piano with missing keys. Here and there rotten, jagged pilings stick out of the water. I follow her—rather gingerly, I might add, because I'm much heavier and more awkward—while Merle skips across the pier and works her way skillfully over the missing boards. I'm more deliberate. I'm thinking to myself that I'd rather be on land than in the water. By the time I catch up to her, she is already peering into the first bucket and talking to a fisherman, his hands crusty with old bait. He is peeling off the bait like dry skin as he speaks to her.

"Look," Merle turns to say to me. "They have a couple of halalū in here." She points at the fish for my benefit. After all this time, I still can't tell the different varieties, even if she has explained it to me before. "The halalū must be running. Nice sized ones, too." She's pleased that the fish are biting.

All I see are two not very large, overturned-on-their-bellies, big-eyed silver fish in the bucket of water. "Look here, let me explain again," she says, seeing that I don't get it. "Shad? I think that's what they call it in English—the haole name for this fish. I'm not sure . . . but anyway, they're adolescents of the akule—the grown-up versions of the halalū that you see in this bucket. You can catch akule only at night. If you catch them during the day, they're halalū," she explains.

I scratch my head. "Okay, I think I get it," I say to reassure her, but I'm still confused as to why one type ran at night, and the other during the day, especially if they were the same fish. I wonder about when the fish decide on making these reversals.

"Aaron. They're just like the 'oama and weke. Remember the small fish, in schools . . . the old ladies with the big hats and bamboo poles . . . at Ala Moana beach, waist-deep . . . the time you tangled up their lines?" she asks, a bit exasperated at this point, knowing I'm still puzzled. "The ones, Aaron, we use for bait—to catch pāpio. You know which ones." There's almost a plea in her voice.

"Oh yeah, I think I know what you're talking about," I say, a victim of my own disinterest. But before I can sort the differences in my mind—halalū or akule, 'oama or weke—a cowbell rings insistantly from the head of the pier.

At the sound of the bell, Merle dashes off to where the sound is coming from. A gray graphite rod, striped with red and yellow thread to hold the eyes of the line guides, is dipping actively. Three elderly men pole fishing at the end of the pier also rush toward the lurching rod. Two of them are limping, having risen too suddenly for their old legs. "Yoisho!" one of them exclaims.

Something big.

When the fish strikes, I have no idea who these men are. All I want to do is to get out of the way so I don't knock anyone down or get called a "dumb haole."

Later, I learn it's Masamune "Masa" Ishikawa's second strike for the day. Two of his friends, Jackson "Jalopy" Igawa, and Suburo "Sub" Endo, are shaking their heads in disbelief.

"God damn lucky sonovabitch. I try all morning, fo' nothin', and who get the strikes?" says the man called Sub, a round-faced fellow, who also sounds the most intense.

By the time we get close enough to the commotion, Masa has his pole out of its holder and is playing with the fish to work it in toward the pier. Merle, wanting to be quiet and unobtrusive as the man brings in his catch, has her mouth open in order to catch her breath so as not to make a sound after having made her way over quickly.

"What—?" I ask as I come up to her side.

"Shush," Merle says, putting a finger to her lips to stop me from saying anything at the moment—a matter of courtesy to the fishermen. Sacred fishing moment, the hush dedicated to the struggle.

Everyone stands around Masa to watch him horse in his fish. "This bugger feels like a mullet. Very heavy," he says, negotiating the drag. As the fish rises, it suddenly cuts across the water with more vigor than ever. Flashes of silver in green water.

"Eh, what you think, Jalopy?" asks Sub. "Look mo' like one halalū, yeah?"

Like two little boys the men are leaning over the pier, looking into the water, straining to see what Masa has caught. The guessing evolves into a game, the men relying on years of fishing experience. For a moment, each one's guess is as good as the other's.

"Saa," says Masa, then inhales between his teeth as if he is sipping the cool ocean breeze. He appears a bit winded from working his Daiwa reel and arching his body back and forth. "I don't know. Can't be a halalū because it looks too big. Hard to say what it feels like. To me, it feels like a mullet. Has a lot of pull for the bottom. You know how a mullet drags."

"Nah, no can be one mullet. Not season, this time of yea. Besides, yo' bait not limu," says the man called Jalopy, mopping the top of his bald head, sweeping his hand across it as if he still had hair to run his fingers through, and squaring his cap on his head as he tries to make a better guess. When he straightens up after peering into the water, I see that he is rather lanky and tall but crooked in his legs. "Mullet—they no fight l'dat. They mo' sluggish."

"How you know, Jalopy? When you wen eva catch one mullet? Long time eh, since you even catch one fish? So what you talking?" taunts Sub.

"No get smart, Sub. You just as bad as me. Whitewash, every time."

The two men watch Masa and the water, intently. Sub, who is short and the stubbiest looking of the bunch, has his rough, calloused hands on his knees as he peers into the greenish water.

"One pāpio, you," Sub yells out, slapping his thigh like a sumo wrestler and scolding Masa. "Dat one pāpio!" There's envy in Sub's voice, as he retrieves a small gaff and net from an old khaki bag and goes down a short ladder on the side of the pier to wait for Masa to bring the fish around.

"This fish," Masa says, as if he can already taste it, "will make a nice plate of white-meat sashimi. My wife can prepare it for us. The head and tail sections, she'll fry. Makes good pūpū to drink with beer."

Merle claps when Masa slips off the gaff and takes the fish out from the net. With two fingers inserted in the gill flaps for all to see, as if he and the fish were being photographed, he holds it up. "Look close to being one ulua, you," Sub whines at Masa, irritated at his friend. "You doan even know you wen catch one pāpio," he says, amazed.

As I watch and listen to the men, I notice that Sub is talking about another one of those fish distinctions: one between a pāpio and ulua. The difference between the two stages of this fish is quite puzzling to me. I could never remember how many pounds the pāpio had to be before it became an ulua. Five? Ten? I remember Merle telling me once. Sub then opens the cover to a blue Igloo cooler so Masa can toss in the flapping, silver fish.

Jalopy now turns his attention to us. Addressing Merle first, which I think he does because she is Japanese and I am haole, Jalopy jerks his thumb and cocks his head toward Masa and says, "This bugga, all his life he lucky. By right, even when he supposed to ma-ke, he doan ma-ke. Yeah, Masa?" The friends laugh, amused at themselves and their inside joke. They beam at us, their newfound audience. They know they have kindled our interest in them.

The men tease each other a while longer for our benefit. Their repertoire is filled with crude jokes about two-legged "land kūmū" and other namecalling. Masa ribs his friends, "So far you buggers are all mullet."

Not long into the conversation, Sub says he wants to change his fishing spot and casts his line in another direction. "Maybe dis time, they goin' bite," he says and winks at Merle and me. "Then you goin' see how 'mullet' us guys. No listen to Masa. Sometimes we catch mo' fish den him. He pretty lucky but not *that* lucky that he wipe us out all da time."

"Sub, you got to understand, hates to lose," Masa says to us. "Don't go by his looks, look in his eyes. You want to *shine* don't you, Sub? You want to impress these kids, right?" A having-caught-a-fish-contented Masa scratches his side.

"Nah, I just like catch one fish. You wait, I goin' show all you guys I can catch someting," says Sub.

While waiting for the fish to bite, Merle talks like a real pro to the men about fishing—spots on Kaua'i and the other islands, the kinds of bait, the different fish to catch and what was running where and when. "What kind of palu are you guys using today?" I hear her ask with an ease I can never have.

I stand on the side and wait, relaxed, the wind blowing pleasantly as Merle continues to talk with the men. I am amazed at how much she knows about the sport even if she has never fished since I've known her. I don't know why she doesn't go fishing. I had told her a long time ago that I was not against her fishing, if she found companions to go along with.

While I am thinking about encouraging Merle to take up fishing again, Sub says, "Eh, why you guys no come fish with us tomorrow?"

"I don't fish," I say.

"Your wife can come," he says.

"I can? But I need to buy a small reel and pole," she says to me, excited at the prospect.

"Ask them where you can buy your pole," I encourage.

Merle goes over to ask the men. I notice that Masa is off to the side and listening to the conversation that Merle is having with Jalopy and Sub, but not really participating in the small talk, so I move over toward him and direct a comment or two his way. Rather casually, so as not to make it seem as if I am a "know-it-all kine haole," I ask, "This used to be a big harbor before, right?" My question makes Masa look at me and raise one gray eyebrow like a slow slug. A quizzical look.

He takes a long, deep breath. He leans back on the guardrail, rests his dried and wrinkled elbows on the top of the railing, and expands his already wide, muscular chest. A nostalgic look sweeps over his face. "Yup. This used to be a pretty big harbor all right—at least that's the way it looked to us. This is where we all left from—me, Jalopy, Sub—some of the other guys from this area."

What it is that makes him nod to his friends and soon call out a "hey you guys, come here" statement, drawing their attention to show us that he wants to get to know us better and introduce ourselves to them, I have yet to decipher and understand. But once the introductions make their way around, everyone shaking hands and nodding to each other, the polite air is loosened. Jalopy says, "Eh, you like one?" and gives me a beer. A good sign, I've been told, about people offering you beer. That means these Japanese locals trust you, somewhat, I think to myself.

Everyone turns toward Masa to hear what he has to say. "This was a busy place, once upon a time. When we volunteered to fight for the army, we didn't know much about what was going on, but we were fired up because of Japanese pride. Hell, we were so young. The war was going to get us out of this place. So we enlisted. We all went up together. You see, over on this side?" Masa points to an area near the pier.

"I see it," I say and turn my body toward where he is pointing.

"The ships were tied to the docks there—well, I shouldn't say ships. They were more like cattle barges. That's where we boarded."

"Had all kine hula dancers. Our families bring us leis. My madda, she cry up," Sub says.

"Yeh, my family dem too," Jalopy says.

"First, we sailed to Honolulu. Then we went to San Francisco and took the train cross-country. How monotonous it was, going to Mississippi," says Masa.

"That must have been Camp Shelby," I say.

"Camp Shelby? How come you, one haole boy, know about that?" asks Masa, surprised. "Hey check this kid out, you guys," he says. "Not everybody knows about Camp Shelby, you know." The men have surprised looks on their faces.

I feel my own face grow red. "I read a lot about the war because I was a Japanese history major at UH and I was curious about the 442nd and the 100th Battalion. Well, you know, being that I grew up in the islands, I knew several men who fought in the war. My father's friends."

"Oh so, you're a local haole. I guess that explains it," says Masa.

"I was born and raised here."

I try to be modest and self-effacing. I notice that Masa begins to see me differently. There's a big difference between being local haole and mainland haole, which gives me a seal of the men's approval, like there's a big difference, I reckon, between small fishes and big fishes, pāpio and ulua, halalū and akule.

"So what are you and your missus doing on Kaua'i?" Masa wants to know.

"We're both teachers in Honolulu. We had a few days off from school so we came to Kaua'i," I say.

Masa is happy to find that we are a regular local couple—schoolteachers and all—and that we find Kaua'i a nice place to vacation. When he learns that my family had come originally from Kaua'i, long before even the Japanese were in the islands, he says, "No wonder you know a lot about us—more than most people," he says appreciatively. I see that he is somewhat convinced that I am a different sort of haole, a regular local, perhaps. But I see a wariness, a skepticism that makes him hold back. I'm guess I'm still different, and as Merle often says, "gaijin," to point it out.

My face colors for them. I hope they don't see the sudden flush as I am a bit embarrassed for the men by the way they accept me. But I'm glad to know that I'm more or less taken in by them, as a friend, and that I don't come across like a know-it-all haole, so far. And I know that I'm on target with these men because Merle is relaxed, not giving me that "don't-be-so-haole-in-front-of-the-Japanese" look that she sometimes gives me.

Masa and I talk more about the war. While Sub seems interested in the war stories, he is also intent on catching a fish while we are there—to show up Masa and to show off to us, too. And Jalopy, as if he'd heard the stories many times before, is happy to listen in, commenting only when Masa misses a point, or a name, in recounting the wartime stories they had probably heard over and over in their infantry reunions or family get-togethers. Nothing could have been new, in rehashing the old times.

I learn that the men were originally with the 100th Battalion and that they had seen action in Italy and France. "All ova," according to Jalopy's interruption.

"We started in the 100th Battalion. Later, they combined us with all the other guys and formed the 442nd," says Masa. We fought hard. "'Bus ass' us guys as they used to say." The other two men solemnly agree.

"Were you guys," I ask, "under General Almond when the 442 was part of the 92nd Division, the one with the popolo regiment?"

"Ah ha, you really one local haole, eh?" Sub and Jalopy declare—almost together. They exchange an "eh, this guy all-right" look. With this, the men are doubly impressed because they know that not many people remember these details about the war, especially who General Almond was and his role with the Japanese American troops.

Jalopy whistles. "How you know dat? Nowadays, nobody remembers dat stuff. Not even my kids. Too good, you," he compliments. The men look at me with surprise and I am even more embarrassed, my face getting redder. I see the approval in the men's eyes and feel a bit more comfortable talking to them.

"Did you folks leave from New York?" I ask.

"Yeah, we went to New York from there and caught the ships. We were packed like sardines. The boat ride was scary because there were rumors flying around about German submarines and U-boats. Boy, I was a poor sailor. Sick all the way across. The best time for me was when the war ended and we gave cigarettes and candies to everybody. Talk about appreciation. The people still invite us back," Masa rambles.

"Was the fall of '43, yeah?" Jalopy rubs his head and mumbles. "Cassino, I tink, was the big fight."

"Den the 100th wen hitch up with the 442nd Regiment, remember? Or wuz afta. Boy I forget, awready. J'like dey neva know wat fo' do with us. They send us any kine place," says Sub.

"They neva know what fo' do with guys like *you*," Jalopy jokes. "Anyway, after I come back home from the war, I wen open my own business. My girl-fren, she wait for me so we got married, had a couple-a kids, send them school."

"Me, too," says Sub. "Same ting."

"And you, Masa?" I ask. "What did you do?"

"Me? I came back home, then went to UCLA on the GI Bill. That saved my life. I came back here and opened an accounting firm. Now, my boy is a comptroller for the company."

"Masa was always lucky. He get one good head," says Sub.

"You didn't do so badly for yourself Sub," Masa says. "Everyone uses your plumbing company."

All the more so, Sub wants to catch a fish for us. "Next pāpio for you guys," he says to Merle and me. In the background, as I am talking to Masa and Jalopy, Sub is trying his best to hook a fish. He casts and retrieves his line. He does this several times, to look for a good spot. He finally settles on what he feels is a likely area.

Jalopy continues. "We almost the first ones out in Italy—all us Japanese, I mean. It's a wonder we went through all dat and we still living. Somehow us guys damn lucky. As I was saying befo', you take Masa—this guy suppose to ma-ke uku billion times. The bugga, when young, he take plenny chances, but he still live. I don't know why, this ugly bugga. He just lucky, I guess."

"When you *stay* lucky and you live, okay, but you sure see funny kine stuff, too," says Sub reflectively, watching the tip of his pole that is shaking. While he talks, he is looking up and taking up the slack on his line by slowly winding his reel. "Yeah, Masa? You no tink so too, Jalopy?"

"Of course, man, we sure wen see all kine stuff. Sometimes, cannot forget," Jalopy says.

"Yup. I think it was in France," Masa says. "I had the worst time there. I was wounded by a Screaming Meemie that exploded nearby my position."

"You got it all wrong, Masa," Jalopy says. "Wuz one Bouncing Betty, not one Screaming Meemie that wen get you. I saw the whatchamacallit bouncin' toward us. I wen duck, grab my head. Boy, I wen dig in fast. Masa was ahead of me. He always in the front line, eh, and I wen see him fly back and no could do nothing. Yeah, Masa was lucky he not hurt some mo'. At least he neva lose his family jewels," Jalopy says. Masa's face reddens.

"Yeah," Masa says, nodding his head. "I was hit by shrapnel in my arm, my leg, and on my side." He lifts up his baggy khaki pants to show me the wound on his leg. The scar is rough and ugly with a purple discoloration running through it like a bruise.

"I wanted to go home that time, so badly. I wanted to cry, but we buddha-heads, so we have to hold back. Not even a whimper. We needed to be tough," Masa recalls. "I wanted them to ship me back to the States. But they didn't give me any chance. Next thing you know, as soon as I was well, I was back in the front. When I went back out, that's the time, I felt everything was poho. I was so sick of it. Mud everywhere. The other guys were all suffering, too, the Hawai'i boys not used to the cold. Everybody had trench foot—it was so stink—I got sick of everything. That time, I really wanted to go AWOL. I almost did too. I would have run off with any girl in the area."

As Masa makes this confession, the cowbell rings on Sub's pole. It has a tentative ring to it. Although the men go on talking, all eyes move up Sub's pole. Something plays with his 'ōpelu bait.

"After Italy," Masa goes on to say, all eyes riveted to the tip of Sub's pole, "we went to France and were involved in helping to save the Texas Lost Battalion." He describes to me how they all were blasted by the Germans but had pushed on. "I just can't tell you how it was," he tells me, "especially when, left and right, all your buddies die."

He looks as if the pain of loss is just as fresh in his mind as it was back then. He appears to be contemplating the luck of the draw. I can only nod my head. I don't know what to say.

"But it was before that . . . I think it was in France. You know something funny? After all these years the goddamn thing *still* bothers me. A small thing when you consider the war, but maybe it was because the boy was so young. Maybe it was the way his face looked when he died that I can't forget it. I don't know. Anyway, it was while we were—it must have been on a forest sweep—in a small wooded area. Wow, talk about unlucky."

"It was early in the morning. I came across this young German soldier, a kid, sitting on the john—the door wide open, just like one of the old plantation outhouses—like the ones we had here. The kid was reading something and laughing to himself. It looked like he was reading the comics. Anyway, I was point man and crouched down behind a log. The other guys—Jalopy, Sub, some guys from the other company—they were all in the back of me. The kid had no idea we were watching him. I figure, I let the poor bugger at least finish taking a crap before I kill him, right? But before I know it, from behind me, I heard this crack. The bullet zings past me and the poor kid huli. Just like that."

Masa pauses, overturns his hand to show the boy toppling over, and pats his shirt pocket as if looking for a cigarette—the gesture of a longtime smoker. "Every once in a while, I think about that poor, unlucky son-of-a-gun. Incredible. So young and dead. You know, the funny thing is, after all these years, I still don't know who killed him."

Sub has a surprised look on his face. "Whatcha mean you never know who wen kill the kid? You mean to say, you neva know all dis time?"

"Yes, I don't," answers Masa.

"Sure you know. Everybody know. Was me wen kill the kid."

"I didn't know that!"

"I no believe you," Sub says and shakes his head. "Here I thought you knew all along. Not that we wen keep sco-wa, if you know what I mean. How come you neva say nothing before, when we shoot the bull l'dat, reunion time?"

"It never occurred to me," says Masa. "It was sort of private for me. I felt sorry for the damn kid."

"Me, I figga, if we don't kill um, he going turn around and kill us. So, I wen kill um," Sub says as he shakes his head.

I want to ask Masa how he missed knowing this and how come they had never discussed it before, but before I can say anything, Sub yells out. "Look!" He's pointing to the tip of the pole. He grins and says, "Someting playing with my bait, again. Bite, you ugly bastard!"

"I should have guessed it was you, Sub. I should have known. It's just that—oh, never mind. I just didn't think it was you, that's all. I guess it just never occurred to me. You know how these things happen. Besides, there were so many other guys in the woods. The place was crawling with soldiers. It could have been any one of them. I actually thought it was Mits from Fox Company. And to think I let it bother me all these years. I let it hang over my head." Turning to Merle and me he says, "Imagine, finding this out, only now—after almost fifty years. Unbelievable!" Masa shakes his head. "Even back then, Sub, you just didn't want to lose. I should have known."

"Yup. Us or them. Fish or whitewash; pāpio or ulua; halalū or akule. You know what I mean?"

"You son-of-a-gun," says Masa. "I can't imagine how this got lost to me. Eh Jalopy, what about you? You knew this?"

"Yeah, I knew, but . . . was no big thing."

"Surely, you must have known something—" I start to say.

Masa shifts his eyes to me with sudden rock eyes. They are cold. I stop talking. His eyebrows take on a Jōmon hood that tell me I should hold my tongue. He then slowly moves his head to look out at the sea.

With this bit of exchange, our little group is drawn into silence. In the silence it is as if I am pulled away from their intimacy and put back to my place once more as a mere acquaintance. What has been disclosed was not supposed to have been privileged for my ears. I had walked into something private and the men felt uncomfortable with me there. I was, after all, still an outsider. It seems as though some things are better left as myths, and if the myths were to be shattered, not shared with others.

I am reflective about what I have learned about fate and luck, the reversals in fish, in life, how the man called Sub could be cold and ruthless. Most of all what brings people together or tears them apart. I, too, stare out into the ocean.

"About tomorrow," Masa says to Sub abruptly. "I don't think I can be here to fish. I forgot. I have an appointment." Sub, catching the drift, says he can't make it, either.

"Well, if you guys not going be hea, I not coming, too, den," says Jalopy. He turns to Merle. "Sorry. Maybe, nex' time we can go fish."

"Sure," Merle replies as she glares at me.

After a while, I tell the men how much I had enjoyed talking to them, "But it's really time for me and Merle to head back, hit the right road," I say. They look relieved.

"Come back again," Masa says with a hollow ring. We all shake hands, knowing we would never see each other again.

Merle and I pull out of the pier area. In my rearview mirror I see Sub hastily reeling up his line. He has his back turned to me. I wonder if he's caught a fish. Merle looks over at me. "You spoiled my chances, you know."

"I know. I'm sorry about that."

"Tell me why. Tell me why you have to be so—" she asks, her voice low and halalū.

Web

Mary Kato approached the long, low building nestled below the Koʻolau mountain range. She rang the buzzer at the entrance of the state mental hospital. A small window in the door slid open and the lips of a mouth appeared. They moved mechanically. A voice asked, "Yes? Who do you want to see?"

"My son, Tommy Kato."

Mary waited a while before the main door, creaking lightly on its hinges, swung open. When she stepped into the cool hallway, a woman clanged the door shut. "Sign in," the woman said and pointed to a huge open log on a low metal table. Mary looked around. Everything was muted pink in color.

Soon a wide-shouldered male orderly appeared. He told Mary to wait, then made a call somewhere in the building. He, too, disappeared. Shortly after, another nurse came into the waiting area. She was hefty and had a no-nonsense attitude. "Follow me," she said and led the way to a separate lockup. Keys jangled on the woman's thigh as she fiddled first with one key, then another, in order to open one more door in a series of ironclad doors.

"He's in there," she said as she pointed with her chin down a semi-lit corridor.

"Aren't you coming with me?" Mary asked, anxious at the thought of having to go in by herself. She didn't know what to expect.

"Don't worry, honey," the woman said in a high voice. "There's another orderly inside. And the doctor's there, too. Besides, the patients are not violent. They're on some pretty heavy stuff."

Tommy was Mary's only child. Strangely, she did not feel connected to him in the same way mothers were supposed to feel toward their children. She felt detached from him as if she had never *reached* him in all her life. When she was a young girl, she remembered using the outhouse of her grandmother's house in Pāpaʻikou, where the brown widow spiders swayed on their webs, carrying their white sacks of spider eggs under their bellies. She felt as close to her son these days as the spider did for its children in the sack, she thought guiltily. Love was not the web that necessarily tied them together. Motherhood was no automatic guarantee that she would feel close to the child she had nurtured.

Nobody told her these things when she was growing up.

Today was the first time Mary was going to see Tommy at the hospital. Although she had not smoked for many years, she wished she had a cigarette to calm the nervousness in her stomach. She took a deep breath and thought of how thrilled she had been when she first learned to French inhale in the backseat of Tommy's father's car. In her ex-husband's metallic-red '56 Chevy, the smoke hovered over her top lip and moved like jet streams up into her nostrils. Taking up smoking and getting pregnant with Tommy was part of her own delinquency years ago. She was a Japanese good girl trying to be bad. It was so minor, the smoking and occasional drinking, but a big thing back then.

Mary guessed that she first smoked because it wasn't what a proper Japanese girl should be doing. Her mother constantly told her when growing up that good girls didn't smoke.

"Only loose kine women smoke in public," she said. Loose women also pierced their ears and wore anklets, like Mary. Her mother was not smart enough to figure out that by harping on Mary about what was not proper, her greatest fears would become a reality. Mary wore pierced earrings and anklets only because her mother didn't like her wearing them. "You look like Aladdin," her mother said after Mary pierced her ears, and in sarcasm added, "You might as well make your head bolohead, too!"

Mary remembered her mother having to fan herself and sit down when Mary took out a cigarette and first smoked in front of her. Her mother was further astonished when she told Mary's father about the smoking and he said, "Nemmine. She old enough. Whatchu going do?"

"Right on," Mary had said, but saw a hint of betrayal creep over her mother's face because of her father's response.

Earlier that morning, before going to the hospital, Mary had slipped a T-shirt over her head; pulled on some Levi's; combed her damp, bulky hair that threatened to frizz—especially the wild, white hair that had started to grow in. She fluffed her hair with her hands, waxed on some lipstick, and smacked her lips on a tissue before crumpling it and throwing it into the wastebasket.

She felt a pang of guilt at her wastefulness, remembering the lengths her mother went through to save money in order to buy Mary what all the other Japanese girls had. To keep up. Gold bracelets, friendship rings, Saint Christopher medallions, black Chinese medicinal dried lemons at Kawamoto Store, dried abalone, kokeshi dolls, woven basket handbags, artificial flowers for her hair, ivory plumeria earrings. Having something different all the time and bringing it to school was one way to be popular.

Her mother never threw away Kleenex tissues after just one use. Instead, she draped the tissue she was going to reuse, the one with several lip imprints already on it, over the turquoise green lid of Ponds cold cream and a green bottle of witch hazel. As a child, wanting to, but forbidden to play with her mother's lipsticks, Mary would take the Kleenex tissue, fold it over where her mother had folded it, and place her lips on the colored imprint. She imitated the way her mother rolled, puckered, and smacked on the tissue—the round O of her mother's lips radiating like the thin lines of a spider web.

"Thank you," Mary said as she squeaked by the orderly who showed her the way in. She felt ashamed that she had assumed that all patients there would be crazy looking. She couldn't bear to look at their faces.

Mary walked down the corridor. Several women appeared from a room off to one side and approached her. One came up to her and fingered the sleeve of her blouse. Mary stepped back slightly and tried not to shudder or show any disgust, after which the group of women looked at each other and roared in laughter. Mary wondered what could have been so funny about her blouse. But she knew that they were making fun of her because they sensed her discomfort. It was like walking nude, with the fine line between sanity and being crazy becoming fuzzy in her own mind.

Mary saw shadows of people in the other rooms she passed. She knew they were watching every move she made. She then wondered if she would recognize Tommy, wondered if his mental condition had changed his looks in any way, or if the changes were so subtle that only a mother could notice. She was afraid she wouldn't be able to tell.

The corridor opened into a wide, well-lit courtyardlike room. A fountain in the center burped weakly, surrounded by struggling monsterra and anthurium plants. Mary could see men and women milling about. She stood on the side. But the people in the room weren't merely milling around as she first thought. They were going around the fountain in a loose circle, following each other like elephants in a circus ring. Nose to tail.

"Hail Mary full of grace. Blessed is thy womb, Jesus—" one woman with her head dipped to one side and a paintbrush of hair on top, prayed loudly. She didn't finish the prayer. Other women chorused, "Amen."

Mary looked around for Tommy in the circle and saw him coming toward her as the circle rotated her way. He had his head down. He was talking to himself. She could hear his voice among the others. Coming closer to her, she heard him much clearer. He sounded as if he were barking, but the sounds were not *real* barks. Mary was relieved. They only sounded like barks in the staccato of whatever he was saying. As he drew closer, Mary heard him say, "I'm no fag, you think I'm a fag? I not a fag. Yeah, you—you think I'm a fag? I not a fag. Shit all of you, if you think I'm a fag."

Mary watched intently as Tommy repeated this litany. He pounded one fist into the other as he said each word. It was strange watching him. She called the orderly. She wanted to know why he was saying such things.

"Don't worry," the orderly said. "We are adjusting his medications and what he's going through is quite common."

"Oh, I didn't know. It's hard—"

Mary moved away from the corridor entrance into the room and waited until Tommy made another circuit. He was standing almost directly in front of her before she called out to him.

"Hi," Mary greeted in a feeble voice, interrupting his chanting. Tommy looked up. Hair slid over his face, and his eyes looked dull. He nodded his head at her in recognition and stepped out of the ring. He walked the few steps over to where she stood.

"Howzit," he said, his tongue heavy because of the medication.

"Hi," Mary said, not knowing what else to say.

"Eh, you gotta get me outta here," he said and reached out for her arm in jerks.

He stared at her, then walked back to the circling ring of people and stepped in as if more comfortable there. He motioned Mary to fall in with him and the group. Mary complied. She and Tommy walked together in the circle. Though they hardly spoke, Mary sensed a mounting anger in Tommy the longer they walked.

"You see this?" he finally said. He lifted up his green hospital gown. "They give this shit to people they think going run away. This stuff glows in the night so they can spot you. Trippy, eh?" He looked at Mary straight on. "You think I'm a fag, too?"

"Of course not! There never was any question," Mary said, showing her best indignation. "You're not a fag."

"You see? You see, everybody? My mother said I not a fag." He shouted what he said, but no one looked up.

The bright green surgical-style shirt had an iridescent glow to it. Mary didn't know if she was imagining the color since it wasn't even dark. Suddenly feeling overwhelmed and hemmed in as if in a straightjacket, Mary wanted to get out of the ring.

"Look, I'm tired of walking," she said to Tommy. "Mind if we sit down?"

"No, I don't mind," he said, shrugging his shoulders. "We can sit down over there," he pointed. When they approached a bench, they moved out of the circle to sit down.

"How are you—really?"

Tommy made no attempt to answer her. He simply put his head down. Here, there were no courtesies, no rules. After a long while, he lifted his head and said, "You stupid or what? How do you think I'd be? You think this funny?"

"Of course I don't," Mary said, defensively.

"Why you looking at me like that, then? You think I crazy?"

Mary didn't know what to say. She felt inadequate and apologetic and the words she wanted to use all seemed fake, and they crumbled like a bitter pill in her mouth. She could only sit there and say nothing and feel stupid. She sat on the bench, rooted there by fear, not understanding anything.

After what seemed like an unbearably long time, Mary made a move to leave. Tommy looked at her angrily. His eyes accusing, piercing. He looked at her as if she were abandoning him.

"You were always running away, leaving me," he said.

"That's not true. You have no right—"

"Right? You're the crazy one. They should put you in here. You never could face up to anything. You the one, always running away. You never stood up for me."

"You have no right—to judge," Mary started to say, wanting to defend herself, but she realized that it was useless to argue with him. Yet Mary could not erase the niggling feeling that this may have been true. She had wanted to be away from him. She was *there*, but never there; he had sensed it growing up. She had occasionally disappointed him, she had to admit, after having made promises to do something special with him. But what parent didn't?

"It's true. You cannot tell me it's *not* true, you were always pushing me away."

"Okay, maybe you're right, so calm down. And I'm sorry," Mary said to placate him.

Tommy only became more agitated. He suddenly looked large. She was afraid he was going to explode, get violent. A strange look rode the corners of his eyes. His voice began to get louder and he started pounding his fist into his palm. An orderly stood by watching, but did nothing to interfere.

Mary soon motioned to the orderly that she wanted to leave and the man nodded. She picked up her purse and jacket and stood up. It was suddenly very cold in the lockup, a chill making Mary grab her elbows and cradle herself.

"Look, Tommy, I'll be back to see you again, okay?"

"Yeah, yeah, you always say that." It hurt Mary to hear Tommy say the things he did. Self-doubt about being a good mother once more crept into her heart.

She started down the corridor, slowly at first, then briskly. She had to get out of there. She no longer wanted to hear what Tommy had to say. "Quick! Quick!" she said to herself and couldn't move fast enough away from these rooms of guilt. But Mary heard Tommy in a drug-shuffling walk behind her.

"Ma, wait!" By this time Mary was almost on the run. She needed to get out. "Take me home," Tommy said. "Please Ma, I wanna go home."

He caught up with her. He tried to hold onto her arm. His hand felt cloying, sticky, like a cobweb. He was like a spider weaving its web around her and Mary had to peel off his hand to push him away. By that time an orderly had come from behind Tommy and grabbed hold of him. Restrained him.

"I'll come back later, okay?" Mary said, as soothingly as she could. Soon, other staff members came by. One held a syringe and gave Tommy a shot in his arm. Tommy let out a curdling yell.

"You FUCKAAAS!"

With Tommy sufficiently subdued, his hands swept behind his back, he was led writhing into a nearby room with its high ceilings and high barred windows.

Mary flew out of the old building. She had never experienced anything like that in her life. She clenched her stomach and held one hand to her mouth and made a dash for the car. The sound was muffled, but she could hear Tommy screaming.

What made her do it, she didn't know, but she turned around to look back at the building. And she saw him. He had scaled the bars of the window in the room and had attached himself like a spider, to look down at her. His mouth was wide open in a scream. She was horrified by the howl.

Mary thought she, too, was going crazy. She saw multiple figures in his silhouette—images of his father, her parents, her grandparents—swaying in his form clasped on the window. Mary could not bear to look at him.

She drove off, stabbing her foot on the gas pedal, but not before she heard him wail: "Ma, don't leave me!"

On her way home from the hospital, Mary decided to stop over at her parents' house for a minute. Her mother had called the day before, wanting her to pick up some pickled vegetables made of Chinese mustard and head cabbages. Her mother prided herself in not making the vegetables too salty—all of the family members having to fight high blood pressure these days.

Mary also knew she had to say something about Tommy. He was her parents' only grandson. But what could she possibly say about his condition without her mother feeling ashamed about it, getting weepy, and feeling sorry for the family? Between her father's obstinacy and her mother's wounded bird behavior, it seemed that they were never able to discuss or resolve their problems.

Mary felt she better say something to her parents, however. She did not want them finding out about Tommy some other way. In all probability, had she not said anything, they never would have known, and while she was sorely tempted not to say anything, she knew silence was impossible. She was trying to get away from hiding things from the family. She no longer wanted to spare their feelings. She was tired of it.

After Mary took off her shoes, she lined them up on the porch as neatly as the rest of the shoes there. She pushed in the front screen door and adjusted her eyes to the darkness of her parents' small living room. A mosquito coil burned in one corner. She made out her father's Naugahyde recliner and the old sofa, then walked down a short hallway toward a well-lit, cheerful kitchen. Her mother's room. Her mother stood dicing an onion on the cutting board.

"Hi," Mary said, looking around. She then seated herself on a plastic red-patterned chair, part of a Formica kitchen table set. She picked up a magazine from a rack near the counter and started turning the pages of *Elle*. She had to look at the cover again, surprised that it would be in the kitchen of her parents' home. The girls in the magazine looked plastic, too beautiful for real life and the truth in it.

"Who gave you this?" asked Mary.

"The magazine? Why I ordered it from—oh, you know. The one you can win plenty money."

"Oh, Mom." Mary continued to turn the pages as her mother talked. Mary interrupted the chatter. "Where's Dad?"

"Who, Daddy?"

"Who else?"

"I think he went out with the Konishi old man. They like to shoot the breeze—the two of them, so they went for coffee. King's Bakery, I think. Good for them get some exercise."

"So, what about you? Why don't you go out with some girlfriend and exercise, too? You stay at home all day just to cook for Daddy—to make him something he wants to eat. Boy!"

Mary wished she could take back what she had just said. It must have been hurtful, as her mother did not have any close friends. Her mother had only her family, which was narrowing; all of her sisters and brothers were either dying or too busy with their own families.

"So, how come you not at work today? They don't need you, or what? Try not miss work. Japanese get ahead because, before time, they don't miss work. They sick, but they still go work."

"Then they were crazy. Don't worry, I'm not going to lose my job. There are enough people where I work. Besides, when you work for the state, the work just keeps on coming. There's no end to it."

"Lucky you have state job. That's what we wanted for you. Cannot beat the retirement."

"True."

"Plus, you have plenty vacation. So lucky, you. Other companies not like that. Japanese companies the worst one. Your daddy had so small pension, even though he worked long time for Ishii Company. Make me mad. Only one gold watch at the end. That's how they treat you."

Mary didn't say anything. Her mother could go on talking about the injustice she felt about her father's retirement. She needed little prompting, and Mary did not feel like listening.

She put the magazine away and watched her mother in silence. Her mother was scraping some carrots for the surimi dough. "You just have to try my recipe, Mary," she said. "Tommy would like this style fish, too. Put little curry powder inside. It's so ono like that. You try. I give you some when you go home."

"No need to give me some, Ma. I'm going out with Jon."

"You and Jon eat out too much. Not good. You too lazy. But you still got to cook for Tommy, right? He's got to eat—so bring home some."

"Ma, Tommy's not at home. He's in the hospital."

"What you mean? What happened? What hospital?"

"He's not in a regular hospital," Mary explained. "He's in Kāneʻohe."

"You mean he—? Must be mistake. You sure?"

"It's no mistake. He had, uh, a mental breakdown." Mary went on to explain to her mother the circumstances of Tommy's illness. Her mother had a hard time understanding it.

"It just happens," Mary said. "Nobody knows why. They say it could be partly genetic, too."

"What you mean 'genetic'?"

"Passed down through the family. Plus, I think he took some drugs. He had a bad reaction."

"Well, cannot be our side. We never had anything like that in our family. Must be his father side."

Mary said that she probably knew just as much as her mother did about the cause of Tommy's problems. "Maybe, long ago, somebody in the family we don't know about—in Japan, perhaps—could have had a mental problem and nobody knew. No one in Japan would have confessed to having problems, right? They'd be too scared. Who'd want to marry them in Hawaiʻi?"

"Who else beside us know about this?"

"Only us. Why?" Mary asked, interested to know what her mother was driving at.

"None of anyone's business."

"Mom, it's not as if I'm going to broadcast it around. But why not? There's nothing to be ashamed about."

"What you mean. What if he act funny. What if he stick out his tongue like I seen pupule people make. Shame that, the tongue sticking out. What our friends and auntie folks going think when they see him like that, doing that kine stuff."

"Shame? Oh Mom, let's just forget I told you anything. I better go. I thought at least you and Dad would understand and go to see him. It's pretty clear where *you* stand. I'm sick and tired of all this stuff about shame."

Mary got up to leave. She saw tears piling up in her mother's eyes. She always got teary eyed whenever she and Mary had a disagreement. "Mary, don't say anything, okay. We look bad, bum-bye. People—they just not going understand."

"Understand? You really mean it, don't you? I'm going home. I'll talk to Dad later."

Her mother's body shook when Mary mentioned her father. This time, her mother's tears spilled from her eyes and rolled in two unbroken streams down her cheek.

"What is it, Ma? You don't want me to say anything to Daddy, either? Boy, you're something else—a piece of work."

"What you mean?"

"Nothing, Ma, nothing! I just hate this attitude you have. No wonder we're so screwed up!"

"You marry that kine boy, that's why."

"Oh, you mean Tommy's father. I'm sure he is somewhat to blame for this, but that's all so long ago. What if I said that the illness comes from *our* side of the family—then what? And Tommy's dad was pure Japanese, too! You were always telling me, 'Marry Japanese, marry Japanese.' So I married Japanese. Oh, what's the use of explaining."

"So now you going marry one Hawaiian-Filipino boy."

"Be careful, Mama, of what you say. Be *very* careful."

Mary's mother shook her head and faced the stove. Exasperated, Mary picked up her jacket from the back of a chair, walked heavily down the short corridor and walked out of the house, slamming the screen door shut. When Mary went back to her car, she again wished she had a cigarette with her. While all that transpired with her mother was *not* unexpected, Mary felt infuriated, blood throbbing at her temples.

That evening her boyfriend, Jon, said, "Lighten up. Give your parents time. They'll come around. News like this is hard to take. Besides, the Japanese aren't the only ones who hide things and let things go unsaid. Filipino families, Hawaiian families, all the same."

A week later, Mary got a call from her mother to come over. Mary was hesitant, but she knew that this was her mother's way of making up. Mary could no longer remain angry.

When she went over to the house—under the pretense of picking up more pickled vegetables—Mary reluctantly walked up the stone steps. Twice she thought of turning and leaving, but once on the porch, she put her slippers away, flat palmed the screen door, and moved in with it. Adjusting her eyes, she saw her father on the recliner. Hearing her come in, her father put his paper down, which sounded as if he were crumpling it.

"Oh, I wen think was you, wen I hea the car," he said, looking above the top of his glasses, "but you neva come up for long time, so I figa you went home."

"Hi Dad," Mary said and tried to be cheerful in her greeting. "I had to straighten something in the backseat, that's all," she lied.

"That you, Mary?" her mother said, poking her head out from the light in the kitchen to the darkness of the hallway. Mary saw only her mother's silhouette, the light behind her mother making her face look hazy.

"Yes, it's me, your wayward daughter."

"Good, good . . . and no need talk like that!"

Her mother shuffled about in socked feet and lau hala slippers. Mary noticed the socks were her father's old maroon ones, one side sagging, the elastic all stretched out. Mary's mother was surprisingly cheerful as she hurried over toward Mary, wiping her hands on a half apron, which looked gray from washing and use. Years ago, the apron had been spanking white. Mary felt sad at its shabbiness, her mother practically living in the kitchen, becoming as dowdy as her apron.

"Hey," her father said. "We wen fo' see the kid the other day."

"Oh?" exclaimed Mary, a bit surprised, but glad.

"Hats," her father said, which was short for her mother's name, Hatsuko, "tol' me what happen to the kid. At first, she neva like tell me. But I tell her, 'Why you shame fo'?' No shame, already. Pau, that.'"

"But you the one, long time go, who tol' me—" Mary's mother said.

"What I tol' you?" asked Mary's father. Her mother made no reply but stood fiddling with her apron. "See, you cannot tell me what I tol' you."

"Buuut—"

Mary's mother was not able to say that it was because of the way he dictated things that they did what they did or felt what they felt, including how they saw the "mental." Mary understood what her mother was trying to say—that her father wouldn't have tolerated Tommy's illness before.

Mary did not side with her mother, however. She wanted her mother to defend herself, say for herself what she couldn't say. But the moment passed and her mother was already ahead of what Mary felt should have been corrected. Mary let out a sigh.

"I neva like go," Mary's mother said. "But I figure if Daddy had a change of heart, I go with him."

"Change of heart? What you talking about? You no make sense," Mary's father said sharply to her mother. "I never have one 'change of heart.' You twisting everything."

"So, what happened?" asked Mary.

"So, nothing. The kid not that bad!" Mary's father said. "Talk little bit funny, but not too bad. You know why we went? After your motha tell me about Tommy—this was coincidence, you know. You remember Konishi old man? You remember him, right? Anyway, the other day, I went his house. His mother get Al . . . Alzhima."

"You mean Alzheimer's disease, Dad."

"Yeah, that's the stuff. Funny disease. Anyway, Konishi say, 'No shame. Come inside. Go eat. Get plenny food. Here, put this on your plate, no enryo. Get plenny rice, too.' But me, I had hard time for eat, afta I watch his mother. She drop all the food from the mouth, like one kid. I feel funny, watching her. But this get me going. I think to myself I can get like that, too, yeah? What you say? So, son-of-a-gun, that's wen I told Mommy we better go see the kid."

Mary nodded her head, touched by her father's account. Going to the hospital was probably the closest thing to an "I love you" from him. This was his way of showing her how he felt.

"Pupule now. Pupule later. Who knows," Mary's father continued, rustling the paper on his lap. "But we take kea, Mary. No worry. Us family—got fo' stick togetha deese days. What you say?"

"Thanks Dad," Mary said, choking, trying to hold back her tears. "How come Ma told you about Tommy in the first place?"

"Your Ma cannot keep secret." He winked and looked up at Mary's mother. "Eh Hats, go make some coffee for us."

"Cream? Shu-ga?" she asked, as her father nodded. "What about you Mary?"

"I'll go with you to the kitchen," she said to her mother. Mary got up from the chair, looked toward her father who had already put the afternoon paper in front of his face. Mary followed her mother into the kitchen.

"Your father, so strange. I never expected. Ten years ago would have been so different."

"Well, that was always part of the problem, wasn't it Ma? Always trying to shield us from things."

"Why, you blaming me?"

"No Ma, I'm not blaming you. I'm just saying that's what happened, that's all." Mary went over to her mother's side, dropped one arm around her shoulder, and gave her a squeeze. "I think many families are caught in the same way. We're not the only ones."

"Why Tommy wen get sick, anyhow?"

"I don't know, but sometimes there are no reasons. Things just happen and it's not bachi, you know."

"I didn't say."

"But you were thinking it, I bet." Mary's mother smiled a sheepish, weary smile. Mary smiled back. "This is not a payback for—for lord knows what somebody in the family has done. Sometimes it's good to let the old thinking go to rest."

"Mary?"

"Yeah, Ma?"

"You're a good daughter—even if you give us big headache sometime," she said as she turned to kiss Mary on the cheek.

In the car, before driving off, Mary looked at herself in the rearview mirror. On her face, she saw the red imprint of her mother's lipstick on her cheek—that same perfect circle, the lines radiating from it like a spider's web—reminding her of the Kleenex tissues draped over the cosmetic jars those many years ago.

Anniversary

In remembrance of someone dead, the Buddhists mark certain anniversary years with a church service: the first, third, fifth, seventh, and so on. Two weeks before the thirteenth anniversary of my grandmother's death, my mother makes a frantic phone call to me in Honolulu. These days, all of her calls are frantic.

"Jenny," she says. "Can't have Grandma's service on the day I told you."

"Oh, why not?" I ask, not really caring.

"Auntie Kay and Auntie Yuki can't make it to Hilo. Ayaa!" she wails. "The week afta that don't look too good eitha."

In her old age, she has taken to dropping the rs at the end of her words, as if having no time to bother with them. I gather from her cry that she's looking at her KTA Supermarket calendar. She continues. "They say they have tickets to the university football game. They going tailgate. I *have* to change the time. Okay with you?"

"Look, Ma, anytime is okay with me. Just let me know when it's going to be. I'll work my schedule around it."

"You such a good daughta. We all set, then."

"Next time when you do something like this, make the service whenever you want to have it. Have Auntie folks decide whether they want to come or not," I say in a scold. "I can't see you running around, trying to please everyone."

My mother has four sisters and a brother. Along with my mother, two of her sisters and their families live in Hilo. They are my Auntie Mit-chan and Kiyono Uncle; Aunty Toshie and Moss Uncle. Moss Uncle used to be called Hilo Uncle, but most of us call him Moss Uncle nowadays because he's slow moving. My mother's explanation is that, in Hilo, if you stand around too long, "you going get covered with moss."

Two other sisters and their husbands live in Honolulu. They are my Auntie Kay and Auntie Yuki and their husbands. The only boy in the family, Uncle George, lives on Kaua'i. A confirmed bachelor, he sports a goatee, a shaved head, an occasional girlfriend.

Several days later, my mother calls to see if I would call Uncle George in Kaua'i for her. As an afterthought, she wants me to call *the gang* in Honolulu, too. "Tell them I made the church service for the end of the month, on Saturday. That should satisfy everybody."

A few weeks later, the day before the service, my husband, Jim, and I fly to Hilo. When I arrive at my parents' home, I see that Uncle George is already in town from Kaua'i, and my aunties from Honolulu have also arrived. Several boxes of omiyage are scattered on the dining room table.

"Who's the mochi from?" I ask, opening the lid to the box and popping into my mouth a soft pink-and-white rice cake covered with silky potato starch. "Mm-mm. This tastes good. Did you try it, Ma?"

"Uncle George brought that. Auntie Kay folks brought the manapua—curry chicken and cha siu pork. Auntie Yuki brought the apricot bread," she says. "You and Jim—eat. Sweet stuff no good fo' Daddy. He look at the food and he want to eat everything. He shove in his mouth what he not supposed to eat when we not looking. Bad habit, him."

"Before we do anything, better put the manapua in the refridge, don't you think so?" I say.

"Go ahead. No, no, wait. Pack them inside the Ziploc bags, four each, then put in the freeza. But first, don't forget to go Freitas house to give them some." My mother feels indebted to Mrs. Freitas, a neighbor, because the woman watches my parents' home whenever they go out of town.

"Freitas lady—pua thing. Can't go anywhea. Nobody to take kea her."

My mother sighs and laments her friend's situation. I know that when she says things like this, she is dropping hints about her own welfare. But she is oblique in expressing her wishes, never clear as to what she wants me to do for her or how she wants me to take care of her and my dad.

Over at the Freitas's, I thank the woman on behalf of our family. When I get back to the house, I find my mother reconfirming reservations for the dinner that is scheduled after we hold the church service.

"Where's this restaurant?" I ask. "Never heard of it before."

"Called Yone's. People say, not bad. So I make the reservations."

"But you never went there?"

"Whea, Yone's? No need to. I take people's word."

"I don't know about this, Ma," I say.

The day of the church service is a busy one for my mother. She must cut anthurium flowers from her garden to bring to church. She needs two bouquets: one for the altar in the columbarium, and another for the main temple. She also has to have her hair done at Kay's Beauty Salon. Since her time at the hairdresser will run through the lunch hour, she leaves me with a long list of instructions on how to feed my semi-invalid father, who is annoyed because he doesn't like it when my mother leaves him alone for any length of time. He makes a big face and is uncooperative during lunch.

"Why Mommy gotta go do her hay-a?" he asks, whining, dropping food down his shirt. He makes curlicues around his ears with his good hand to indicate that she's crazy to leave him like this.

Before she leaves, my mother had says, "Make nice-nice fo' me, 'kay? Big baby him, that's why." But I'm surprised at the extent of mollifying that needs to be done.

After my mother gets back, she puts money into several envelopes she has set aside for the priest, the service, and the church donation. She then decides she wants to get to the church as early as possible. We leave the house at 2:15 for the 3:00 p.m. service. My father grumbles, saying that it's too early to go. When we reach the church, however, all of my mother's sisters and her brother are already there. "Nissei time," my husband says, leaning into me. "Everyone early—way before time."

"See?" my mother says. "I told you we should have come early—even earlia would have been betta."

"Mom, you came home late from the hairdresser, remember? So it's okay," I pat her hand and wink. "Besides, Grandma's not going anywhere." My mother gives me an I-don't-think-that's-very-funny look.

"I going be hea, too, soon enough," she says.

The Honpa Hongwanji Temple in Hilo is of Spanish mosque design, a large dome covering the temple. It still stands as one of the tallest structures in that section of town. Hairline cracks inside the building wander across the thick concrete walls and ceiling because of a large earthquake that once rocked the island. Aside from the cracks, the church has remained unchanged since my childhood.

On the right side of the building, a long hallway runs parallel to the main hall and altar, at the end of which is the columbarium. My mother hurries down this hallway with the two bunches of anthuriums, carrying them like torches in her hands. Her sisters are already there, paying their respects at their mother's niche. I take one bunch out of my mother's hands and tell her not to worry, that I would take care of the flowers for the main altar.

While my mother and aunts are busy in the columbarium, I walk with Jim to the main altar. I notice that my father and Kiyono Uncle, who like my father is semi-invalid, are sitting on one of the pews and waiting for the service to begin.

After putting the flowers in a vase, I find room next to my father and sit with him and my uncle. We wait. Jim is interested in the architecture so he roams about the place. From where I sit, I then see my mother, aunts, and uncle troop down the hallway, but they are walking away from where we are. I watch them go into a small, one-room family chapel across the way. Concerned, I leave my father and Kiyono Uncle and head over to where the other family members are seated.

"Is this where we're having the service?" I ask when I get there.

"I think so," my mother says. "Earlia, when I went to the office, the reverend said to meet him hea. Why?"

"It's okay, I suppose. I don't care, but Dad and Kiyono Uncle are waiting in the main temple. Let me go back and bring them here."

I walk back to the main temple and tell my father and Kiyono Uncle what is happening—that the church service is going to be held in the family chapel across the hallway. My father is distressed. "I staying right hea," he announces and points to his seat. "I staying hea—one au-wa!"

Kiyono Uncle nods his head in agreement. "Me too!"

"Wait here," I instruct and walk over to the family chapel again.

In the smaller chapel, my mother and her sisters are busily talking. My mother looks up at me when I walk in. "Whea's Daddy?" she asks. She covers her mouth and looks at her sisters, sheepishly. "Oh my! I forgot all about him." The sisters laugh and bring their bodies in like conspirators.

I tell my mother what my father had said, and the kind reverend who overhears the conversation and learns of our predicament comes over to my mother. "Don't worry," he says. "It's no problem. We can shift places."

"So hum-bug, Daddy. Always making it hard on everybody."

Picking up his prayer books, the reverend snuffs out the candles, puts a lid on the burning senkō in the incense burner, and soon has everyone following him across the hallway.

We get seated with a lot of scuffing of heels and rustling of clothing, each family on different pews—where men and their families, then women and theirs are supposed to sit according to birth order. Uncle George does not have a family so he sits in the first pew by himself; my mother, father, Jim, and I sit in the second pew; it goes on down the line.

In the back of the altar, the reverend is rushing about, lighting the candles. A gas wand with a pale blue light hisses and ignites the wicks. The candlelight brightens the room as if the sun had suddenly come in.

After the short service, we move out of the church to take some pictures. We congregate at the bottom of the stairway that leads up to the church. Soon, everyone is milling around at the foot of the steps—all except Auntie Mit-chan and Kiyono Uncle.

"What's taking Kiyono Uncle folks so long?" my mother inquires of no one in particular. As an aside, she tells me, "I wish I don't get like Uncle—whea I cannot take kea myself no mo."

"Can't help it, though, if it happens," I say, quietly. "What do you want me to do?" She steps aside and doesn't answer me.

At this time, the reverend comes down the steps and says that the Kiyonos are on their way. He had them use the church elevator in the back of the building. Kiyono Uncle is using a walker, not his wheelchair, and it has slowed him down. Everyone turns to look at the walkway that leads from the elevator and we watch Kiyono Uncle lurch his way up to us. Someone in the family sighs. It takes Auntie Mit-chan and Kiyono Uncle several more minutes before they reach us.

Once everyone is together, we take the customary "all the gang" picture. My father becomes impatient with the whole thing and wants to be included in only a few shots. Soon after, he is seen limping his way to the car.

The sisters really get into the act, then. First, they want pictures with their only brother. Next, they want a picture taken with all the women and their spouses (my father excluded). Then one with the girls only. They line up like Ziegfeld chorus girls. They suck in their breath, throw out their chests, fling back their shoulders, smile broadly, as if one action precipitated the other, and they face the camera. For fun, they kick up their legs in unison. Except for my mother, all the others have jet-black hair.

After the picture-taking session, my mother gives the directions to Yone's Restaurant. When we reach the place, a red truck and a couple of sedans dot the parking lot.

"Must not be busy tonight," my mother says.

"That's a bad sign," Jim says in a whisper. I squeeze his hand.

Outside the restaurant, we watch koi circle an artificial moat that surrounds the place. My father is delighted to watch the fish. He perches his head to one side, old memories of being a weekend fisherman seeming to cross his mind—schools of fish before his eyes. "I wish I brought some bread so Daddy can throw to the fish," my mother says.

"I don't think that's such a good idea," I say. "It clouds the water."

"Why? Only lilibit—make Daddy happy," she says with that "so what—we not going to live long" or the "let us do what we like" look of hers.

"That's true." I concede and wonder if I would be able to care for my parents with all their idiosyncrasies.

Inside, the restaurant is dimly lit. I see one or two people walking about. Our table is a long one under a graceless chandelier, and the area is dark because some of the bulbs on the chandelier are burned out or clouded over by dust and oil.

My mother directs everyone where to sit. Her siblings all listen. "You thea, Kay. Ova this side, George. No, no, this side, I said. Mit-chan, you come sit by me."

The menu is plate-lunch style. Saimin, loco moco, three-choice platters with rice and salad. My father, I notice, begins to get agitated. His diabetic condition makes him hungry and he needs to be fed at appropriate times. He wants a bowl of saimin.

"Saimin? Not nourishing, Daddy," my mother admonishes. "Get something mo filling than that."

"Neva mind, you," my father says and pouts.

Everyone gives an order for drinks to the waitress. The men start with a round of beer, the women with wine coolers, others soft drinks. My dad has some iced-tea with NutraSweet.

My Aunt Mit-chan hits a glass *ting, ting, ting* with her spoon. "To our mother," she says in a toast.

"Kampai," we all say.

After that, we sit around, relax, make small talk, and sip our drinks while waiting for our dinners.

The orders arrive slowly. "What they doing?" Moss Uncle asks. "Killing the beef?" Light laughter sprinkles across the table. By this time, he's had several rounds of liquor and is getting louder. My Auntie Toshie nudges him with her elbow.

Opposite Jim and me, my father's face looks angst-ridden. Finally, everyone gets served. All except my father. Somehow, the restaurant has forgotten his saimin. I see him tap one of the waitresses as she passes by. When she looks at him, he pounds the table and says: "How come no mo?"

The waitress, red-faced, apologizes profusely and scampers quickly into the kitchen. We can hear her shout to the cook: "Eh Kam, where's da saimin? You wen forget da order or what?"

By this time, my father is on the verge of a temper tantrum. He is raising his voice at my mother. "I like eat!" he is saying.

"Dad," I say. "Look, your food's here." And, just in time, a steaming bowl of saimin soup arrives, the waitress placing it before him. My father dives into the noodles with his chopsticks. By now, most of us are through eating; our heads turned his way, watching him slurp the noodles.

"Drink some wata, Daddy," my mother urges. "You going choke."

"Come up for air, Uncle," one of my cousin teases, the one who's never without cracking a stick of Spearmint gum, wearing a Hale Niu yellow bowling shirt with black velvet lettering.

After rushing to eat at the beginning of his meal, my father quickly slows down. He doesn't eat much. By this time, he is overtired and cranky, his hunger having passed.

After dinner, the family congregates at my mother's house. They troop in with pies and stacks of pastries from KTA or Robert's Bakery, the boxes piled high on the kitchen counter.

"What we going do, yeah, with all this pastry? Look at this," my mother says, sweeping her hands across the boxes. "No wonder we get so momona. Look at my fat 'ōpū," she says as she pats her belly.

She serves coffee and tea, and I cut a sliver of each pie for each paper plate: chocolate, jello, haupia, guava, and lilikoi chiffon. We sit in the living room and watch television while we eat on small, low tables on the floor.

My father is watching a Japanese movie. We try to follow it but can't understand what is being said.

"Change the station, Daddy," my mother says. "Change to one English program."

"Let's watch the Miss America contest. It's on tonight," Auntie Kay says.

When my mother takes the remote from my father's side and changes the station, the bathing suit competition is on. My aunties and cousins begin making snide comments about each contestant: "Look at that—the hips too big on that one." "That one, ho da bow-legged—gotta get straight legs, yeah, if you run." "Her chin some long. You see that—look the jaw—like one witch, no?"

Kiyono Uncle, disgusted at listening to the comments, says, "Why you folks gotta run everybody down for?"

"It's okay, Papa," Auntie Mit-chan says to her husband. "This is home. Not like we saying this outside. Here, we can say what we like, yeah?" She looks at her sisters for approval.

"Just like you guys perfeck," Kiyono Uncle says.

"Enough, already," my aunt says, clipping his arm with a soft slap. They continue arguing on the side.

The rest of us go on with our running commentaries—our severe judgments. "That's local Japanese style for you. Even if we can never do better, we criticize everything," laughs Auntie Toshie.

As the night wears on, most of the men drop off to sleep. Uncle George has his head back on the sofa and is snoring loudly. My mother, noticing him, shakes him gently. "Eh George, mo' betta you go back to the hotel fo' sleep," she says.

Once Uncle George gets up to leave, the rest of the sisters decide that it's time for them to go, too. In large paper plates to be covered by sheets of aluminum foil, my mother divides the pastry among her sisters to take with them.

"Thanks, Nesan," they call out. "Let us know when—the next one."

"Seventeen yee-a service—the next one. But skip that one. No need. Go fo' the twenty-five. Most likely I be dead by that time, too, anyway," laughs my mother. "Jenny, you going take kea everything for me, right?"

"Oh? Thanks a lot, Mom, for volunteering my services," I say.

At last, everyone is gone. I help my mother clean up the kitchen and hurriedly go back to the living room to view the remaining portion of the Miss America contest. I'm just in time to see the ending. *There she is, Miss America, my ideal.* The winner holds on to a wobbly crown perched on her head and walks down the ramp with an armful of red roses. The program ends. As the credits go up, the girls swarm the winner like bees, hug each other and cry, relieved that the pageant is over.

"Time to go sleep," says my mother who is watching the last part of the program with me.

"Yeah, I think we'd all better turn in. Jim's already gone to bed. It's been a long day."

"Shu-a was, no?" my mother says. She is tired but goes around to straighten things in the house. "Daddy, you betta go sleep, too," she says.

"What you mean," he slurs. Getting up from his chair, his body bent over, unable to straighten out, he stands to face her. He stomps his feet. "I no *like* sleep!" he shouts.

My mother shrugs her shoulders. "I don't know why you have to act like one baby!"

"Go you!" My father says.

"Go, mom. Go to your room," I say. I take her hand and walk her down the hallway. By this time she is half-crying, half-laughing.

"Funny to be old, yeah? But you take kea of us, you hea? Even if we get pupule in the head. And don't forget our anniversaries, when we ma-ke," she orders.

"Don't worry, I'll do my best to take care of you, and I'll try not to forget what needs to be done."

Without thinking, I had made a commitment to care for my parents. The thing that surprises me the most is how easily the obligation had been imposed, and met. Almost casually. I can't believe how it came to be, how I didn't fight the idea, when all the time, up to that moment, I wasn't at all sure I could take care of them or even wanted to. In that short moment, I had even agreed to do their anniversary services, and this for the *rest* of my life.

I walk back to the living room. "Dad, what's the matter with you? Don't treat Mom this way."

Inside of myself, I feel an anger, which is quickly overtaken by pity. He looks helplessly at me and in a faltering, stroke-hindered, sputtering speech, he says, "I mad 'cause I no can watch what I like."

"Oh, Dad," I say.

I'm at a loss for words at his not understanding that it was only for one night, and that no one would have understood the Japanese program he was watching. "Well, you watch what you want to right now if you can't sleep," I say.

By this time, my mother is back with us again. "Mom, everything's okay. Why don't you go back to bed. I'll take care of things out here." But she waits for me at the doorway to the hallway. I settle my father down and walk with my mother down the hall again.

"I won't blame you one bit, Jenny, if you send Daddy straight to the nursing home and don't make anniversary services for him when he dies," she says. "I release you. You don't have to do anything for him. He give everybody too much trouble."

"Don't worry about it, Mom. Good night." I give her a tight hug.

Soon everyone is asleep. I cover my father, who has fallen asleep on his recliner, with a blanket. He is fast asleep. He has his mouth open—"catching flies," as my mother would have said.

I turn off the television and all the lights in the house.

The Grandfathers

The feud began because of a bait-well. Sachi M's new grandfather-in-law, Grandpa Sam, said that he felt slighted by her and her Japanese family. As he grumbled to Tom, his grandson, "The Jap side got first crack" at making the bait-well for the boat, even if he were equally capable of making it.

One day while bottom fishing with her father-in-law just outside of Honolulu Harbor, Sachi M thought about the "bait-well fiasco." She felt the pettiness of the incident drain away as she hooked another red weke.

In the late afternoon sun, the glassy surface of the ocean shattered into a million dazzling pieces. Although the light on the water reflected on their faces, the heat was mild and comforting as they drifted out to sea. Sachi M took off her hat and nodded to her father-in-law when she saw his hand-line grow taut.

Her father-in-law lifted his face into the wind. Looking at him as he raised his gaunt face, she could see how frail and delicate he had become. These days, his body assumed a protective curve around his chest. Even under the armor of the pumpkin-colored life jackets, she could see the hollow that his body made. He coughed mildly into his hand.

When they moved past the last buoy in the channel, her father-in-law started the engine and signaled Sachi M to pick up her line. He drove the boat as they headed inland toward the mouth of the harbor and was careful about skirting the backside of the shore breakers as he pointed them out to her.

"Stay clear of them," he said. "Give them lots of room to break. They're unpredictable. You can overturn the boat if you're not cautious." Sachi M nodded her head. "In stormy weather, they start breaking farther out," he shouted in a sudden gust of wind, his mouth filling with air.

Stopping near the opening of the harbor channel, Sachi M dropped a sea anchor, which caused a drag to slow the boat down. The anchor gave the boat a slight jerk and spin before settling into a drift. She dropped the line from her pole and let it free-fall from the reel into the water. Her father-in-law slipped his hand-line over the side. Together, they let the shiny monofilament nylon line run quietly into the water, connecting them to what was below.

The run of the lines had their own momentum, like the flow of a river. Once the lines hit bottom, the two of them lifted, then dropped their lines—almost in unison—as they rocked with the rise and fall of the waves. They did this steadily, the pace never changing, unless one of them had a bite. Even then, the other person did not break motion. Fish were caught, but the overall rhythm to which the sea held them was not interrupted. When one of them caught a fish, nothing much was said. They unhooked the fish and placed it into the new bait-well.

In her first marriage, one of her sons, in teasing her, called her Sachi M, saying that the name sounded like Auntie Em in *The Wizard of Oz*. The logic was somewhat skewed but the nickname stuck. Since then, everyone called her Sachi M. Her married name was Mukai at the time, so it was fitting that people called her Sachi with a capital M. But when Sachi M divorced her husband, her mother complained to people that the *M* in Sachi M was not the *M* of her maiden name—for Miyamoto—but the "junk" husband's name. She wished it stood for their family name.

"Just think it's for Miyamoto," Sachi M told her mother, exasperated over such a trifle.

But her mother was stubborn. "Not same," she said. "Not when *I* know."

"Oh, Ma," was all Sachi M could say at how illogical her mother appeared.

When Sachi M and Tom decided to marry, her mother felt that Sachi M should tell her Grandpa Asa, first, and in person, as a courtesy, if she also wanted his approval of their marriage. Sachi M couldn't see why, but as her mother said, "If anyone is going to have a difficult time with the marriage, it is bound to be your grandpa. Our family, slow. Nobody married gaijin, yet. So I don't know what Grandpa's going to say. You never know with him."

About a month before the wedding, Sachi M drove up to her parents' home in Mānoa. Grandpa Asa, her mother's father, now lived with her parents after having moved to Honolulu from the Big Island. Her grandfather hated to lose his independence but had settled into his new home quite easily, letting his daughter and her husband indulge him.

Sachi M parked the car on Oʻahu Avenue, walked into the house, and tapped her mother's miniature terrier on its head as he sniffed her legs. "Are you hungry?" she asked the dog as he licked her hand. She stuck her head into the kitchen, which was neat but cluttered with piles of packaged goodies—potato chips, kakimochi, roasted peanuts, ika—closed with twist-ties or clothespins.

No one seemed to be around. She walked out back, then went through a side door that opened onto the lanai. There she found her grandfather repotting a dendrobium plant on a table.

The older man was perched on a vegetable box like the ones Sachi M's mother had reprimanded him for bringing home from the supermarket. "Termite food," she had scolded her father. "House going fall down one day."

To Grandpa Asa, it was wasteful the way the supermarkets threw the boxes out into the rubbish bins. He had railed about the matter to the family. Having lived in poverty most of his life, where saving and using everything was a matter of survival, he just could not let a good piece of string or wood or pipe go to waste, let alone the boxes. "Look all the junk in the garage, Papa. Throw them out," Sachi M's mother had nagged her father. Sachi M reminded her mother on those occasions that her grandfather did not have much longer to live, and, when the time came, her mother could get rid of all the junk he had accumulated.

"I guess I have to live with it," her mother acknowledged.

Sachi M walked over to where her grandfather sat. "Aaa, Sachi ka?" he said when he saw her. He motioned her to grab a vegetable box in the corner and gestured for her to sit down with him. An old-man smell greeted her—the smell of garden dirt, perspiration, tobacco, Mennen's aftershave lotion.

"Did you see Ma folks? Do you know where she and my papa went?" Sachi M asked.

"Me, no pololei," he said as he shook his head. He then explained in Japanese that he had taken a nap in the afternoon, and when he got up no one was home. "Today," he said, "I moe-moe long time. Makule, eh, me?" He laughed, as if he had told a joke.

Sachi M wanted to protest and say, "Oh no, you're not old, still young at heart," or some such stupid thing, but she knew her grandfather would see through it and raise one of his eyebrows at her nonsense.

"I come to see you. Me and Tom, my haole boyfren, you know, we going get married. Married, kekkon, wakaru ka? I letting you know." She explained in the best way she could.

"Oh," he said, mulling over what she had just said. "Ano gaijin, ka?"

"Yes, the gaijin." A bit annoyed, Sachi M answered with a short tone.

After a pause her grandfather said, "Yoroshī, all right," and slapped his hands on the face of his thighs. He sprang up from the vegetable box, which wobbled under him.

"Grandpa—" Sachi M started, but did not continue.

She was not sure what he felt, so she didn't want to press the matter. She had notified him and that was that. Besides, no matter what anyone said, she and Tom were planning to get married. No question about it. But she wanted to extend the personal invitation out of respect and courtesy. Too, Grandpa was special to her. Her mother had been right to say that Sachi M should go to see him.

"So you come, Grandpa, okay?"

"Where you mally?" he asked.

"We marry downtown—Chinatown—at the court."

"Not Hongwanji?"

"Tom's a Christian, Grandpa . . . Kirisuto."

"Soo ka," he said, sounding disappointed.

When Sachi M left her parents' home that day, she wasn't sure what to make of her grandfather's reaction. He didn't disapprove, outright, but it wasn't as if he were particularly happy, either.

Tom had troubles of his own. First of all, his mother wanted a get-acquainted party for the two families before the wedding. Later, Tom told Sachi M how he had nixed the idea. Tom's family, especially his grandfather who had bombarded Tom with far too many questions, was a bit apprehensive about meeting their new *Japanese* in-laws. The emphasis was his grandfather's, because Tom had cautioned his Grandpa Sam about using the word "Jap." At any time! He also warned Sachi M that if his Grandpa Sam *did* make a slip when they met, it was unintentional. "While it's no excuse, it's a generational thing," he tried to explain; his grandpa's generation had grown up using the word. "They never thought anything of it in their day and age. I don't understand it, but . . . so ingrained, I guess."

"It's okay, Tom, my family's the same way to the point of embarrassment. I guess we just have to live with it. My parents are always talking about haoles or gaijin or ketō, hair people, as if Japanese men don't have hair on their chests. My dad has plenty on his."

All went well at the wedding. As soon as the introductions were made, the wedding began, which left little time for social interaction among the guests. It was only after the wedding that Tom and Sachi M held their breath. But everyone was civil, so the couple did not have to worry much.

Sachi M's and Tom's parents found they had some mutual friends, which made it easier for them to have a pleasant conversation. Sachi M heard her mother say, "Small world, Hawai'i," to Tom's mother and she sounded relaxed talking to her new haole in-law. But Sachi M's mother kept bowing to her new in-laws, until Sachi M had to take her mother aside and say, "Mom, you don't have to keep on bowing to these people."

Her mother giggled, her hand across her mouth, and said, "That's right. They haole, yeah? Habit—me."

As for her father, Sachi M felt embarrassed at the ever-effusive and genial Tosh, who loved to play host. In front of haoles, he always tried to speak perfect English, the affectation which made him sound unnatural, weird. Sachi M cringed.

"Act natural, be yourself Dad," she said, coming up to him as he went about talking to different groups of people. To make an impression with the haoles, he put rs or exaggerated the sound in all the wrong places and sprinkled a nasal "hunh" once too often. "Howr are you, hunh?" he'd ask shaking hands.

"I just making the rounds," he said to Sachi M with a wink.

"Dad, don't try to act haole, okay?" Sachi M said.

"Okay, okay." He gave her another wink. "But mo' shame, eh, if I talk any kine way, no?"

"No. Better to be natural. No need to put on airs. Makes you sound silly."

Sachi M saw that Grandpa Sam and Grandpa Asa just stood around in the background, letting the young folks circulate, as they waited for the wedding get-together to end. The two had met each other, briefly, and stood by straight and formal. When they could, they eyed each other. The two men seemed as familiar as people they had worked with over the years, but unfamiliar as family members. Nevertheless, whatever they felt inside, the atmosphere between them was one of utmost respect.

Largely due to her mother's urging, Sachi M consented to having a small wedding reception at her parents' home, the evening of the wedding. The Japanese side of the family who could not attend the wedding earlier in the day wanted to meet the haole side of the family. But at the party, all the haoles gravitated to one side of the long living room and the Japanese, shy, hung around at the other side.

"Bad idea," said Sachi M as she passed Tom, who rotated between the two groups with trays of food. Gradually, people began relaxing and intermingling. Sachi M soon saw her mother take Tom's mother into one of the bedrooms to show off her collection of crocheted dolls. By this time, too, her father and Tom's dad were talking amicably. Sachi M's father was behaving more like his usual self, and the two fathers-in-law had found a common interest: fishing. They talked about fishing spots and all the ulua that got away, the stories getting more and more exaggerated as time passed.

"Das the spot I wen ketch one big ulua. Ask Sachi M," Sachi M heard her father say.

Don't drag me in, thought Sachi M. *I can't corroborate your story. The fish wasn't that big.*

Not very long into the gathering, Sachi M saw Grandpa Sam follow her Grandpa Asa out onto the patio and garden. She called Tom to the window to watch, which made him arch one of his eyebrows in surprise.

Grandpa Asa first took Grandpa Sam to look at his orchid plants—the fragrant purple and yellow 'okika honohono flowering on hāpu'u stumps near a lighted tile wall. Then Grandpa Asa took him into his workshop off the garage. There, the two men found a common interest. Both of them appreciated good tools and both of them liked to work with wood. Grandpa Asa had been working on a koa table and the grain on the planks intrigued Grandpa Sam, who ran his hands over the hard-to-come-by curly koa. They talked with a lot of pointing and gesturing. Watching them, Sachi M felt relieved.

"Come inside," Sachi M urged after awhile, sticking her head out of the kitchen door that led to the workshop. "Have some cake and coffee."

In the house, Grandpa Asa sat stiffly next to Grandpa Sam who crossed his ankles, unbuttoned his coat, and took out a cigar to chew on. "Just like a haole," Tom said to Sachi M.

"At least he took off his shoes," Sachi M said. The couple laughed.

Sachi M's mother had taken out her Noritake dishes and stainless steel flatware just for the occasion.

"Bet Tom's folks use silver, eh, Sachi M?" asked her mother on the side.

"So?" replied Sachi M.

Grandpa Asa and Sachi M's father clinked their cups loudly as they stirred their coffee with their teaspoons. Sachi M's father drank his coffee like soup with his spoon, and her grandfather sipped his coffee like tea with a lot of loud smacking of his lips. Everyone tried to make-believe they didn't hear the noises, but Tom's mother made a face, as if she had smelled something bad.

Back in the kitchen with Tom, Sachi M said, "Boy, I never thought of my parents as ill-mannered before, but next to your family, my family looks crude."

"Are you embarrassed for them?"

"Somewhat. I shouldn't be, but they seem so *local*."

"In my eyes, my family seems so *haole*. I cringed several times today. Don't think I didn't catch my mother's face when she heard your grandfather slurping his coffee. I'll have to explain to her it's just Japanese style. And my grandfather, refusing to take off his shoes at first. But it's okay. Everyone's doing fine."

"Yeah, I suppose so. I wish I didn't feel so on edge. It'll be okay as long as my father doesn't totally relax and start eating with his fingers. Or worse, break out the beer and the stink, dried cuttlefish and the kakimochi. Then again, why not?"

"Yeah, why not?"

At one point, in making a conversation with Sachi M, his father, and father-in-law, Tom said, "Dad, didn't you have a sampan of your own? Didn't you go fishing a lot in Kailua Bay when you were a young boy?"

"Yes, that's true. It was good then, not many people living on the Windward side. Flat Island, Mōkapu Island, my fishing grounds," his father said.

"I used to like fo' go fishing, too," Sachi M's father said.

"Boy, do I miss fishing," Tom's father said.

Tom, brightening, suggested, "Hey, then why don't you two guys buy a boat together and go fishing?"

"No, no," Sachi M's father said. "I go golf deese days. Go ask my daughta. She the one love fo' fish."

Two weeks later, Sachi M's father-in-law bought a boat so the two of them could go fishing. Tom preferred to stay at home, glad that his father and wife found something mutual to do.

Tom's father outfitted the new twelve-foot Boston Whaler with a forty-five horsepower Evinrude outboard motor and a small, spare twenty horsepower for emergencies. He also installed a two-way radio, bought all the fishing gear and life vests. He even had the boat blessed by a Shinto priest and christened it the *Sachi M*. It was at this time, without thinking, that Sachi M had asked her Grandpa Asa to make a bait-well for the boat. And it was this asking that caused Grandpa Sam to feel angry about not having been asked.

"I guess, from now on, you can't ask one without asking the other," said Tom. "We'll always have to consider both sides' feelings."

"Boy, I never thought a simple bait-well would cause this much trouble."

Sachi M's father provided the rationale: "Just like the two of them competing, eh, with each otha—to see which one you guys like betta. Not much they can do, eh, nowadays? No can drive, their frens all dead or half ma-ke—that's why they ack up. Like they all ga-ga already."

"Hush," Sachi M's mother said. "You're no better these days."

Sachi M and her father-in-law went fishing on Sundays in the late afternoons, when the sun was not too high and most boats were coming in. Near sunset, they spent two or three hours fishing. They launched the boat at Kīhei Lagoon, cut across Honolulu Harbor, took a left at the first buoy, cut the engine, let out their lines and drifted out to sea. It was a comfortable outing—just the two of them—hardly speaking but enjoying the sport. They caught good-sized fish at this hour: red weke, maru, uku. They took only the larger fish home and let the small ones go. Even at that, everyone's freezer in the family soon filled to capacity with fish. Later, Grandpa Sam and Grandpa Asa became all the more popular among their friends because of the abundant fish they gave away.

Even after the doctors diagnosed Sachi M's father-in-law with cancer, the two of them fished almost every chance they had between his surgery, the chemotherapy and radiation treatments. Any time he felt better, the two of them were, as usual, out in the ocean, fishing.

Around this time, Tom's mother said to him, "I need another chest of drawers—something like a tansu—for your dad. With him ill, I need more space for his clothes and medicines."

Sachi M just happened to mention needing a tansu in a conversation with her parents at their home, whereupon her Grandpa Asa, hearing about it said, "I make one for the nice-u haole man."

Sachi M was not averse to the idea of her grandfather building the chest for Tom's father, but she felt that Grandpa Sam would only get offended again. After all, it was *his* son. Sachi M's father, in his own enlightened way about the two old men, said, "Tell dem build the stuff together. That way no fight. Let em build the stuff hea."

"You're right, Dad," Sachi M agreed. "That may be the solution."

At the beginning of the project, Grandpa Sam said, "I like maple—what you say Asa?"

"No, mo' betta koa," Grandpa Asa said. Long discussion. A lot of pointing, grunting, gesturing. Outcome, koa.

Then Grandpa Sam said, "Let me buy the nails."

"Nails? Make dis Japanee style. No need nails."

"Japanese way, humbug,"

"Kāpulu use nails." Another long discussion. Outcome, no nails. Dovetails.

For both men the last straw was when they actually started working on the chest. Grandpa Sam started in on Grandpa Asa's old-fashioned tools.

"Asa-san, if you use your old tools, it's going to take too long to build the chest."

"How you know? This way mo' pololei. Izu show you how make this tansu."

"You, show me how? I know how!"

Back and forth it went.

"Hey Tom, it's very hard for me to work with Asa. The ole Jap is hard-headed," he grumbled.

"Shhh," said Tom, "Sachi M can hear."

"So pākīkē, the haole ole man. No good him. All-u time talk-talk," Asa grumbled to Sachi M.

"Shhh," said Sachi M. "Tom will hear you."

How was the complicated joinery to be made without a lathe and more modern equipment? How was the Japanese old man going to make anything with such old-fashioned tools?

According to Grandpa Asa, things really began to get bad when Grandpa Sam eyed his tools with disgust, "giving bad looks." Grandpa Asa thought it was so rude of the haole. He just didn't like the idea that Grandpa Sam didn't say anything, but insinuated with his eyes that Grandpa Asa was an old-fashioned carpenter.

"I quit!" Grandpa Sam said one day. He started up his truck and left.

"No come-u back hea," Grandpa Asa shouted after Grandpa Sam in the driveway.

Grandpa Sam and Grandpa Asa quit working on the chest, altogether, both in a huff over how they were going to divide the job. That was the end of the partnership and their shaky relationship. Neither Tom nor Sachi M could talk the men into resuming their work.

One Sunday afternoon Sachi M's father-in-law, although very frail by this time, indicated that he wanted to go fishing. Above his wife's and Tom's objections, he insisted. "Take me out, Sachi M."

"Okay, I'll take you out," Sachi M reassured him, knowing this was probably the last time they would be fishing together.

This time, her father-in-law let her pack the equipment and do most of the work. She drove the truck and even launched the boat by herself—something she had never done before. When she climbed into the boat, she noticed that her father-in-law had taken her seat and motioned her to take over the steering. Before she could say anything, he gave her the keys and motioned with his hands for her to take the boat out.

"Go on," he encouraged, "you know how to do this."

He now moved as if his body were not his own. Sachi M recognized how illness and pain could make one feel that way—to the point where even one's limbs no longer belonged to the body.

The sun was comfortable but a bank of dark clouds was gathering in the sky. Sachi M looked up but was not unduly concerned. She'd seen worse. The clouds were high and far off.

Once out at sea, the two of them fished silently, each content in the motion and rhythm of the ocean, their ease with each other due to the understanding that came from enjoying something together. Occasionally, a bird's cry cut through the sky and her father-in-law looked up. The whites of his eyes had a gray cast to them. Sachi M grieved for this soft, gentle man as she looked at him. He was not very old.

Lost in the act of fishing, they had forgotten about the time and had drifted farther out than usual. Before long, Sachi M felt a few drops of rain on her forearms. The wind had picked up slightly and began a low howl. The sea, suddenly feathered with whitecapped waves, began cresting higher. Wind hissed past their ears and sea spray whipped their faces. Sachi M had heard how the weather at sea could turn without notice, but this was her first encounter with this kind of sudden change.

"Papa," Sachi M yelled above the wind. "I think we're going to have to ride this one out. I don't think we'll make it back in." Her father-in-law nodded his head.

By this time, she couldn't see any of the buoys or landmarks. The squall had hit suddenly, and it now hid the shoreline. Visibility poor, Sachi M peered into the mist and rain. The temperature had also dropped, the air growing cold. Sachi M noticed that her father-in-law had started shivering. Uncontrollably.

"Here, papa, wear this jacket." She threw her jacket at him. "You better tighten your life jacket, too." He nodded, slow in his response.

Sachi M revved the engine. She whipped the boat around, headed out and away from the direction of the shore breakers. It was better to be farther out than near the coastline. She had never done anything like this before in her life, but she knew enough to keep the engine on and the boat headed into the waves. She had to keep the boat as far away from the shore breaks as possible.

Waves began towering over the small boat. "Plough in, plough in. Head right into the waves. Don't get hit broadside," her father-in-law shouted between chattering teeth.

Water poured over the sides and into the boat. The wind seemed to be carrying them farther and farther out to sea. Sachi M needed help. The boat did not respond readily to her steering. It was taking in too much water.

"Here, bail!" she commanded her father-in-law, tossing him a Clorox bottle that had been cut into a bailer. With great effort, the shivering man threw his body into each scoop and tossed the water out as if he were losing himself to the sea.

The hull slammed into each crest. Pitched high, it headed down, steeply, into the troughs. The boat lurched and dropped and banged them about. Sachi M's arms ached and she thought the struggle with the waves would never cease. She was willing to give up the fight but kept on in the same way that her father-in-law kept on in his fight—the struggle to live stronger, becoming something of sheer necessity and, as Sachi M thought of it later, human will.

They rode out the storm.

Soon the storm clouds moved past, driven on by the trades. In the west, the sun was barely visible, sinking fast near the outline of the Wai'anae coast. Sachi M heard her father-in-law give a sigh of relief. No one was ever ready for death, she thought, no matter what his condition.

When Sachi M finally had a moment's respite, she looked over at her father-in-law who sat hugging himself. Once in a while, with great effort, he forced himself to bail more of the water, working around his legs. Lips purple and quivering, he gripped the neck of his jacket tightly. Sachi M threw the engine into idle, retrieved a plastic rubbish bag from one of the compartments and ripped the top off the bag. She slipped it over her father-in-law's head and took the bailer out of his hands by peeling away his fingers.

"It's okay, Papa, you can let go. And let's go in," she said. He took in a huge breath and closed his eyes. "Look, it's getting dark real fast."

Looking up and ahead of them, toward land, Sachi M saw the far-off stretch of city lights ran down the hillsides like lava flows.

A soft moon rose as they chugged back in toward the small-boat harbor. They were farther out than Sachi M ever imagined. A frightening thought crossed her mind—that they could have been lost at sea. She choked back a sob.

They entered a sea smooth as glass near the harbor, the lights from land wavering and playing off it as on mirror. Schools of silver flying fish sailed over their tiny boat as it moved toward the harbor mouth, the fish shining like silver tinsels. That beautiful.

Sachi M's father-in-law gradually stopped shivering and she saw him look up at the moon, huge and yellow. There, on the water, Sachi M felt as if they were the only travelers in the world, now on their long journey home.

Late that night, Sachi M and Tom received a phone call from Tom's mother. "I'm at the hospital," she said. "Your dad collapsed and he's in a coma. He's not going to make it. Hurry down," she said.

Grandpa Sam was beside himself at the funeral. To him, his son had broken one of life's rhythms. "It's hard when the young ones go first. The old ones supposed to go first," he said to people who offered their condolences.

Grandpa Asa did not approach Grandpa Sam at the funeral, except to take off his hat and bow when he passed him in the church reception line. Despite the differences between the two men, Grandpa Asa had taken a real liking to Sachi M's father-in-law, the man who was awfully "nice-u for a gaijin."

The chest of drawers the two grandfathers had begun but never finished lay untouched for several weeks before Sachi M's father-in-law's death. And it remained that way for several weeks after his death.

One day, Grandpa Asa called Sachi M to pick him up. "Sachi M," he said. "You take-u me Sam-san house."

"Oh? What for?"

"Must-u speak to him. Izu have some bizu-nes-su with him."

Sachi M was curious but did not press the matter. When her grandfather did not disclose what he was going to do, it meant he wasn't going to explain anything.

The day Sachi M brought her grandfather to talk to Grandpa Sam, Grandpa Sam was out on the lanai, smoking a cigar, his legs propped on another chair, his belly showing. "Come in, come in," Grandpa Sam directed when he saw Grandpa Asa and Sachi M coming. He tried pulling down his short shirt over his belly.

Grandpa Asa acknowledged Grandpa Sam by bowing as if the ceiling was too low in the room.

"Sit down, sit down," offered Grandpa Sam. "So what brings you here?"

"Anno . . . tansu, ne? What to do?"

"M-m-m-m. Funny, I've been thinking about it, too. What you say?"

"Izu think so, mo' betta we finish."

"If we finish it, who shall we give it to?"

"We give to Tom-san and Sachi M."

"Of course. That makes sense," agreed Grandpa Sam.

A few days later, the two men resumed their work on the tansu. One day after work, in the late afternoon, Sachi M and Tom went to Mānoa to see how their grandfathers were getting along.

Sachi M's mother was in the yard on her knees, digging up some weeds under the mock orange hedge. "Shhh," she said and pointed toward the garage. "They working nicely now. Before this, they were fighting. Go peek inside, Sachi M, see what they doing. Tom, you come with me. I need you to carry the potting soil."

Sachi M walked slowly down the path toward the doorway on the side of the garage. Halfway over, she stopped to listen. She could hear someone sawing a piece of wood. She then heard Grandpa Sam cough.

"Wassamalla you. Go docta, you," she heard her grandpa say.

"Never mind me. Just hurry up and cut that piece so I can join it here. When you're through you gotta hold it for me like this."

"Moloā style, dat."

"You try then."

When Sachi M finally peeked in on the grandfathers from the doorway, she saw the two of them held in the palm of a soft sepia light streaming into the room from a side window. It bathed the two men in repose, their intent for the moment graced by accord and purpose, as they worked with their hands and the wood.

Rock Fever

Sandra Ota Carter had been helping to care for her husband's mother for six years, and she was tired of it. She wanted her mother-in-law, or Mama as they called her, placed in a nursing home but felt guilty wishing for it, not wanting to hurt her husband, Rick. When Mama became ill with Alzheimer's disease, she had promised Rick she would help him. After all, he had helped to care for her mother before she died of cancer. What Sandra had not realized, however, was how long caring for Mama was going to take and how different and difficult it was going to be.

Just the other day, when Mama said *I have to think to think*, it was about as clear a statement as Sandra had heard since Mama entered the late stages of her aphasia. Once in a while she would say something clear that wrenched Sandra's heart, but these utterances were becoming rare, the window of coherence closing shut.

Sandra felt trapped. There were days when she wanted to jump into her car and drive forever. The island was closing in on her. People in Hawai'i called this condition "rock fever." It could cause you to go stir-crazy, the feeling that you could only go so far, and whichever way you went, you'd wind up where you began. It was impossible to drive endlessly as when she and Rick were first married and traveled across the States. Even then, they were soon back in Honolulu to help their parents. Sandra began to feel more hemmed in the longer she and Rick took care of Mama. They were caught in a circle of care.

Sandra didn't mind the hassle while growing up on the Big Island—getting up early in the morning, her father saying, "Eh, everybody ready? C'mon, we go!" and everyone piled into his old, beat-up truck. They lurched out of their garage, the bed of the truck packed high with an old tent and futon, the charcoal broiler, the lunch her mother had prepared, inner tubes for swimming, and her father's fishing poles and smelly bait. They would leave one end of Hilo Town on a Friday morning of a three-day weekend to fish at Spencer Park or South Point on the other side of the island, and they would return in the evening two days later, coming in from the other side of town. "Circle island too-ahs," her father called these excursions. But now, being on an island felt like a noose around Sandra's neck.

The night she and Rick went to see the Samsara Trio in concert at the Hawai'i Theatre was supposed to offer them respite from their caregiving. In part, because of Sandra's urging and Rick's own ambivalent feelings about whether or not he should put his mother into a nursing home, the evening was not as relaxing as they had hoped it would be, the tension between them palpable as they sat in the theater and stared straight ahead, barely touching each other.

In their latest discussions, Rick had been hesitant about making the move, saying that his mother still made sense to him despite her aphasia. "She must be understanding something," he reasoned. *The weather is too Roy*, she'd say if it were raining. Or she'd say something like *Is she pilting and falking again?* to ask Rick if Sandra was sulking again.

Sandra had to agree that Mama still made *sense*. If there was some cognition left, Sandra reckoned Rick couldn't just dump his mother into some nursing home. "And notice how beautiful her sentences are," Rick pointed out. Sandra had to agree that Mama often sounded poetic.

Life was full of little glitches, irritations, the unexpected. Sandra found that she couldn't get away from them. Take the concert that night. Sandra noticed the plight of the young page turner when she caught the disgruntlement on the pianist's face. The page turner had mistakenly turned one of the pages too soon and had almost lost the woman's place in the music. The piano player had been keeping time by deeply nodding her head in a particular passionate segment of adagio cantabile in Beethoven's Trio in E-flat major, Op. 1, No. 1, which was mistaken by the page turner as a cue to turn the page. Sandra felt sorry for the young girl when the pianist looked up and glared at her small, round face.

Not too far into Schoenberg's *Verklärte Nacht*, a few strands of the violin player's bow became undone. The strings wafted into the air like a puff of smoke. The violinist, balancing the violin on her neck and chin, used her fingering hand during pauses to try once, twice, thrice to catch the fine strands of hair. Finally, she ripped the cobweb-like floaters off the end of the bow. She smiled at the audience as she lifted her fist in triumph.

Things just happened. They always did. And Sandra proved herself right. While she was having these thoughts, the A-string of the cellist snapped. The woman waved her hands to stop the music. She apologized for the group and the trio exited the stage to fix the string, their satin gowns rustling as they walked out. Rick leaned over and said, "How would she have explained a G-string snapping?" Sandra buried her head into his shoulder to half-cry and half-laugh at the absurdity of his off-color joke.

"That wasn't bad," Rick said after the concert.

"It wasn't bad at all," Sandra said as they walked arm in arm up to their apartment in the clear, cool night. Rick murmured part of the music into Sandra's hair.

When they reached the door he said, "Thank you for everything—especially the years with Mama. It has been a difficult time for you. But I'll make it up. I swear. And thanks for the nice evening."

"Yeah, while it lasted." Sandra immediately felt sorry for the barb. "All I know is that you'll have to make some kind of decision about Mama. I don't know how much longer I can last."

Sandra felt Rick's warm breath on her scalp and longed for some answers. Sandra wanted to linger outside the doorway in Rick's arms, but she could already hear Mama jabbering, her words as distinct as they had been in health. *Perfort me finny first*, she was saying.

"I think we better go in," Sandra said. "You know what bothers me? I think I understand Mama perfectly well. Right now, for instance, she wants us to come in. She wants us to think of her first."

"I think you're right," Rick said, as he opened the door to the apartment.

"Yep. And the longer we think we still understand her, the harder it is to let her go, isn't it?"

Sandra sat on the chair in the foyer and took off her shoes. She lingered in the last movement of the music still playing in her head. She sighed and walked into Mama's bedroom. Karen, Mama's sitter, was walking Mama up and down the room, Mama babbling incoherently, agitated in her day-night reversals.

"How was she tonight?" Rick asked Karen.

I'm shopping my up. I have been recrimbed from both sides.

"Not you, Mama, I'm asking Karen," Rick said.

"Oh, she was good," said Karen. "Ate all that I gave her. I gave her a Buspar after dinner, but I'm afraid she's still wide awake. Hope you guys get some sleep."

You are leaving a shut too much. Don't make it look sery. Is this for a wackering long one?

"I think she's got to pee," said Sandra, putting a finger on her chin, cupping her elbow with the other hand, marveling at the humor of Mama's words. Sandra took her mother-in-law to the bathroom.

Rick walked to the door with Karen to pay her. From the bathroom, Sandra heard bits and pieces of Rick's and Karen's conversation above the slow and steady stream of Mama's urine. She heard Rick giving Karen something extra for her time and Karen saying something about having to mash Mama's food these days, Mama having more difficulty swallowing. She was at another level of decline. "But she's mild compared to most," Karen said. Mild? thought Sandra. Others must be murder, then. She supposed she should be thankful that Mama wasn't as difficult, but she felt only resentment.

She's got to get a peasant at the animal.

"She certainly does," said Sandra, pulling up Mama's diaper. "You're right on the nose. So what else is up?"

Be careful of the oifins. The beets are belled up on the road.

Sandra smiled at the warning. She then walked Mama to bed and settled her under the covers. "Try to sleep Mama, okay?"

With Mama reasonably settled, Sandra joined Rick and Karen. "Your mom's in bed," said Sandra. Rick said good-bye to Karen and went to his mother's room to say the nighttime ritual of prayers he said with her. Sandra lingered on with Karen.

"Thanks. You've been such a big help. We're going to be needing you again in a couple of days."

"Anytime." Looking up at Sandra, Karen said, "It's time, you know."

"I know, but I feel guilty pushing it. It's up to Rick." Karen gave Sandra a long hug that was full of sadness.

Sandra went back in to join Rick. He sat talking to his mother and was brushing back her fine white hair with his fingers. It was already eleven o'clock. Rick's mother's blue-gray eyes were wide open but they seemed far away. Empty.

Fid is a piddy layer.

"Yes, whatever it is, it is a pity," replied Rick. "So did you have a good night with Karen?"

Her lips are quicker than a doer.

"I would say that, too, but Karen is a doer. Now be a good girl and go to sleep. Good night, Mama."

Mama looked up at Rick and said: *Daddy, your pain is plain as dark.*

"That it is, Mama," Rick said, agreeing.

Sandra and Rick went into their bedroom. The intercom crackled with the static of Mama's voice. Sandra turned it down, slumped into the chair beside the bed, and pulled an old afghan around her legs. Rick sat on the bed.

"Boy, I'm tired," Rick said, weaving his fingers through his hair in anguish.

"*You're* tired? You have that wonderful ability to fall right back to sleep when you get up for your mom at night. It takes me hours."

"I'm sorry. I don't mean to sound so selfish."

"We both don't, but how long, Rick? It's been six years of going downhill. All I know is, I hope she sleeps tonight."

"Yeah. I hope she sleeps."

There passed a long silence. Sandra said quietly, "I really think it's time. Don't you?"

"I just can't, Sandra. Not yet, anyway. Please understand. I'm having a hard time with this."

"What about me, Rick?"

"You'll always come first, but—"

"But what? You make me feel like a nag. What's holding you back?"

"I don't know. I can't right now, that's all."

"I remember, a long time ago, you said that when your mother forgot your father that would be the time to put her into a nursing home. That time has come and gone. 'Now tell me again. Who's this young man?' she asked when she looked at your father's picture, remember? That was supposed to be the sign, but she's still here."

"I know I said that."

"Your taking me here and there to a concert and movie doesn't make up for the burden of helping to care for her. Damn. You make me feel small!"

Rick said nothing. He blinked and held his eyes on Sandra. It was at times like this that she wished that she could just hop into her car and drive on forever. Never look back.

That night, in its deepest pocket, Rick rolled over to her side. "I'm sorry," he said, drawing her into the circle of his arms, "that I'm not doing any better by you." He made overtures of wanting to make love to her. Sandra responded—each of them compacted into each other's ball of hurt. Sandra burst into tears at the height of their lovemaking, and the way Rick gave way simultaneously, it was as if he were letting go of his grief in her. Sandra felt a little crazy inside.

After making love, Sandra walked down the hallway to check on Mama. She ran her finger under Mama's clothing to her diaper and found that Mama was soaking wet. Thank goodness her bedclothes are dry, thought Sandra. I don't have to change those.

You're leaving a shut too much.

Sandra went back down the hall to their bedroom to fetch Rick. "I think she still needs to go to the bathroom. Help me to take her?"

"What time is it?" he asked, as he staggered behind Sandra.

"About two."

"Oh, lordy!"

Bathroom chores filled their lives. The next morning it started all over again. They woke to, *The waining of the twaining of the train.*

Sandra helped Rick maneuver Mama onto the toilet. Right on time.

Mother's on the button book on the boy box.

"You're good at this," he said to Sandra as he turned to his mom. "Are you through?" he asked her.

Let's get it at least half past Europe, she said.

"Small consolation to be good at something like this," Sandra answered in between.

"But, can you call it. You almost always hit it on the nose. She moved like you said she would. You know how messy it can get if we don't catch it."

Why in the world would anyone want to be good at something like *that*, thought Sandra. She didn't want to be good at deciphering what Mama said. If she could understand Mama, caregiving could become her *whole* life. She would have to quit her job; she would have to give up going to an occasional movie with friends. Taking care of Mama was smothering her. Her whole body screamed in itself.

Sandra brushed Mama's teeth, dressed her, and got her ready for Rick to take to adult day care in Nu'uanu. *Are you going to kerkle the key?* Mama inquired as Sandra put on her shoes. Sandra was brusque and more irritated than usual. *You got the mimps?* asked Mama, as if she knew. Day care helped a bit, but Sandra knew it wasn't going to last. Mama's condition was way beyond the help day care could give her.

That evening after supper, Sandra had a terrible bathing session with Mama. She had given Sandra a left hook to the jaw while Sandra was washing under her arms. The punch had come before Rick could stop Mama's hands, his own hands holding a soapy washrag. It took two to bathe her these days.

With the punch, Sandra had staggered and nearly blacked out. Angered, Rick shouted, "This is the last straw, Mama. I'm putting you into a nursing home. You just can't hit Sandra."

"Hey, cool it," said a groggy Sandra, defending Mama. "She didn't mean to hit me. She doesn't know any better."

"Precisely. She no longer knows any better. I guess that's what I needed to know inside myself."

"It's good you're finally thinking of a nursing home. But it doesn't have to be today *today*, okay? You can still think about it."

"You do want her to go, don't you?"

"Yes and no."

"Now what kind of an answer is that?"

"I know it sounds crazy, but I would miss her."

"You're always complaining that you have no life. I don't get it!" Rick said, exasperated.

"But don't you see? It was you who has to want it. Not me."

Rick wiped Mama down. He dressed her in pajamas and brushed her hair. *Eeeee!* she squealed between strokes. Sandra cleaned up the bathroom, picking up the clothing and towels strewn on the counters and floor. Bathing Mama was a big production.

In a quiet moment when all was done and Mama was clean, Rick sat with his mother on the sofa in the living room. Sandra looked at the two of them from the bathroom door, towels still bundled in her arms, and she saw Mama take Rick's face into her hands and kiss Rick on the forehead. She then heard Mama say in an almost inaudible voice, but with amazing clarity: *I want to die, but I don't know how.* In the next minute, her words turned to gibberish once more.

Sandra backed herself into Mama's bathroom. She dropped down heavily on the toilet seat. She sat and wept into her hands.

Once Rick put his mind to getting his mother placed in a home, there was no stopping him. He called the doctor and the doctor put him in touch with a placement center.

They didn't have to wait long. A week later, Rick received a call from the placement center stating that there was an opening at Maunalani Hospital if they wanted to take it. An unexpected death. Rick called Sandra that day and picked her up after school to look at the facilities. They found the place clean and the inhabitants well cared for. Then Sandra and Rick talked to the social worker, and they signed the necessary papers.

"How soon?" asked Sandra.

"Two days," the woman said. "If you don't take it, we will find another tenant."

"Two days? That fast? I thought we would have at least a couple of weeks."

"The demand is great. I'm sorry, but I can't give you more time.

You have to take what you can when it is offered. Rooms are hard to come by."

Sandra hadn't considered that Mama could be gone that soon. It didn't feel the same as when their son Kent went to college. She had time for the letting-go rituals: shopping, going out to dinner, giving him extra money (aside from what she and Rick had decided on) and packing a care package filled with his favorite snacks. She wouldn't have time to do much fussing for Mama.

Sandra managed, nonetheless, to buy Mama two pairs of Isotonic slippers and called Karen to cut Mama's hair and do her nails. Sandra also bought a nice pink bed jacket for Mama to wear, along with some housedresses, new underwear, and toiletries. But that didn't hide the guilt she harbored. I guess we're never satisfied, thought Sandra about this nuisance human condition. She wanted Mama to go, but now that the time was here, she was sad and felt sorry Mama had to leave home. There didn't seem to be enough time to say an adequate good-bye.

Rick packed Mama's bag with every item marked with her name in indelible laundry ink the day they were to take her to the hospital.

"Is one o'clock tomorrow okay with you? I want you to accompany me to the hospital. I need you Sandra. This is hard for me."

"I thought maybe you wanted some privacy and time with your mom. But that's fine. I'll wait at home for you."

On the way to school that morning, Sandra plugged in a Samsara Trio tape. She could barely listen to the music, remembering the crestfallen young page turner, the violinist with the wayward bow strings, and the cellist with the broken A-string.

She rushed home from school after teaching her classes and gave Rick a hurried call.

"What time do we have to be at the hospital?" she asked.

"I said one, but the office closes at five. Why?" answered Rick.

"Can I meet you there at 4:30 instead? I'll pick up Mama and bring her with me."

"Sure, but what's going on?"

"I'll tell you later. Can't explain now. I have to go. See you at the hospital."

"Hey, wait a minute—"

Sandra had little time to waste. She tossed Mama's bag into her trunk and drove to the day-care center to pick her up. A line of patients extended their last good-byes. "How come you wen lose your brains?" Ida Mae, one of Mama's friends called out. "We'll miss you," chorused the others.

One and one and one is white, Mama said as she waved good-bye. *Can you fudge with my glad?*

"I sure can, Mama. That's exactly what we're going to do—fudge with your glad."

Sandra strapped Mama into the car. She headed down to the old Chun Hoon Shopping Center to the Yami Yogurt store, where she bought two ice cream cones, the one for Mama loaded with rainbow-colored sprinkles. "Pile it on," Sandra ordered the girl making the cones. She knew Mama felt the excitement, too. *I have to go to the light of the fire.*

They finished eating their cones and Sandra said, "C'mon, let's go. I'm taking you for a ride around the island."

As if she knew where they were going, Mama clapped her hands. She waved a long good-bye out the window. She looked at Sandra and said, *I don't want to go any place but you.*

Juliet S. Kono has written two books of poems, *Hilo Rains* (1988) and *Tsunami Years* (1995), which were both published by Bamboo Ridge Press. She has won the Elliot Cades Award for Literature, the American Japanese National Literary Award, and the Ka Palapala Poʻokela Award for Excellence in Literature. She was a recipient of a US/Japan Friendship Commission Creative Artist Exchange Fellowship in 1999. Born and raised in Hilo, Hawaiʻi, she now lives in Honolulu and teaches English at Leeward Community College.